C000228491

YELLuw
TAPE

YELLOW TAPE

A GRAY GIRLS MYSTERY

ALICIA ELLIS

YELLOW TAPE

Cover design by Miblart

Published by Figmented Ink in Atlanta
First Publication, July 2024
Trade Paperback ISBN: 978-1-939452-60-3

Library of Congress Control Number: 2024913427

This book is about siblings,
so it is for my brothers,
Jacob and
the one who doesn't want his name mentioned.

CHAPTER 1

IVY

My phone's shrill cry jarred me from work.

It was my dearest husband. Again. What would my excuse be if I didn't answer?

My weekly conference with my supervisor was due to start in a moment, and I would usually be prepping. The meeting was canceled, but Derek didn't know that.

He also didn't know I'd spent the last month working in a rented workspace instead of my usual FBI field office. I had sneaked my personal laptop out of the house every day for weeks without notice.

Now, I didn't have to sneak. To the left of my computer sat two stacks of papers—one with documents I'd read three times and the other only twice. Progress was slow but steady.

I accepted the call. "What can I do for you?" I switched to speaker and set my phone on the desk to the right of my laptop. Farther right, a dark-haired man with kind eyes looked up from a photograph. I touched his face before returning my fingertips to the keyboard.

This was the third version of my statement. The previous ones were unacceptable—according to the higher-ups— leaving me languishing on administrative leave.

"I tried you twice already," Derek said.

"Can I call you back in twenty-one minutes? I should be ready for a break by then."

"Why haven't you signed, Ivy?"

Derek Lawson, the man of my dreams, grew up in a middle-class family south of Los Angeles and catapulted himself to the lower rich by his mid-twenties. His wide-set eyes, symmetrical features, and movie-star smile won him most negotiations before he opened his mouth. Women in his social circle considered him the catch of the century.

I used to agree.

"I haven't had time to review everything," I said. "I have a lot going on." Derek wouldn't like that answer, but it was the best I had. Our disagreements had become a push-and-pull dance of two people who hated to love each other—or loved to hate each other. It was hard to tell at this point.

The pause stretched across the line and burst. "I thought we were on the same page."

I rubbed the headache forming behind my eyes. "We are. I'm going to sign as soon as I make sure the terms are fair."

"I intercepted your gift for Jess from the mail," he said. "Our divorce is going to be tough enough for her. I don't want her confused."

I turned away from my document to glare at the phone. After three steadying breaths, I kept my tone flat. "It's her birthday." At ten years younger than Derek, his sister Jess had known me since she was small. I'd never skipped her birthday.

His voice rose. "This is not what we agreed."

Beeping alerted me to a call waiting. The caller ID said *Gray Investigations* in Willow Lake, Georgia. I swiped it to voicemail and returned that half of my attention to Derek.

"Look," I said, "I'm sorry. You can say it's from you. It's a personalized phone case. I ordered it months ago, but they were backordered, and then the customization took time. I don't want her to miss out because you and I are . . . you know. I have a mountain of work. Can we finish this later?"

"Fine. Avoid this conversation. Avoid *me*. That's your specialty." The line went dead.

With a groan, I pressed the heels of my hands into my forehead. The throb intensified.

The phone rang again—Gray Investigations. If he was going to keep calling, I might as well get it over with.

"Dad?" I snapped.

"Thank God. I thought you might be on a case." It was a female voice.

"Who is this?"

"It's Anna."

Anna Baxter worked part-time as a self-employed accountant and part-time as my father's assistant. The latter was only because he'd begged. They were best friends since grade school in small-town Willow Lake. She had been keeping his secrets since they were kids, which was why I wanted nothing to do with her.

The size of my irritation doubled. My father couldn't even call me himself. He needed his longtime friend to do his dirty work.

"I don't want to hear from him." I aimed my finger at the button that would end this call. "Can you tell him not to call—and not to have *you* call?"

"He's missing."

My finger stalled. "New mistress?"

"No, Ivy. He's *missing*." A long pause, then, "I haven't seen him since yesterday. He said he would be back after lunch."

"Did you check with the new wife?"

"Pearl hasn't seen him either—and they've been married for nine years. He's not answering calls from me, her, or clients. Feel how you want about him, but he takes his work seriously. I found—"

On my computer, my document disappeared. My chest went numb.

I couldn't lose this statement. Anna was still speaking, but this was more important. My dream career was on the line. This job was the only thing that had gone right over the last few years.

"He's been missing for half my life," I said. "I have to go. Nice to hear from you."

"Wait!" Anna shouted. "We're family, Ivy. I need you. Caleb needs you."

I laughed. "There's no blood between us."

"Family is the people you choose. I didn't always do a great job of choosing you, but I hope to change that. Life is too short to be at odds with people you love."

"I have to go. When you find him, let me know where he was . . . and who he was with." I disconnected.

I hit the keystroke to undo whatever I just did, and my file reappeared. I closed my eyes in thanks. Losing this document would be what I deserved for not giving it my undivided attention.

A voicemail notification popped up on my phone. With a sigh, I played it.

"Hey, Ivy. It's Anna."

Right, I had declined her first call. I reached to delete the recording.

"Caleb is missing. I found blood on the letter opener on his desk."

I let it play.

Anna's voice trembled. "The sheriff doesn't care because it's only been a day, but I'm worried. Maybe you could pull some strings at the FBI and get someone to take a look. It's an emergency. Please call me back... Please."

The message ended, leaving me cold.

I'd hung up on her too soon. I should have let Anna explain. If she wanted the FBI, there must be more to this story.

I called Gray Investigations. The line rang five times before voicemail picked up. "Anna, this is Ivy. Call me back."

I tried again. Still no answer.

Bringing in the FBI wasn't an option.

In the hallway, a trio of laughing men in business casual clothing passed my glass door, each holding a steaming mug of caffeine. Outside my window, the West Coast skyline greeted me, and sunlight blinked off high buildings.

My life in Los Angeles wasn't perfect, but it was the one I chose. There was still a chance to get it on track.

The life I'd *escaped* was back in Willow Lake.

CHAPTER 2
ROSE

POUNDING BASS DID A TAP DANCE ON MY BRAIN THROUGH THE CEILING of my studio apartment. I mashed my pillow over my face. Except for nearly suffocating me, it didn't help.

Suffocation would be a sweet release from the hell of my upstairs neighbor's eardrum-rattling music.

I tossed the pillow and charged the door. On my way, I grabbed two pizza crusts from last night's box on the counter. I'd go out for groceries later—after getting some decent rest.

My puppy, Rusty, hunkered his 110-pounds-and-growing, furry brown frame in the doorway and refused to move until I opened it wide enough for him to follow. I dropped a crust, and Rusty snapped it up before it hit the floor.

Stuffing the other one in my mouth, I ran up the hallway stairs and pounded on my upstairs neighbor's door.

"Hey!" I banged again. "Keep it down."

Rusty scratched at the door beside me and whined.

Harold yanked it open, and music spilled out. Marijuana-scented smoke swirled out and slapped me in the face.

"Rose, hey!" He cast me a lazy grin. "Did you bring food?"

"I'm not staying."

He spotted Rusty and pushed the door to only a crack. "What's up?"

"Your *music* is up. I'm trying to sleep."

"It's eleven in the morning."

"I had a long night."

"Trying to save the world on your computer?"

"Just trying to pay the rent. IT stuff."

He stared, head cocked, waiting for the punchline.

"Seriously," I said. "I'm doing freelance information technology now. I have business cards and everything."

"No shit?"

"No shit."

"Bummer." He shook his head. "I should turn it down, huh?"

"Go with your gut." My body swayed, and I widened my stance for balance.

"You look like you're about to drop. Better get some sleep."

I pointed at my ears.

"Right, the music! Oh sure, my bad." He grabbed his phone and hit a button.

The noise softened in a blissful instant. The echo of it still throbbed in my head, but it was a start.

"That okay?"

I pressed my palms together. "Bless you."

"I don't think I like the new you." He shut the door in my face.

I stared at it, tempted to bang again and demand to know why I couldn't get my life together without facing his judgment. But I didn't need his approval. I just needed sleep.

I flipped the bird at the door, and Rusty led the way down to my apartment. As soon as we got inside, the music blared again.

I screamed at the ceiling.

A scream answered from above.

Harold was so high he probably thought I was cheering his taste—as if anyone would call that earsplitting cacophony of screeches and bangs *music*.

Rusty whined.

"I know, baby." I rubbed his head. Time to take matters into my own hands.

My cozy apartment fit my bed, a massive desk with dual monitors, and not much else. I could've afforded more space if I spent less on gear, but no regrets.

I dropped into my chair and checked for available Wi-Fi. Because this was an apartment complex, the list was long.

Given the weed smoke upstairs, I guessed the one called *HighFiWiFi* was Harold's. It was password-protected, but I could handle that.

I tried the usual suspects—*password, admin, letmein*—and threw in *cannabis, gethigh*, the name of the router, and a few others. All losers.

This wasn't going to be easy, but it wasn't going to be hard.

I had deleted all my tools the last time I turned over a new leaf, but I navigated to a website and downloaded a password-cracker I'd donated to the public ages ago.

It used a basic dictionary-attack algorithm that occasionally swapped out letters for numbers and special characters and used an artificial intelligence API to get recommendations on what to try next.

After starting the program, I fed it what I knew about Harold: age, hobbies, where we lived. Then I let it rip.

Twelve seconds later, I had access to his Wi-Fi and a peek at every connected device.

I drummed my fingers to the beat of his awful music.

On his network, he had a phone and an audio receiver. The two weren't linked, so his phone was probably transmitting to the receiver over Bluetooth, and speakers were attached to the receiver. Easy fix—I turned off the Bluetooth.

Sweet, blessed silence.

Harold cursed. I grinned, but I wasn't done.

Some people liked whale sounds or rain when they slept. Me? I preferred white noise. I reactivated the Bluetooth, connected my phone to the audio receiver, and hit play on my favorite static.

The sizzle-pop-fizz of white noise poured from the ceiling.

With a grin, I slid from behind my desk and crawled into bed. I pulled the covers tight over my shoulders, letting my eyes drift shut. Rusty curled up beside me.

My phone rang.

"No!" I snatched it up and checked the display: *Gray Investigations.*

Interesting. Dear old Daddy Gray suddenly realized I existed.

I stared at the screen as the ringtone played. After ten seconds, it went to voicemail. Maybe I should have answered.

It rang again.

"Hello?"

"Rose?" A woman's voice. Definitely not my father.

"Is he dead?" Not my most compassionate moment, but I hadn't spoken to Caleb in twenty-three years, since I was five.

"I hope not. I need your help."

CHAPTER 3

IVY

THE ADDRESS OF GRAY INVESTIGATIONS WAS A TWO-STORY, BRICK office building. It stood out among the mom-and-pop shops and restaurants that occupied Willow Lake's charming downtown.

I parked in one of the gravel lot's many open spaces. Anna's worried voicemail still clung to my nerves, and I tried not to worry about the empty space beside me with a sign saying it was reserved for Caleb Gray.

In the alcove, a placard identified the businesses inside. I found Gray Investigations and noted the floor and suite number.

My feet creaked up the wooden steps and down the hall to the frosted-glass door. Gold lettering proclaimed this the site of Gray Investigations, my father's private investigations office.

I gathered my resolve while my stomach did gymnastics. I hadn't seen Dad or Anna in over a year. Part of me needed this to be a true emergency, worth my time and worry. The rest of me wanted to go inside, find nothing of note, and book my flight home.

I pushed the door open.

A ceiling fan with a trio of bulbs lit the waiting room's mismatched upholstered chairs and a squat table covered with old magazines. Beige walls held framed newspaper clippings behind Anna's reception desk.

Anna's desk was empty, and beside it, the door to Caleb's inner office stood cracked open.

I stood still. "Anna?"

No one answered, but goose bumps popped along my forearms.

A faint metallic scent hit my nose as I reached for the inner door, and my pulse spiked.

"Dad?"

I pulled it open and stepped through. The smell slapped me in the face, turning my stomach. My mouth filled with sour-tasting saliva. I staggered back and slammed into the doorframe.

Anna was slumped backward in Caleb's chair behind his desk. Her wide eyes stared at everything but saw nothing. Her sandy-colored hair hung in dark red clumps that dripped onto her shoulders. The bullet through her forehead had sprayed blood and gray matter against the wall behind her.

My stomach flipped inside out, and I doubled over, my hand clamped over my mouth to keep from hurling. My eyes watered and burned, but I willed my stomach not to purge itself. Despite the silence in the room, my internal panic was screaming.

"Keep it together," I muttered. The sound of my voice comforted me. Solid. Steady. Just like I always was.

Some people thought the FBI was all gunfights and serial killers, like in the movies, but most of us had never fired a service weapon in the field and certainly never stumbled onto a scene like this. Three years on the job, and I'd only ever seen dead bodies in photos and videos.

Until now.

As if I might startle the corpse back into motion, I eased a trembling hand into my purse and extracted my phone. My sweat-damp fingers fumbled, and the phone fell to the dark carpet, bounced, and tumbled deeper into the room.

Great, now I'd have to go closer. "Keep it together."

This time, the words did nothing to ease my pounding heart stampeding in my chest.

I pressed my shaking hands to my stomach and stretched out one foot to toe my phone. I succeeded only in pushing it farther away.

"Holy shit!" came a shout behind me.

I screamed.

I barreled past the phone and dove toward the desk. I snatched a silver letter opener from its surface and spun on the intruder. "Stay there." My voice quaked, and I silently cursed myself for not keeping it together.

A brown-skinned woman a few inches shorter than me, with thick coily hair in a ponytail, slid backward toward the doorway. She looked about my age, late twenties. Her eyes watered. Her mouth gaped.

She was standing between me and the only exit.

"She . . . she . . ." The woman pointed a trembling finger at my father's desk.

"She's dead," I filled in.

The woman's gaze landed on me and went even wider until the white was visible on all sides. "Hey, whatever happened here has nothing to do with me. I didn't see anything." She slapped a hand over her eyes and stepped backward. "Totally blind."

She lowered her hand and inched over the threshold into the waiting room.

I registered the panicked look. "No! I didn't do this. I just got here and found her."

"Right, of course. That's what we'll tell the police."

Why was I the one defending myself? She was the stranger. "What about you?"

"Oh, sure." The woman nodded, but sarcasm seeped into her tone. "I shot her in the head." She licked her lips and swallowed. "Then I came back to accuse whoever found the body. Very logical. I'm not the one with a weapon."

"She was shot—and not with a letter opener." Still, it was reckless of me to have moved it. I'd have to tell the sheriff exactly where it had been on the desk.

The woman nodded down at my hand.

I followed her look and, for the first time, saw the blood along one sharp edge of the opener. Instinctively, I tossed it. It thunked on the floor between us. We stared at it and then back at each other.

The woman folded her arms over her stomach and shrugged. "The gun could be in your purse."

"So despite having a gun, I grabbed a *letter opener* when you walked in?" Now I was the one with the sarcasm.

She scanned up and down my body, taking in my straight dark hair and brown eyes, my now-empty fingers.

I pressed my hands against my legs to steady them. Neither of us had killed Anna. But someone had. A murderer had been in this office and could still be nearby.

I pointed at my phone, which was still on the floor between us. "I need to call the police, and both of us need to wait outside so we don't damage this crime scene even more."

Her eyes narrowed. "Of course, the golden child of Caleb Gray first accuses me of murder and then of damaging a crime scene when she's the one snatching up bloody weapons."

"Do I know you?" Then it hit me.

I'd searched for her across the web on days when my curiosity won out, but I never found much. Now, when I examined her face, I saw my father in the shape of her eyes.

She swept my phone up from the floor and held it between her thumb and forefinger as if it were diseased.

I accepted it. "Rosaline?"

"Ivy," she said.

CHAPTER 4

IVY

WE STARED EACH OTHER DOWN. WHAT DO YOU SAY TO THE HALF sister you've had for twenty-eight years and never met?

According to my research and what my mother would confess after multiple glasses of wine, Rosaline Gray was born three months after me. At the time, my dad was making frequent trips to Atlanta for conferences. Five years later, my mother discovered evidence of the affair with Rosaline's mom in the form of a lease for an apartment in the city—with one adult female occupant and a five-year-old.

My dad had carelessly left the lease locked in the top drawer of his desk.

"I go by Rose," she said.

"How did you know it was me?" It was a stupid thing to ask, but there wasn't an etiquette book for these situations.

"Your former law firm makes its lawyers' profiles public—which seems like a really bad idea, by the way."

"I only worked there for six months."

"Before joining the FBI—I know." She tapped her temple. "The internet remembers. Privacy is so important."

"I guess that's why I couldn't find your photo anywhere."

Her lips twitched upward. "You looked?"

"Didn't find much."

The smile widened. It fell an instant later after Rose seemed to remember we stood ten feet from a dead body.

After another minute of us staring at each other, Rose's attention shifted to a framed town map hanging on the left wall. Mostly monochrome, it featured splashes of color for the lake, the sky, and a spotting of trees with reddish and brown leaves. A glossy black frame highlighted the piece, which was the only artwork in the room.

"So this is Willow Lake," she said, her tone thoughtful.

"Not much to it."

Her gaze slid downward to a pair of tall filing cabinets below the map. She walked over to them, grabbed the top drawer, and yanked. The lock clicked.

"Hey," I said. "This is a crime scene."

"Uh-huh." She tried the next three drawers in quick succession. All locked.

I slipped my phone into my back pocket, gripped her shoulders, and pulled her away. As we moved, she grabbed the top drawer of the second cabinet and checked it too. *Click.* Also locked.

I guided Rose back to the threshold of the waiting room and stood between her and the rest of my dad's office. "Crime scene," I said again, more slowly this time.

"You think the key is on her?" Rose jerked her head toward Anna's corpse but kept her gaze on me.

"Probably. Or in my dad's desk."

"Our dad's desk."

"Whatever. You're not touching it. Or her. Or I swear to God I'll tackle you to the ground and hold you until the sheriff gets here."

Rose shut her eyes for a second as if preparing her nerve, and then flicked her attention over to Anna's body behind the desk.

I grabbed her arm. "We're waiting."

She pointed at the phone sticking out of my back pocket. "Have you called them yet?"

I stared at her for a second, debating whether I could trust her if I left her alone. I didn't have much choice, though. The longer I waited to contact the sheriff's office, the longer anyone would take to get here. I dialed 9-1-1.

"What's your emergency?" came a crisp voice when the call connected.

"This is Ivy Gray. I'm at Gray Investigations." I rattled off the address. "Anna Baxter is . . ." I paused to keep my voice from trembling. Anna and I hadn't been on good terms, but I'd known her forever. For every moment of my life, Anna Baxter had existed.

Still facing me in the doorway, Rose gave me a curious look.

I turned my face away and continued. "She's dead. Gunshot to the head." The dispatcher asked more questions, and I answered in a daze.

Rose squeezed past me toward the desk. She balled her hands into fists, nodded once, loosened them, and then opened one of the desk drawers.

"Rose," I hissed.

She rummaged inside the drawer and opened a second

one. She kept her face cranked at an odd angle to keep the body out of her field of view.

"I'll see them when they get here," I said to the dispatcher before ending the call. "What are you doing?"

"Exactly what it looks like." Rose stood, leaving the drawers hanging open. "There's no key. It's probably on the body."

I circled behind the desk, giving Anna's corpse as much breadth as possible, and started shoving drawers back where they belonged.

"Relax. I won't hurt anything. I just want a peek at what Caleb was working on."

"I will not relax." My voice had gone high-pitched, and I struggled to return it to a reasonable range. "Ever heard of *tampering with evidence?*"

"Is that your favorite band?"

It took me a second to parse that question because of its ridiculousness. "It's a crime—is what it is. Let the sheriff's office do its job when they get here."

Rose huffed. "How about a compromise? You go to the waiting room and watch for the sheriff, and I'll do what I came here to do—find our father."

Since she wouldn't move, neither would I.

I crossed my arms over my chest and glared. Anna's body sat only feet from me, so on second thought, I shifted farther away to resume glaring.

Rose pulled the keyboard toward her on its rotating swivel, careful not to touch the body tipped backward in the chair. She turned on the computer and squinted at the screen. "It's password protected."

"He's a private investigator. He knows about security."

Rose checked the desk surface and lifted the oversized paper calendar to look under it. She dropped it with a grunt and crawled under the desk.

"What are you doing?" I asked.

"Looking for the password." She felt around on the underside of the desk. "Sometimes older people write them down, like on a sticky note."

"He's not that old," I said. "And again, private investigator. He knows better."

She popped back into view and scrambled to her feet. "It was worth a shot. Do you know the Wi-Fi password?"

"Why would I know it? I haven't spent more than fifteen minutes with him at a time in the last ten years."

Rose tilted her head. "Why's that?"

This wasn't the time—and the room with Anna's corpse was not the place—to get into the string of lies he'd told me over the years as he hid one affair after another from my mom and me. Eventually, she divorced him. He remarried and even made peace with my mother.

I hadn't forgiven him for the lies.

I shrugged.

"I haven't seen him since I was five. Is that a *no* on the password?"

"Yes," I said. "No."

"Okay. Next option." Rose marched from the office into the waiting room. I followed.

She dove into Anna's desk, throwing open drawers, feeling every surface, and fumbling through papers.

Any second, the sheriff would burst through that door and find Rose with her grubby paws all over evidence in a murder investigation. Sister or not, I wasn't ready to drop my hard-earned savings on her bail.

"Rose," I said, my voice strained but measured. "The town is about this big." I snapped to illustrate how not-big it was. "The sheriff's substation is only minutes from here."

"Trust me." She squatted to get a better view of the desk's underside.

"I don't even know you."

"What's your favorite color?"

I squinted at her, hesitated, but decided it couldn't hurt. "Blue."

She pulled a face.

"What's wrong with that?"

"It's not very interesting."

"You're judging me by a color?"

"Do you have hobbies? Are FBI agents even allowed to have hobbies, or does their official restriction on fun prevent that?"

"You see the dead body, right?" I gestured toward the next room. "It's not the best time for chitchat."

Rose felt inside the bottom drawer, grinned, and withdrew a neon-green sticky note. She waved it at my face. "Taped to the top of the drawer."

I sighed.

She slapped the note onto the desk beside her and typed the password. She hit the Enter key with a flourish, and the lock screen disappeared, revealing a wallpaper of Anna and her husband George, their smiling faces so close to the camera lens that this had to be a selfie.

"This computer is already on the Wi-Fi," she said as she opened a new window on the screen. "I see Caleb's computer on the same network, so I'll try to get in from here. I'll still need his password, but I should be able to try out options faster this way rather than from his keyboard. What do you think the chances are it's a simple password, like a one-word phrase?"

I craned my neck to see what she was doing, but she deftly angled the screen away. "Private investigator," I said again, enunciating each syllable.

"So you've said." Rose squinted at the display.

The door to Gray Investigations banged open, and my heart did a skydive into my shoes. I jumped away from Rose and the laptop and put both hands up to shoulder level, palms out.

"Deputy Sheriff!" a gruff voice bellowed. The words rang through the small office like an alarm.

Rose locked the computer with two quick taps, her face a mask of innocence.

Two deputies strode into the room.

CHAPTER 5

ROSE

A FRESH-FACED KID STOOD IN THE DOORWAY, HIS HAND HOVERING over the gun at his waist. His wild look flew between Ivy and me and back again. The badge over his breast pocket labeled him a deputy, but he looked barely out of high school.

A dark-haired woman wearing the same badge and gray uniform squeezed through the door behind him and placed a hand on his shoulder. If either of them had itchy fingers, it was the kid. I kept my attention on him.

"We found her like this." I threw my hands up and jerked my head toward Ivy. "She's the one who called 9-1-1."

Ivy slid in front of me, palms high. "I'm FBI Agent Ivy Gray, and this is Rose Gray. Like she said, I called it in. We found Anna Baxter dead from a gunshot wound to the head." She pointed toward the open doorway into Caleb's office.

The body was visible from here, and the kid paled.

The woman squeezed his shoulder and held out her hand. "I'm Deputy Leila Ramirez, and this is Deputy Sam Marks."

The kid relaxed enough that his fingers stopped hovering around his gun. He straightened up and shook Ivy's hand next. Neither of them bothered to shake mine.

"Marks," Ivy said. "As in Sammy Marks, little brother of Stephanie Marks?"

"Yeah." He squinted at her.

"Your sister and I used to hang out in high school." Ivy snort-laughed. "You used to sneak into her room shirtless, and we would try out new hairstyles on you."

His face went rocket red, and he scrubbed a hand through his closely cropped dark hair.

"Small towns," I muttered to myself.

"You're telling me," Marks said.

Ramirez nudged his shoulder. "Check on Anna."

Marks looked like he might lose his lunch. "Her brains are on the wall."

She glared at him until he eased into the office and toward the body. He walked on tiptoes like heavy feet might disturb her. He licked his lips, then lifted her wrist and checked her pulse. Shaking his head, he hurried to glue himself back to his partner's side.

She moved over to put space between them. "Would you ladies step into the hallway for us, please?"

We obliged, moving past them into the dimly lit corridor. I expected at least one of them to accompany us. Instead, Marks stuck his head out, mumbled an apology, and shut us outside.

Muffled voices started on the other side of the door—mostly Marks's voice, high-pitched and frantic, cut occasionally with calmer, steadier words from Ramirez.

Ivy and I exchanged a look. She was all sharp angles and tight lips, her lawyer-slash-FBI mask firmly in place. I tried to match her expression instead of betraying the rising panic in my stomach.

"So . . ." What kind of conversation was appropriate for half sisters meeting for the first time over a corpse? "You see a lot of bodies in the FBI?"

She sucked in a breath.

Deputy Marks emerged from the office, his face flushed. He motioned toward Ivy. "Ma'am, I need you to come with me outside."

As I started to follow, Ivy put her hand on my shoulder. "They're separating us. It's protocol."

"You can sit if you want." The deputy gestured toward a bench against the wall farther down the hall. Instead, I chose the one directly across from Gray Investigations.

He paused, as if considering whether to object, and then led Ivy down the interior stairs. "What's it like in the FBI?" he asked her.

"Ask me another time," Ivy said.

Their voices faded down the steps and out of the building, leaving me alone. I hugged my arms around my waist.

A few minutes later, Marks reappeared with a duffel in one hand and a roll of yellow crime scene tape in the other.

I stood. "How long will I have to wait?" I might not have been able to see Anna's dead body anymore, but it was still only feet beyond that closed door, a hole through the forehead.

"Deputy Ramirez will be out to question you in a moment." He cracked the door open and slipped through before closing it again.

Soon, Ramirez stepped out of the office.

"I'm going to take your statement now. Would you feel

better sitting in my cruiser?" She kicked the hard bench I was sitting on a moment ago. "This can't be comfortable."

I'd been in a cop car once before and had no desire for a repeat. "I'm good."

We sat, and she extracted a flip pad from her breast pocket. "How did you know Anna?"

"I didn't," I said quickly. "She was my dad's assistant, so I knew *of* her."

Ramirez's pen paused over the pad. "Caleb Gray is your father."

"That's what my mom says."

"Don't get cute." Ramirez squinted and scanned my face, taking in the brown skin, the broader nose, and the eyes and chin that Caleb, Ivy, and I all shared. She struck something down on her pad. "You're estranged?"

I grunted. "You could say that."

"I was under the impression Caleb had one daughter."

"Is that a question?"

Ramirez cocked her head and resumed in a monotone. "Were you at the party last night?"

"I got to town today and came straight here. What party?"

"You're not here for Anna's birthday?"

"I told you. I didn't know Anna, let alone when her birthday was." I hoped she had the time of her life, though, because what I saw inside was a terrible way to celebrate.

Ramirez eyed me, her pen hovering over the pad. "Then why are you in town?"

"Anna called me this morning, said Caleb was missing, and asked me to help her find him."

"Why didn't she call the sheriff?"

"Maybe she did. How should I know?"

Ramirez squinted at me and wrote something down. When I tried to peek, she angled the notebook away. "Tell me exactly what happened when you arrived."

I took a deep breath and told her my version of events, starting from when I arrived in the parking lot and finishing with convincing Ivy not to stab me with a letter opener. I skipped the part where I tried to break into Caleb's computer.

"How did Anna have your number?" Ramirez asked without looking up.

"Excuse me?"

"You didn't know her, but she called and demanded you come running?"

"She didn't demand . . . I don't know, but it's not a state secret." I heard the defensiveness in my own tone and pulled a long breath to steady my nerves.

"Why are you in town?" She kept her gaze on her notepad as if the question was unimportant, just making conversation.

I didn't buy it. "I told you. Anna called me."

Ramirez looked up. "If I got a call from my estranged father's assistant saying he was missing, I wouldn't necessarily drop everything."

"She wouldn't call me with such a big ask unless it was important."

"So you *did* know Anna?"

I forced my mouth to slow so my brain could catch up. "Do I need a lawyer?"

"Do you think you need a lawyer?" Ramirez shot back.

"I had nothing to do with her death if that's what you're implying."

"No one said you did."

"This interview is over." I jumped to my feet. "I just want to go home. This place is trouble."

The deputy snapped her notebook closed and stood. "We would appreciate it if you could stay in town in case we have more questions."

"I'm not under arrest, so I can go where I like."

"Of course you can." She locked eyes with me. "But we would appreciate it. Around here, people take care of each other."

"I'll keep it in mind." I didn't have much in my account to sink into a hotel, and it might be tough to find IT work around town as an outsider. Plus, Willow Lake wasn't turning out to be a dream trip so far.

"You're not from around here," Ramirez added. "You'll see." She gave me a nod and headed down the stairs.

Since I was on my way out, I followed at a distance. Outside, Ramirez found Ivy and headed toward her. I felt Ivy's gaze on me as I hurried to my car and peeled out of the parking lot.

CHAPTER 6
ROSE

THE STEAM FROM MY COFFEE CUP FOGGED UP THE WINDOW OF Mugged, the town's one and only coffee shop.

I stuck out my tongue at the sunshine-yellow mug in my hands. Its round bowl shape warmed me while its molded smiley face grinned. Willow Lake might still be a question mark, but with my cozy window seat, the gentle buzz of conversation, and tasty lattes, Mugged was a winner.

My phone vibrated against the wooden table, blasting the *Super Mario Bros* theme. I checked the caller ID, hesitated, then answered anyway.

"Ivy?" I set down the mug and got serious.

"Are you still in town? I need a favor."

"How can asking for a favor be one of the first thousand words we've ever exchanged?"

I could practically hear her grinding her teeth. "Hi, Rosaline. How are you?" Her tune was sickly sweet now.

"I'm good. I found a hotel I can afford for a couple days,

decided to stick around until my money runs out, discovered the coffee shop—"

"How many words are we up to?"

I stifled a smile. "Tell me what you need, and I'll consider it. I don't promise favors until I know what I'm promising."

"Could you—please—go to the sheriff's office and get an update on Dad's case? Please?"

"Yes, I could . . . Why can't *you*?"

A too-long pause and then, "My ex is a deputy."

"And?"

"I don't want to see him."

"You haven't lived here since high school. You're scared of a guy you dated a decade ago?"

"I'm not scared. I just . . . How do you know that?"

"I majored in computer science. There's this advanced technique. It's technical, so I'm not sure you'll understand it. I turned on a computer, opened a web browser, and ran a search for your name."

"You're hilarious."

"I think so. You're an FBI agent. How are you scared of a high school boyfriend?"

"I just don't want to get pulled into a conversation about ancient history."

"Speaking of work, how long are you sticking around before you have to get back?" In theory, I could do freelance IT work anywhere if I could find the customers. I doubted the FBI was so flexible.

The line went silent except for a low crackle of background noise.

"You there?"

"I'm on extended leave."

From what I'd learned about Ivy online, taking time off didn't seem like her thing. "Why?"

"Can we get to two thousand words before we start spilling secrets?"

"Fair." I had no plans to share mine with her either. "Why don't you call and ask? I assume deputies don't man the phones."

"True. But they're going to want to know who's asking. They probably know me over there, which means they know about Jay and me and will probably call him to the phone anyway. Small towns are like that. And you can't call because they don't know you and won't tell you anything over the phone."

"Fine. I'll go down there, but you owe me." It couldn't hurt to have an FBI agent in my debt.

"Great! The sheriff's name is Dan Foster. Ask him these questions." Ivy paused as though waiting for me to grab a pen. "Who is handling the case? Do they have any suspects or leads? Can I help them in any way? When will they clear Gray Investigations for me to go back there?"

"Uh-huh," I said.

"You want me to repeat that so you can write it down?"

"If you want." I rapped my fingers on the tabletop while she gave me her questions again.

"Got it?"

"Yup."

"Let me know what you find out."

We ended the call. I gathered my things, dumped the rest of the coffee into my mouth, and clawed at my throat as it scalded its way down.

A woman tapped my arm as I headed for the door. "Can you drop me at my house? It's on your way."

She was a Black woman, probably in her late sixties. A chain necklace with a chunky stone pendant hung over her red blouse.

I searched her face for the joke but found none.

"Sorry." She stuck out her hand. "Vera Watkins. You're headed to the sheriff's office?"

Still stunned, I shook her offering. "Rose Gray . . . Yeah."

"You're not from around here." To the rest of the coffee shop, she shouted, "Could you assure this young lady I'm harmless?"

Laughter and a couple yells of "That's Vera" and "No harm there" met her request. She turned back to me with an expectant look.

"Why not?" I jerked my head toward the door, and we stepped into the warm fall air.

The parking lot was large for a small-town joint and nearly full this morning. Fallen leaves in shades of red and orange crunched underfoot as I led Vera to my compact black sedan.

She clicked her tongue at the scratch running along the passenger-side front fender and then slid into the seat.

I started the ignition. "Where to?"

"Just head to the sheriff's substation. I'll direct you on the way."

I propped my phone into its holder and started the navigation app.

Vera slapped my hand away. "If you don't know the way, just say so."

I blinked at her. In less than five minutes, she'd stunned me twice.

Vera touched the side button to put my phone screen to sleep. "Take a right out of the parking lot and stay on that road for a minute." She popped open the glove compartment and rooted through it.

I didn't keep anything private in there. I kept my registration in my wallet, just in case someone broke in—no need to give them the registration and my home address on top of the car itself. Still, boundaries were a thing, and I was fond of mine.

I leaned over and shut the compartment.

She huffed. "What brings you to town?"

I chewed my lip and decided no harm could come from this. "My father is missing—maybe. Could be nothing."

She twisted in her seat to stare at me. "Missing, huh? Is that why you're heading to the sheriff?" Before I could answer, she pointed ahead. "Left up here."

"Do you know Caleb Gray?"

"Is that the PI?"

I nodded. "The only one in town—I assume."

"I don't know him personally, but I've heard he's good."

"Any thoughts on who would know what he's been up to?"

"I take it you're not close."

I bit my lower lip.

"Maybe try his wife." She gestured as if reaching for something. "What's her name?"

"Pearl," I supplied.

She pointed ahead. "Left up here."

I turned into a neighborhood. By now, everyone would know about the murder, so no need to hold back. "Me and my sister found Caleb's assistant's body after—"

"Stop!"

I slammed my brakes.

"No, no, no. Keep driving. Take the next right, and it's the house at the end of the cul-de-sac." She gestured me forward, her eyes squeezed shut and her head shaking. "I don't want to hear about Anna Baxter. I've gotten enough of it from every Tom, Dick, and Victor who want to gossip. Terrible, terrible."

"Small town," I said.

"Don't I know it." She pointed to a yellow cottage-style house at the end of the street. "There."

I stopped the car.

Vera stayed put.

I made a show of hitting the automatic unlock button, and all four doors clicked as the locks flipped.

"You should come to the Autumn Festival this weekend," she said. "It'll be a good place to meet people for an out-of-towner."

"Who says I want to meet people?"

"Suit yourself." She popped the door open and stepped out. "Lovely to meet you, Rose. Same time tomorrow?"

"No, I can't—"

She slammed the door and wiggled her fingers goodbye before hurrying to her porch. I watched her until she was safely inside and then started the navigator app on my phone.

Three minutes later, I slid out of the car at the Willow Lake substation of the Oak County Sheriff's Office. It featured a beige stucco exterior and utilitarian design.

The inside gave more of the same—beige walls, a linoleum floor that had seen better days, and the hum of fluorescent lights.

A receptionist with a tight bun typed at her computer, her

fingers a blur. Beside her stood a female deputy in a crisp gray uniform. They looked up as I approached.

"I'd like an update on Caleb Gray's disappearance and the murder of Anna Baxter, please."

"You are?" The deputy's face was impassive and her tone flat.

"His daughter."

"Is that so?" The blank expression stretched into a grin. She called over her shoulder, "Hey, Jay! We've got someone pretending to be Ivy."

A man appeared from behind a divider. Dark-blond hair, hazel eyes, and an easy smile that didn't hesitate. Very home-grown. Very next door. Not my type, but possibly Ivy's. The ex-boyfriend?

"You're not Ivy," he said, eyes narrowed.

"Never said I was." I grabbed my ID from my handbag and held it out. "Rose Gray."

Jay scanned it and stepped aside to let the other deputy and the receptionist do the same. It wasn't a three-person job.

"Uh-uh," Jay said, as more of a challenge than a declaration. "I would know if Ivy had a sister."

"Maybe you don't know her as well as you think. Do I need to give you a whole family tree, or can you update me on the case?"

The female deputy straightened up, and Jay slinked back to where he came from.

"The sheriff is here and will want to talk to you personally." The deputy gestured to the back of the office. "Take a left back there, and it'll be the one with a name on the door."

It was a small substation with a hallway stretching left and right from the back wall. I hooked left and reached the door that said Sheriff Daniel Foster.

The door was cracked open, but I knocked.

"Come in," called a voice that sounded like a lifetime of leather chairs, hunting lodges, and cigar smoke.

I pushed the door wider, and a broad-shouldered man with graying dark hair and a stubbled chin waved me in.

"Have a seat." Despite his voice and title, Sheriff Foster offered a warm smile. He gestured toward a metal-and-plastic folding chair. "Please."

The chair squeaked as I settled into it.

The room was brown and simple. A large wooden desk worthy of a man his size dominated the space. The walls held framed photographs of an array of people I assumed lived in town. In a place of honor over his head hung a photo of him and the governor decked in hunting gear in the woods.

He leaned back in his leather chair. "I assume you're here about Anna Baxter."

"And about my father. I'm Rose Gray."

"Mm-hmm." No surprise at that revelation, so he'd read whatever reports his deputies from yesterday provided. "How are you finding Willow Lake?"

"It's . . ." I preferred the city, but I didn't want to insult the man. "Cozy."

He laughed with a big boom that came from the diaphragm. When he finished, he raised his brows as if waiting for me to speak.

"So . . ." I tried to remember Ivy's questions, but my mouth went dry. I should have written them down. "What's the status?"

"When did you last hear from your father?"

"It's been a while," I said. "Years. There was a bloody letter opener on his desk. Was the blood his?"

"Too soon to say."

"What's taking so long? Do you have other priorities? You get a lot of murders in Willow Lake?"

"Ms. Gray." Foster's tone and expression went flat. "My deputies reported finding Anna's computer on the edge of her desk. It was locked, but the screen was still on as if it had just been used." He leaned back in his chair. "Do you know anything about that?"

Crap. "I might have used it. Like I told your people, I'm here to find my father. I thought the computer would have something helpful on it."

"Did it?"

"Like you said, it was locked. I couldn't get in." The lie rolled off my tongue like butter.

"Uh-huh." He stared at me until I looked down at my hands. "Because you're family and it may be useful to have your cooperation, I'll tell you our working theory."

I looked up.

Sheriff Foster rose to his feet. His height and width made the cramped office feel even smaller. He could have been a former weightlifter and was probably still a frequent flyer at the gym, with only a slight stomach that showed his age.

"As far as I'm concerned," he said, his gaze never wavering from my face, "your father murdered Anna and ran off. That's the working theory until someone convinces me otherwise."

CHAPTER 7

IVY

I PUSHED THROUGH THE FROSTED-GLASS DOOR OF GRAY Investigations. It had been only three days since I'd found Anna's body, and every fraction of my good sense told me to stay away.

On the day she died, I told Anna we weren't family, but there was no season of my life during which she hadn't existed. She was always there.

Except now.

I owed it to her to find out how she died—and why.

Rose was already in the waiting room. She had commandeered Anna's reception desk and shoved the large monitor aside to make space for a sleek, high-end laptop.

She didn't look up. Instead, she gestured at the closed door to Caleb's inner office behind her. "I suppose you're here to clean up."

I bristled but didn't deny it.

We couldn't just leave Anna's brains splattered on the wall.

It was macabre and traumatic, not to mention unsanitary. Still, I didn't appreciate Rose assuming I was the predictable, law-abiding, goody-two-shoes one.

"The sheriff's office called," I said. "They told me the crime scene was cleared."

Rose grunted. "No one called *me*. I've been driving by twice a day to check the progress. Last I saw, they were wrapping up, so I figured they would be out today."

"That was your cue to come back and snoop around?"

She looked up. "Exactly."

I pointed at the computer in front of her. "That's not Anna's."

"It's mine. Anna's is gone."

"Gone?"

"Evidence, I assume. Caleb's is gone too."

I cursed. I'd hoped they'd leave us the computers, but of course not. In a murder involving an accountant and a private investigator, the digital files might be evidence. "Any word on when we'll get them back?"

"Like I said, no one called me. All I know is what's here and what's not."

I headed past her toward the office. The sheriff had surrendered the space, but what was left of the cleaning was on us. Murder wasn't my specialty in the FBI, but I had colleagues who talked, so I had an idea of what to expect.

I reached for the doorknob.

"I wouldn't," Rose said.

I twisted and pushed. "I've seen it already."

The smell hit me first. The sour, metallic odor seeped into every pore and clung for dear life, digging in with claws. While blood spatters stained the chair, desk, and carpet, the worst of it was the grisly mural on the wall.

My stomach clenched. Hot saliva filled my mouth.

I yanked the door closed. My eyes watered, and the stench still clung to my nostrils.

"Told you," Rose said. Her fingers danced across the keyboard.

It took a moment for me to focus on anything except what I'd just seen. Somehow, it was *worse* now without Anna's body there, leaving just the insides of her on the outside—all over the wall.

"They gave me a number for a cleanup crew." My voice sounded distant, robotic.

Rose pointed to the mismatched waiting-room chairs. "You should sit. Sitting helps."

I sank into one of them.

She propped her chin on her hands. "So you don't usually deal with murders. What kind of cases do you handle?"

"Organized crime."

"Like the mafia?"

"Yes."

She cocked her head. "You don't see a lot of murder in that?"

"Not as much as you'd think. Mostly drugs and guns and money. Most FBI agents never see dead bodies."

"Lucky you then, huh?"

"Yeah," I said sarcastically. "It's an honor."

Rose closed the laptop. "What made you want to be an FBI agent?" She stared at me like she could pry open my chest and see into my soul.

I squirmed. "I should call these cleaning people before what's left of Anna stains the furniture."

"Sure. Yeah." Rose gave me a stiff nod and turned back to her computer. She grabbed a pen from the holder at the edge of the desk and stuck it in her mouth.

Chewing objects was a consoling gesture—like pacifying herself. She probably didn't even realize she was doing it, but I recognized the body language from my training.

I didn't care if I'd hurt Rose's feelings. She and I didn't know each other, and I didn't come here to make new friends. As soon as Caleb came home and explained this mess, I would be back in LA. My administrative leave would end, and my life would be back on track.

I pulled out my phone and dialed the cleaning service the sheriff's office recommended.

A perky voice answered, "Anything Goes Cleaning."

The front door to Gray Investigations burst open, and a woman with jet-black hair strode in on a cloud of Chanel No. 5, which, thankfully, drowned the memory of the smell in the back room.

"I'll call you back," I said into the phone before disconnecting. I shot to my feet. "The office is closed. Can I help you with something?"

The woman surveyed Rose and me like we were subjects in her kingdom. She appeared to be in her late fifties, with faint forehead and mouth wrinkles covered by tasteful makeup. The baubles around her neck, wrist, and fingers shouted *money* so loudly the sound echoed.

"Caleb Gray?" Her voice was as crisp as her tailored suit. Without waiting for an answer, she strode toward the office door.

I hurried to block her. "I wouldn't do that."

She raised her chin a notch higher. "It's been four days since I hired him, and I haven't received a single report."

How many reports did she expect in less than a week? "Really, you don't want to go in there." I put myself between her and the door.

She opened her mouth to object, but Rose slid between us. "Your case is our top priority, Ms. . . ."

"Montgomery. *Mrs.* Isabel Montgomery."

"Mrs. Montgomery, of course!" Rose said. "This is Isabel Montgomery," she added to me, as if that was supposed to mean something.

"I want to speak with Caleb Gray. Immediately."

"I'm so sorry for the confusion," Rose said, oozing charm. She flashed a smile that would blind most people and steered the woman to an armchair. "I'm Caleb's daughter—and business partner—Rose, and this is Ivy. Caleb had to leave town on an emergency, but he put me in charge of his most important cases."

"You are not—" I started.

"You are *not* to worry," Rose cut in, throwing me a look. "He explained that your case, in particular, is a top priority."

Isabel's posture relaxed. The appeal to her vanity seemed to be working.

Rose continued, her tone deferential. "We're here to handle your case with the utmost urgency and discretion. If you don't mind me asking, what is your budget for this investigation? We want to ensure we allocate the appropriate resources."

Isabel straightened her jacket and settled into the seat Rose offered. "As I already discussed with Caleb, money is no object. I will pay his hourly fee for as much time as it takes."

"So if we were to spend, say, twenty hours on this case . . ."

"I would pay you the full three thousand, but I expect it would take more time than that."

"Of course." Rose nodded. A grin flashed across her face and disappeared just as quickly. "Plus expenses."

"Exactly," Isabel snapped. "As discussed. Do we have to go over everything again?"

The more Isabel spoke, the more her reputation surfaced from my memories.

The Montgomerys came from old Nashville money that dated back to a slave-owning plantation. Isabel had married into the family after—as rumor had it—she used every cent of her savings on clothing, etiquette lessons, and tickets to rich events to catch the eye of Linus Montgomery. Twenty years later, she inherited his wealth after a heart attack flattened him, much to the distaste of the greater Montgomery family.

"My apologies, Mrs. Montgomery," Rose said. "I understand this must be frustrating, but we want to ensure you get the best results. That's what we do for our VIP clients."

"We're not—" I started.

"We are," Rose said. To Isabel, she added, "Would you mind detailing your case for us again?"

"I already went over this with Caleb." She raised one finger as if to place us on pause, opened her designer bag, and rummaged inside.

"Mrs. Montgomery—" Rose started.

"I must have left my diazepam at home." She snapped the bag closed. "If Caleb is not here, maybe I should go elsewhere."

"No need. We've studied his notes thoroughly." Rose grabbed the chair from behind Anna's desk and dragged it over to sit directly in front of Isabel. "But it's always better to hear details from the source rather than secondhand."

Rose stared at the older woman with utter respect and attention, and Isabel ate it up like a cake topped with buttercream.

"My painting is missing. A Monet." Isabel let that hang in the air. "A treasure. I bought it at auction eleven months ago. Last week, I noticed it's a forgery. It was signed—now, the signature is gone." Her voice quivered.

Her expression deadly serious, Rose said, "Ivy, can you take notes? There may be important clues here."

I almost refused, but I didn't want to make a scene in front of one of my dad's clients. If all went well, he would be back soon and cleared of Anna's murder. He would be ready to get back to work, and blowing up in front of an influential, moneyed client would not help his business.

I sat at Anna's desk and snatched up a notepad and pen.

"Are you sure it was signed when you bid on it?" Rose asked.

"It was signed," Isabel snapped. She straightened her shoulders. "The auction house certified it as authentic before the sale. This means someone there or, worse, someone in my household stole the original and replaced it with that *thing* hanging on my wall."

"Just terrible," Rose said. "I'm so sorry this happened to you."

"The painting is the dearest in my collection. My home won't be the same without it." Isabel looked up at me and then at the notepad in my hand. To Rose, she said, "Shouldn't your girl be taking notes?"

I scribbled the first thing that came to mind: *I'm going to kill you, Rose!* I snapped the notebook closed and set it on Anna's desk.

"Actually." Rose snorted out the word in a suppressed laugh. "This is Caleb's other daughter."

On second thought, I picked up the notepad and jotted a few facts. This case had nothing to do with me, but that didn't mean it shouldn't be well documented. "What's the name of that auction house?" I asked.

"Lakeview Luxe Gallery. It's the only one in town."

I wrote it down.

"Ivy and I will be working this case together under his supervision," Rose said.

"We will not—" I started.

Rose stood. "Thank you for sharing that painful story with us, Mrs. Montgomery." Her voice was back under control, seeping with exaggerated respect.

"I expect progress soon."

Rose nodded, her expression serious, as she led Isabel to the exit. Isabel gave us one last discriminating look before leaving.

The door shut behind her, and I spun on Rose. "What the hell was that?"

"That"—she pointed—"was our invitation to investigate *everyone* in Willow Lake. And get paid for it."

CHAPTER 8

IVY

LATER THAT DAY, THE FAMILIAR HUM OF MUGGED BLENDED LIVELY conversation and the clinking of ceramic cups. The aroma of freshly baked pastries mingled with rich coffee and chocolate. Little had changed in the year since I'd last been here.

"Here's your Earl Grey lavender latte." My cousin Corina set the mug in front of me. Her messy brown bun bobbed as she moved. "Let that cool for a minute."

"Thanks." I stood to embrace her and then settled back in my seat.

Corina Matthews, my cousin on my mom's side, had managed Mugged for the last five years. A young divorcée with a teenage kid, she dreamed of owning this place or a business like it. For now, though, she managed it with twelve-hour workdays that she navigated with a better mood than I displayed on my best days.

"How long are you in town?" she asked. "Another obligatory two-day mom visit?"

Before I could answer, Rose burst through the door, ten minutes late for the meeting *she'd* called. Out of breath, she threw up a wave as she spotted me. Her messenger bag swung at her side and narrowly missed my foot as she dropped it to the floor.

She flopped into the chair across from me. "Sorry I'm late." She glanced up at Corina, who hadn't moved and was eyeing her with zero subtlety.

"You must be Rose."

"And you must be . . ." Rose side-eyed my way for a hint.

Corina stuck out her hand. "Corina. Manager of Mugged." She gestured to the space around us.

Rose obliged with a handshake. "What has Ivy told you about me?"

"Not a thing, but word travels fast. You've been here three days." She winked. "That means everyone knows you down to your credit history."

Rose's eyes went wide for a split second before a casual expression wiped the look away. "That was a joke?"

Corina laughed. "I'm Ivy's cousin, so I guess that makes me your cousin too."

"Technically," I cut in, "Rose is on my dad's side, and you're on my mom's." I pointed back and forth between them. "No relation."

Corina flicked a hand. "Family is family." She pulled a still-seated Rose to her feet and hugged her.

Rose tensed but soon relaxed and returned the embrace.

"Anyway." Corina released her. "I'll see you both at Aunt Faye's dinner on Tuesday?"

I glared at her, and Corina ignored it. I hadn't decided

whether I was inviting Rose. She technically wasn't my mother's family—she was barely mine.

"Now," Corina continued, "stop bothering me. I'm trying to run a coffee shop." She offered a wink before strolling across the room to another table.

An awkward silence fell between Rose and me, punctuated by the clatter of ceramic cups and the hum of conversation around us. This was the moment I was supposed to invite her to the dinner.

"Awkward," Rose mumbled.

I leaned across the table. "I didn't love lying to Isabel Montgomery, but I assume that's why we're here. What's your plan?"

Rose glanced at Corina, who was chatting animatedly with a group of regulars near the counter. "It's a small town, and people gossip. Investigating Isabel's case will give us plenty of opportunities to snoop, maybe figure out what happened to Anna and Caleb."

"I don't disagree, but Georgia has a license requirement for private investigators. It's illegal to operate like one without a license."

"Who says we don't have one?"

I stared at her for a second, waiting for the joke. But she was serious. "No one's going to believe I'm a PI. They know me. They know I'm an FBI agent."

"All they know about me is I'm your sister. I could have a PI license."

I arched one brow. "Do you?"

Rose grinned. "I *could*."

"Why are you being evasive?"

"I'm not. I'm being one hundred percent serious and literal. I *could* have a PI license. Give me a day."

I sipped my coffee. The lavender scent calmed my fraying nerves. "Are you some kind of speed-reading genius who's going to take the licensing exam in the next twenty-four hours?"

She shook her head, and her lips twitched. "Don't need to."

I set the mug down too hard, and liquid sloshed over the side. I dabbed it with a napkin. "Is this like how you tried to hack into my dad's computer?"

"*Our* dad." Rose reached across the table and pulled my mug toward her. Before I could stop her, she brought it to her lips and sipped.

I gaped at her.

"And I don't know what you're talking about," she added.

When she set my mug down, I grabbed it and dragged it to the extreme edge of the table. "You don't have a criminal record." I didn't appreciate how her grin widened at that. "But I know someone who flouts the law when I see them. If you're—"

"I don't think people use the word *flout* in casual conversation."

"If you're going to pull any more of that hacking shit while we're working together," I said, enunciating each word in a loud whisper, "I'm out. I mean it. I can't be associated with anything that even smells illegal."

Rose held up both hands, palms out. "For the record, *again*, I don't know what you're talking about. I promise there will be no hacking on your watch."

"I'm serious."

"I get that." Her face went solemn. "I'm here to find Caleb, and I could use your expertise."

I didn't know what to say to that.

"I need you," she added.

I avoided her gaze by taking another sip of coffee and setting the mug down in front of me.

"What are your thoughts on this theory that Caleb killed Anna and ran?"

"Doubtful." This was more comfortable territory. No promises about how long I was staying or my involvement in any investigation—just theories about what may or may not be going on. "It's predicated on the idea that Dad and Anna were having an affair. Allegedly, he killed her in a lovers' quarrel, perhaps because she tried to break it off."

"You don't buy that, though. You don't think he's a killer."

"Anyone can commit murder with the right motivation, in the right situation, when the right buttons are pushed." I waved a hand. "Dad and Anna were best friends—that's all. For forty years, they were never more than that."

"Sometimes, friends become lovers." Rose nodded down at my hands.

Without noticing, I'd shredded my paper napkin. I released the pieces, shook out my fingers, and placed both hands flat on the table.

"What's on your mind?" she asked.

"There's a lot of history." I sipped the coffee, mostly to stall while I gathered my thoughts. "Anna felt guilty over hiding his affairs all those years. She lied to me. She lied to my mom. She lied to anyone who stopped by Gray Investigations looking for him when he was out banging some new woman."

Rose waited patiently as I swallowed another pull of coffee.

"Anna called me a few years after I left home. I was in college. She was in tears, devastated over the pain she caused my mother, me, and even those women who my dad led to believe he was serious about them. A lot of hurt came out of his affairs, and Anna knew that. She was in a relationship with George Baxter at the time, and she wanted to believe in true love and marriage and all that." I shook my head. "I doubt she would contribute to more hurt by sleeping with him herself, especially now that she's married."

"That puts a different spin on it," Rose said.

"We have to put aside biases during investigations, so I'll try to stay open to the possibility of an affair between them."

"I trust your judgment," Rose said. "If you say Caleb and Anna weren't like that and he didn't kill her, I believe you."

Seconds of silence followed, which gave me plenty of time to think about Anna's body behind my dad's desk. Despite her faults, she didn't deserve that. No one did.

"Why are you here?" I sipped my coffee and pitched the question casually, despite the curiosity churning up my gut. "Why do you even care?"

Rose stared at the table for so long I thought she might not have heard me. Finally, she said, "Caleb has known about me since before I was born. My mom didn't know he was married. When I was a baby, she thought they were planning a life together just as soon as he could get a job in Atlanta."

My chest tightened. Had he been planning to leave my mom back then?

She laughed. "Don't look so distressed. He would never have left you. He was just some guy stringing *my* mom along until *your* mom found out and set him straight." She tilted her forehead toward me. "Then he told us to kick rocks, and I never saw him again."

I gulped my coffee, and it scalded down my throat.

Rose licked her lips. "I want nothing from Caleb except maybe to kick him in the balls. I'm only sticking around long enough to tell him to fuck himself. He owes me that." The words hung between us like the steam from my coffee mug.

"Fair enough."

Rose pulled my coffee toward her, sipped, and cupped the mug between her hands. "Why are *you* still here? Caleb wasn't the king of dads for you either."

As soon as she set my coffee down, I grabbed it. "I promised Mom I'd stay for a bit."

"Right." Rose reached for the mug again, but I held tight. "You're mean," she said.

"Order your own."

"We share a dad. We can't share a coffee?"

"I never offered to share either."

"I don't know what to order, and I like yours." Rose stared at me until I released the cup, and she snatched it up again.

So far, this relationship was not off to the best start. "So you want to use Isabel's missing painting as an opportunity to ask questions around town."

"Exactly."

"And you need my help?"

"You *are* the expert."

"I don't know how long I'll be in town. While I'm here, I see no harm in assisting you while you look into things."

Her smile beamed.

"If we're going to do this," I continued, "and I'm not saying we are—but *if* we are—we will gather evidence for Isabel, analyze it, and do our best to solve her case."

Rose saluted me. "Yes, ma'am."

"I'm serious."

"I understand. This is very serious." She fixed her face into a mock grave expression. "So what's our move?"

"I'll call Isabel and arrange an appointment to tour her manor. We'll see where she keeps the painting, talk to the people she spends time with. That kind of thing. After that, I'll decide if we proceed."

Rose frowned. "Isabel's *manor*? Is that like a plantation? Did they have slaves? Am I even allowed to go there?"

"It's . . . No, it's . . . I don't . . ." My cheeks warmed.

She slapped my elbow. "I'm messing with you, Ivy. Make the appointment. We have two crimes to solve."

CHAPTER 9

IVY

"Here's how this will go." I steered my rental car up the long, tree-lined driveway to Montgomery Manor. "Let me do all the questioning. Observe and report your thoughts later."

"You want me to shut up and look pretty," Rose said from the passenger seat. She fluffed her hair. "Good thing I just deep-conditioned."

"I want you to cooperate with me so we can get this done."

"Don't worry." She pointed ahead. "I know I'm cute, but eyes on the road."

The three-story Georgian-style mansion loomed over us with white stone and black shutters. A large fountain sat in the center of the circular driveway, and water spouted upward as if welcoming us to a grand event.

I parked the sedan, and Rose and I stepped out.

Flowering bushes lined the walkway through a meticulously manicured lawn. Before we could knock, the front door swung open to reveal a tall, lean man with dark hair and blue eyes.

"I'm Blake, Mrs. Montgomery's assistant." He spoke in quick, staccato syllables. He moved aside and waved us into the foyer.

A gleaming crystal chandelier hung from an ornate ceiling medallion. Beyond the entryway, a pair of grand staircases swept up each side of the room to a balcony with a gold-toned railing. A family crest was engraved on the gleaming tile beneath our feet.

"Rose Gray." She gestured toward me. "And this is Ivy Gray. Isabel is expecting us."

I glared at her and stepped forward. Between Rose and me, I was the one with experience. I still wasn't sold on Rose's plan to work for Isabel while we investigated Anna's murder, but the only way it would work was with me in the lead.

"*Mrs.* Montgomery"—Blake emphasized the name while peering down at Rose—"will be with you shortly." He stood with his hands clasped behind his back.

No one spoke for almost a full minute, but Blake made no move to check on his boss's progress.

"So, Blake." Rose gestured up at the chandelier and down at the polished floor. "This place is something, huh?"

"It has been in the Montgomery family for generations."

Rose leaned forward as if expecting more, but Blake clamped his mouth shut and resumed his stoic stance.

"It's nearly perfect," Rose said.

Blake didn't blink.

"Nearly."

His gaze flicked to her and narrowed.

"It could use a water slide. Better yet, has Mrs. Mont-

gomery considered putting a trampoline in here?" She moved
to the wall, placed the back of her heel against it, and put her
other heel right in front of her toes. She walked heel-to-toe
from one side of the room to the other. "About twelve feet
wide? She could fit a giant one in here. I bet you can jump up to
that balcony."

He blinked in rapid succession.

Rose shrugged. "It would be faster than the stairs."

I stabbed her with my elbow. This did not meet the defini-
tion of *observe and report*.

She looked up at the chandelier twinkling above our heads.
"*That* might be a hospital trip, though."

"An interesting suggestion, Ms. Gray," Blake responded, his
face betraying no emotion.

High heels clacked toward us, and Isabel appeared from a
hallway to the right. Her midnight-blue suit cinched at the
waist and fit her hips and shoulders like it was made for her,
which it probably was. She kept her posture as rigid as the
columns flanking the outer entrance.

"Ah, Ms. Gray and Ms. Gray." Her tone hinted at amusement. "Welcome to Montgomery Manor."

"Thank you, Mrs. Montgomery." I stood plank straight,
mirroring her.

She flashed a tight smile before leading us the way she'd
come. Rose and I followed. Blake trailed behind, his steps silent
even with dress shoes on the hard floor.

Isabel pointed out each room, her voice hushed as if to
show honor. "This oaken door leads to the library, where you
can find books spanning centuries." She gestured as we passed.
"It has over five thousand tomes, many first editions."

"Fascinating," Rose said.

I cringed, waiting for a joke to come hurtling from her mouth. To her credit, her face was solemn and respectful now that Isabel was present. At least she knew when it was time to get serious.

Isabel opened a door to reveal a single armchair and an end table, dwarfed by a massive room with a soaring glass ceiling. "It's a cozy sanctuary." She pulled the door closed. "The windows were imported from Italy."

Rose nodded. "Cozy." The edges of her mouth twitched.

"Come." Isabel motioned us to the left, and I could feel us making a circle around the first floor.

"Mrs. Montgomery," Rose said. "Who else lives here besides you and Blake?"

"The servants don't live here," she said.

I peeked at Blake, and he flinched at the word *servants*.

"I live alone," she continued, "since the passing of my husband. Our children are grown and don't stay in town."

"Your household staff includes your personal assistant, Blake Anderson." I gestured at him. "Your maid, Olivia Williams. Your gardener, Ben Carver. Your chef, René Gobert. Anyone else?"

Isabel paused and examined my severe ponytail, gray blazer, slacks, low-heeled pumps. "You've done your research."

"I have."

"All of them are under suspicion." Isabel started walking again and ticked them off on her fingers. "Olivia can be clumsy, but her cleaning is impeccable. Ben keeps the property beautiful, but"—she wrinkled her nose—"his clothes are filthy."

"Doesn't he work outside?" Rose asked. "In the *dirt*?"

Isabel waved a hand. "Chef René can cook a divine meal, but he talks too much."

"Interesting." I walked faster to leave Rose behind us because she was barely containing her laughter.

"Actually," Isabel added, "you should meet my niece Eliza. Blake, would you fetch her from the guesthouse and bring her to my office?"

"Of course." He nodded so low it was almost a bow before hurrying past us down the hall.

"Blake," Isabel added, gesturing after him, "was a poor hire who I whipped into shape. When I first acquired him, he was unorganized and slow to complete his duties. I thought I'd have to let him go, but we perfected his process after the first month."

"Is he okay?" I asked. "He seems high-strung."

"Sometimes, I catch him popping a pill from a bottle of prescription stimulants." She leaned close. "The name on the bottle isn't his."

I gaped, but Isabel didn't seem to notice. She'd just told an FBI agent that her assistant was abusing prescription drugs in the same class as methamphetamines.

"But he's the perfect helper now," Isabel continued, "so who am I to complain?"

Rose sneezed to hide her laughter.

Isabel snapped her face in that direction. "Do you have a cold?"

"Allergies." Rose snorted, suppressing more laughter.

I glared at her.

"Where exactly is Caleb?" Isabel asked. "Such a shame you two have to start over."

"We've read the file thoroughly," Rose said, finally recovered from her laughing fit.

It was a lie. We'd never found the key to the filing cabinets.

"In our experience," I said, "it's best to speak directly to the source. And in this case, that would be you."

"Even if Caleb was here," Rose added, "he'd want to speak to you again, given that you're one of the town's most esteemed residents and a valuable resource."

Isabel tilted her chin even higher.

"Speaking of which." Rose shot me a look. "Is there anyone else in town we should look at? Is there anyone suspicious or dangerous?" She matched her pace to Isabel's and fell into step beside her.

A painting thief wasn't necessarily dangerous, so Rose was looking for our killer.

"No one comes to mind. My guess is the thief is someone from the auction house. I chose every member of my staff personally—despite their flaws."

"But anyone could come and go at the auction house," Rose pressed. "Is there anyone in town who strikes you as dangerous?"

Isabel peered at her down her pointed nose. "The Lakeview Luxe Gallery is open only to the more distinguished towns-people and visitors. I don't imagine any of its patrons would stoop so low as to steal from me."

"What if—"

"Great." I shoved between them before Rose could keep pushing and raise Isabel's suspicions. "We'll focus on the auction house staff, but while we're here, we might as well interview your people."

"Very well." Isabel picked up her pace.

We transitioned to a part of the building with dim lighting and metal filigree covering the walls. Framed in the covering, a massive oil painting stood out as a centerpiece. The portrait depicted Isabel, maybe ten years ago, and a gray-haired man about her age, sitting in high-backed chairs. Behind them stood four older teenagers, who I assumed were their adult children.

Isabel's eyelids softened as she caught me looking at it. "He was a kind, doting man. I miss him every day."

"And the kids?" I asked, even though I knew the answer.

"Here and there across the world."

Much like me, Linus Jr., Kara, Lorelai, and Brent had escaped Willow Lake after high school. Linus ran a real estate development firm and had an obscene net worth. He and his wife donated to all the charities, and their local news outlets praised each donation. Lorelai was a real estate developer engaged to a graphic designer, a woman whose website was surprisingly down-to-earth given her connection to the Montgomery family. Having found a wealthy spouse, Kara was a stay-at-home mom of two who made regular acquaintance with a plastic surgeon. Brent had changed his last name and, despite that, was backpacking across Europe on his trust fund.

None had stepped foot in Willow Lake in the last year, so as interesting as they were, they were innocent of the painting swap.

We reached a staircase, not as grand as the two near the entryway but still sporting wrought-iron railings. Isabel led us upstairs and down a hallway. The second floor had less extravagant decor than the first, but the occasional vase on a pedestal, backlit painting, or sculpture made it clear the selection was just as carefully curated.

Isabel stopped in front of a pair of French doors and threw them open. "My office. This is where I displayed the Monet."

A camera looked down on us from the end of the hall. I

pointed. "Can we get that footage from the period between when you brought the painting home and when you noticed it had been switched with a forgery?"

"You want a year's worth of footage from inside my private home? That's rather invasive, especially since the switch probably happened before it crossed my threshold."

"It would help us exclude everyone in your home," Rose said.

I nodded at her. Nice play.

"I'll think about it." Isabel led Rose and me into her private office.

I took that as a no.

Art pieces adorned the walls, beckoning from every angle. Glittering, gemstone-studded ornate frames displayed exquisite brushstrokes, and golden sculptures glistened in the bright light.

In a place of honor, a miniature painting hung on the wall behind an enormous glass desk. The painting was no more than eight inches on each side, but the vibrant brushstrokes that captured light scattering across a watery surface told me this was a Monet. I was no expert, but I'd loved his work in my high school Art History class.

Isabel stood still, as if giving us a moment to appreciate the art.

"It's gorgeous," I said.

Isabel's nod told me that was the correct response. "Almost as beautiful as the original. Its value would be higher than the rest of these combined."

"Combined, huh?" Rose asked.

I stabbed my elbow into her side.

To me, she whispered, "How much do you think that is per square inch?"

"Here's Eliza," Isabel announced as Blake appeared in the doorway.

He rested a hand on the small of a woman's back and guided her into the room. I'd place her in her early thirties. Her paint-splattered denim overalls and long, loose hair looked out of place amid the ornate furniture and decor.

"Eliza Thompson," Blake said in his fast, clipped tenor, "these are Ivy and Rose Gray. They are investigators with Gray Investigations, here to recover Mrs. Montgomery's Monet."

She gave him a warm smile and offered it to us as well. "Lovely to meet you." She extended her hand.

I shook it, and then Rose did.

"Mrs. Montgomery." Blake straightened his back as if preparing for a military inspection. "I have class. I'll be back in two and a half hours."

"Actually," I said before she could answer, "we were hoping to speak with all the staff today."

Blake tightened his lips but kept his attention on Isabel.

"Go." She flicked a hand.

He dipped his head and backed out of the room.

Eliza reached her fingertips toward Rose's shoulder but withdrew them before making contact. "I did a little research on Gray Investigations, and I'm hopeful. The Monet was an incredible piece."

"It's certainly something," Rose said.

"The original is even better. I hope I'll get to see it again. I'm fond of it."

Isabel scowled and then resumed her pursed, poised expression. "It's not about your fondness for the painting. It's about loyalty. The auction house stole from me after a decade of business together."

Eliza bowed her head. "Of course, Aunt Isabel." She turned to Rose and me. "Stop by the guesthouse if you have any questions for me."

"She moved in for a short spell after her divorce," Isabel said. In a loud whisper, she added, "Two years ago."

Eliza's smile stiffened. "You pushed me to leave him."

"He was a workaholic who took you for granted. You were miserable. Now, you can start fresh, find work, make a life."

"I sell my art. That *is* work."

"Theoretically," Isabel whispered too loudly. "Now that you're down one rich husband, maybe you should reconsider your career path."

With her painted-on smile, Eliza turned back to Rose and me. "Nice to meet you," she mumbled before retreating from the room.

"Would you be a dear and close the door behind you?" Isabel called after her.

Eliza was long gone, so I shut the door.

Isabel's demeanor became more solemn. She walked around her glass desk and sank into the white leather chair, the false painting above her head. She slung her elbows across the metal armrests like a queen on her throne.

"I've had my contacts research the two of you." Isabel's tone was low.

I sucked in a breath but kept my face neutral.

She gestured at the two chairs opposite her, and we sat.

"You are in the FBI. And you"—she picked up a pen and pointed it at Rose—"are self-employed in information technology. Fixing printers and such, I assume."

Rose pulled in her lips but said nothing.

"The sheriff's office has no interest in my painting, and there are no other private investigators as familiar with Willow Lake as you are." She twirled the pen at me.

"So we're keeping the case," Rose said.

"Mm-hmm. But I am not going to pay you."

Rose's feet twitched like she was thinking of leaving.

"Excuse me?" I asked.

"Not with money. With information. *Indispensable* information." Isabel tapped the pen on the desk and drew out the silence.

I leaned forward in my seat.

"I came upon an interesting note in one of Caleb's files when I spoke with him in his office."

"Not *your* file?" I asked.

"A file that was sitting on his desk."

"You were snooping."

"If you like." She twirled the pen in the air. "He stepped away during our meeting to speak to Anna—such a loss, by the way."

It took effort not to roll my eyes. Isabel didn't give a damn about Anna. If she did, she would have said so during our first meeting when she stood in the room where Anna worked, only feet away from her desk.

"I might have peeked at the file sitting on his desk. In a rare clumsy moment, I knocked the top sheet onto the floor. Caleb returned while I was picking it up, and . . ." Pen twirl.

"You hid the page rather than admit you'd been snooping," Rose supplied.

"Again, *snooping* is your word, not mine."

"What's on it?" I asked.

She shrugged. "That *would* be snooping."

"Let me understand." I leaned back and propped one ankle on the other knee. "You want us to give up our fee for your case in return for a piece of paper that may or may not hold information we want."

"I hired Caleb exactly five days ago—the day before Anna's murder and his disappearance. I think there's a fair chance the file on his desk at the time is pertinent to whatever case he was working when those nasty events occurred."

I cast a look at Rose.

Her shoulders slumped, but no objection.

I nodded. "We accept your terms."

CHAPTER 10

IVY

I cleared my throat and stood. "Now that payment has been negotiated, are we okay to interview your staff?"

Without speaking, Isabel gestured to the exit. Rose and I took our cue, and I pulled the French doors closed behind us.

"What are you thinking?" she asked.

I gripped her arm and led her down the hall until we were out of earshot of Isabel and the hallway camera. "The thief probably made the switch here."

"Isabel seems confident it was someone at the auction house."

"The auction house has security personnel in addition to its surveillance." I waved at the camera. "The manor only has those."

"So let's start meeting people. I'll take the upstairs staff, and you work downstairs?"

"We should stick together."

"You don't trust me to do a little questioning?"

"It's called an interview—and no, I don't."

"You didn't want this job." Rose pointed back and forth between us. "I got it for us, and I expect us to be equal partners. I can talk to people without a babysitter."

I pulled her even farther away from Isabel's office door. "I still don't want it, but if we're in, we're all in. We have to be methodical about this."

Rose grinned. "Great. We're all in."

Did I just get tricked into jumping off the fence onto her side? "I'll start downstairs."

She started to walk away, but I grabbed her arm.

"You'll probably run into the maid. Olivia Williams grew up lower class in a small town south of here. This job is a step up from the ones her parents worked. She's going to be desperate to maintain her current lifestyle. Of all the people in this house, she and Blake had the best opportunity to steal the painting from Isabel's office. She cleans in there when no one is around. If she didn't steal it, she might have a guess at who did. House staff members see more than you'd expect because no one pays them attention."

Rose gave me a bored look.

"If you make her feel insecure, like she doesn't deserve nice things, she'll try to prove you wrong. She might even confess if she's the thief."

Rose narrowed her eyes.

I released her. If she didn't get anything useful, I could always re-interview Olivia.

Rose flicked a wave as she headed down the hall. I used one of the curved front staircases to the first level. At the bottom, I followed the smell of food.

The kitchen hit me with the aroma of meat, bread, and something that smelled like a mix of tomatoes and heaven. The room gleamed with stainless steel and polished wood, reflecting the bright overhead lights. The chef stood at the stove in a white coat and poofy hat, talking with his phone outstretched in one hand.

"Ah, we must end this here." A strong French accent made the word *this* sound like *zis*. He wiggled his fingers at the screen. "*Au revoir, mon ami.*"

He turned to me as he set the phone face down on the countertop. It was a high-end one with multiple camera lenses on the back. I'd heard wealthy people often shipped in their chefs, but hiring one all the way from France seemed over the top, even for Isabel Montgomery. And judging by that phone, she paid him well to boot.

I stuck out my hand. "Ivy Gray, daughter of Caleb Gray, owner of Gray Investigations." I preferred not to lie about myself if I could avoid it, and no part of that introduction was untrue. I never said I was a PI, and I never said I worked for Gray Investigations.

The man eyed my hand and turned his back, focusing on a pot on the stove. A wooden spoon stuck out of it. He stirred as he spoke in that thick accent. "Chef René."

"I'd like to ask—"

"Now that we have met," he cut in before I could say more, "you will find that the door to my kitchen is unmoved from when you entered. I must cook."

"Mrs. Montgomery authorized us to interview her staff about her missing painting. She contracted us to locate it." I pulled out a notepad and pen from the inside pocket of my blazer and poised the pen over a page. "Did you ever see the Monet she bought at auction last fall?"

"It is your job to investigate, and it is my job to prepare dinner for twelve this evening."

An unwilling interviewee—I'd have to dig into my bag of tricks for this. "That's tough work. You have to be pretty skilled to manage that, especially at the level of food you prepare."

He puffed out his chest. "I studied at Le Cordon Bleu."

I'd shown empathy and allowed him to flatter himself. That should soften him up. "A professional like yourself must have so much knowledge to share. I'm betting Isabel reaps the rewards without appreciating everything that goes into your food."

His face remained stern, but he thrust an apron at me and pointed to a cutting board laden with vegetables. A chef's knife lay beside it. "If you want my time, you must earn it."

I took the apron. "Do you know anything about Mrs. Montgomery's missing painting?"

René maneuvered around me, plucked a teaspoon from a drawer, and returned to his spot at the stove. He dipped the spoon in the sauce, tasted it, mumbled to himself, and tossed the spoon in the sink.

"Chef René?"

"Do you require an instruction manual for the knife?" he asked in that thick accent.

His expression held no sign of joking, so I tied the apron around my waist and set the notepad beside the cutting board.

"Are you not going to wash your hands?"

As he eyed me, I flipped on the sink, grabbed the dish soap, and scrubbed up to my elbows. He grunted his approval, and I started chopping.

"This is the first I've heard of a missing painting."

I wrote that down with my right hand and brought the knife down with my left. My carrot skidded across the cutting board. I set down the pen and tried to mimic how I'd seen chefs cut vegetables on TV, folding my fingers under and moving the carrot toward the knife instead of the other way around.

René paused his stirring to watch. Amusement twitched at his lips. "Focus on the vegetables, *madame*. The notes can wait."

I looked between Chef René and my notepad.

"The chopping is payment for my conversation, is it not?"

I folded the notebook and slid it and the pen back into my pocket. I picked up the knife and resumed chopping. "Have you heard about any items going missing from the manor?"

"I stay out of house affairs. My domain is this kitchen. Beyond it . . ." He raised his wooden spoon from the sauce and twirled it in the air before he returned to stirring. "Not my business."

I stopped chopping. "Have there been any unusual happenings? Anything out of the norm?"

"My kitchen runs as smoothly as ever." He glared at me. "Except for the occasional uninvited guest. The rest isn't for me to know."

"What about the rest of the staff? Anyone acting oddly?"

He pointed at the cutting board. "Those pieces are too big, and you are slow."

I got back to chopping.

"Everyone does their job and stays out of house affairs."

"And your opinion on them?" I sliced a carrot with more force than necessary.

"Mrs. Montgomery has not complained." He eyed my work. "She *will* complain if the vegetables are not cooked evenly because they are not chopped to the same size."

"They're even!" I wasn't a master chef, but this task wasn't complicated.

"Drop the knife."

I froze.

"Drop the knife and step away from the cutting board before you ruin my meal."

"They're fine," I grumbled but set down the knife and moved away. "Do you know anything about the Lakeview Luxe Gallery?"

"What would I know about an auction house? It exists. It sells art and old books and unnecessary trinkets for the wealthy." He adjusted the heat below the sauce as he stirred with the other hand.

"Do you know of anyone suspicious or with a criminal history in town?" The painting swap was likely a crime of convenience, but knowing about anyone with a dangerous reputation might give us a start in figuring out what happened to Anna.

"There's some gambling, petty drugs, nothing huge." As an afterthought, he added, "None of those types cross into Montgomery Manor."

"Do you know who runs the gambling, the drugs?"

He shook his head and *tut-tutted* at his sauce.

Time to take a leap. "Did you know Anna Baxter?"

He raised the wooden spoon from the pot, set it on a small plate beside the stove, turned to face me for the first time. "I didn't know her well. She did my taxes."

"Did she do anyone else's?"

"Everyone's. It's a small town. We don't have many accountants . . . and even fewer now." He muttered something in French and shuddered before leaning closer. "Have you heard anything?"

I leaned away. "Why would I?"

"You work for the FBI, no?" For the first time, his attention locked on me instead of his sauce. "And Anna worked for Caleb Gray. Your father, you said, yes?"

I cocked my head.

"As I said, it is a small town." He shrugged. "Ivy Gray, daughter of Caleb Gray, owner of Gray Investigations." They were the exact words I'd used to introduce myself.

I didn't think he'd been paying attention. Chef René was more astute than he looked.

Once again, René smoothly sidestepped me and extracted a small metal spoon from the drawer. He brandished it like a swordsman. "Are we done, now that you've destroyed my food and my good mood?"

This was a *good* mood?

He danced to my other side and dipped the spoon in the sauce. "Perfect." He set the dirty spoon in the sink beside his previous taster.

"Have you heard anything about my father's disappearance?"

He quirked an eyebrow. "Do you not think he killed Anna and ran off? They were having an affair, yes?"

"I've heard."

For a man who claimed not to concern himself with things outside this kitchen, that sounded a lot like gossip.

"If you hear anything about the painting, any stolen items in the manor, or about Anna or Caleb, would you give me a call? I'll write down my number."

"I don't need the number. Gray Investigations is right down the road."

I made my exit and hoped Rose was having better luck.

CHAPTER 11

ROSE

As I wandered the halls of Montgomery Manor, I dragged my fingers along the hip-level molding that led from one overdone room to the next. I ducked into a room with a stone fireplace that stretched across the entire wall. Level with my head, the mantle alone looked like it could flatten an eighteen-wheeler.

I knocked on it and got a flat thud. Definitely not hollow.

That was a lot of stone. Must have cost a small fortune—maybe a *big* one.

Above it, a framed painting of a mythological garden scene spanned twelve feet. I stepped back to take in the whole thing: topless maidens, satyrs, and horned entities galore.

"I bet you cost more than a year's rent," I told the giant eyesore.

My leg bumped something behind me, and I whipped around to catch the side table before it toppled over. The vase on top wobbled. I lunged for it too late—the vase crashed on the polished floor.

I froze.

As if on cue, a figure appeared in the doorway. Judging by her traditional black-and-white uniform and the irritation pinching her dark-skinned features, I guessed she was the maid.

"What broke?" she asked in a tone that was sharp, efficient, but not unkind. Her pressed and curled hair was pinned into a tight bun.

"I'm sorry." I bent and started collecting the pieces. "I knocked over a vase. I didn't mean to—"

"It's fine." When her face relaxed, she looked younger, not much older than me. She brought a duster and dustpan from behind her back and knelt beside me.

"I'm so sorry." I added the shards I'd collected to her dustpan.

"Accidents happen." She flashed me a smile.

"You must be Olivia." I extended my hand. "Rose Gray."

She took a firm grip and shook. "Nice to meet you, Ms. Gray."

"It's just Rose."

I reached for another vase shard, but she swatted my hand away. "You're a guest. This is my job."

Technically, I was a contractor, not a guest, but no need to tell her that just yet. I leaned against the side of a nearby chair with ornamented wooden rails that looked hand carved. "Did you grow up around here?"

She finished picking up the larger pieces and gave me a questioning look.

"I'm new to Willow Lake," I said, "and still figuring out the town."

"No, not here. Hours away." Luckily, she was too formal in

her role to ask me what I was doing in Montgomery Manor. We'd get to that.

"It's nice here, though?" I gestured at the expensive decor. "Lots of breakable things."

She chuckled as she swept up the smaller pieces. "Money can buy nice things."

Contrary to Ivy's proposed strategy, I didn't want Olivia to feel insecure. "My family didn't have much when I was coming up. It was just me and my mom. She worked two jobs, and I helped out after school."

Olivia scanned me, from coily hair to well-loved tennis shoes. "It's not easy. Takes a lot of work to get out and make something of yourself."

"Absolutely. Is that what brought you to Willow Lake? Work?"

Olivia pulled an empty plastic trash bag from a pocket and dumped the contents of the dustpan into it. "I saw the job posting online. Isabel pays well enough, and the hours are reasonable." Her tone was measured, her words picked with precision.

"And you like her?"

She shrugged.

Time to dive in. "I work for Gray Investigations. We're investigating Isabel's missing painting."

In robotic jerks, Olivia brushed the last shards off the pan into the bag and popped to her feet. "I don't know anything about that."

"But you heard it was swapped with a fake?"

"The house is big, but the town is small. I heard."

"You must have access to the office to clean in there. Have you seen anything odd?"

"I'm paid not to notice things, and I'm good at my job."

"But you have access to the office?"

"Only when Mrs. Montgomery is in there. No one is allowed in her office without her." She paused for a second, and then spun toward the doorway. "I'm finished here, and I have other rooms to clean. It's a big house."

She slipped out, leaving me alone again.

I stuck out my tongue at the eyesore painting and left the room too. Isabel said she had four members of her house staff: the chef, the maid, the gardener, and her assistant. The chef would be downstairs in Ivy's domain, and the gardener would be outside.

The assistant must have an office somewhere.

The upper floor was a maze of rooms, each grander than the last. This place could have been a museum.

I opened a door and peeked inside to find a small office, which might have been designed to be a large broom closet. Unlike every other room, it lacked windows and was no more than ten feet on each side.

A sleek wooden desk sat near one wall, with a rolling chair behind it. Behind that, books on business, wealth, and management filled a bookcase. Every spine was aligned with the edge of its shelf. An armchair sat in the corner beside a side table with a reading lamp.

The top of the desk was bare except for a nameplate and a leather-looking pen holder with several blue pens sticking out. I raised the nameplate and read it: Blake Anderson.

I maneuvered around the desk to the bookshelf and pushed two books out of alignment, just for kicks. Blake would be pissed.

I opened a desk drawer to find it empty, meaning Blake

kept his notes and calendars in digital. That made it harder to find anything useful here.

As I left, I closed the door just as I'd found it.

Maybe Ivy would have better luck with the chef, but I doubted it. Olivia seemed well-drilled on minding her own business. The chef had probably received the same training.

Halfway down one of the two main staircases, I reached a massive picture window. Across the property's lush garden, the guesthouse looked quaint next to the manor's over-the-top luxury.

Eliza had not gone back to the guesthouse. I couldn't see her expression or hear her at this distance, but she stood on the garden path. Her fisted hands trembled at her sides.

Her companion had medium-brown skin that caught the sun in just the right way. A black tee stretched over a chest that deserved attention. I leaned closer to the glass.

"Hello, you," I said, even though the man couldn't hear me.

Their conversation, though inaudible, was heated. Eliza leaned forward, and her mouth moved quickly. She threw up an open hand as if to slap him but then let it fall.

The man was ice. He wore an impassive expression as natural on him as his black leather jacket. He kept his shoulders square, feet planted, and arms folded in front of him.

Eliza stomped toward her guesthouse. The man followed at a measured pace, letting Eliza leave him behind.

"Any progress?" Ivy called up from the bottom of the staircase.

I motioned for her to join me. "You first."

She did and leaned against the railing, taking in the garden view. "I spoke with Chef René. He knows more than he says but didn't take the painting."

"I need details, Ivy, not just conclusions. Is that the kind of report you give at work?"

She scowled. "You think you're at the level of my FBI supervisor?"

"I'm at least at the level of your partner." I grinned. It was so easy to push Ivy's buttons that it was almost unsporting.

Her lips pinched, but she nodded. "He claims not to pay attention to gossip, but he perked up and probed for details when I mentioned Anna. He says he knows nothing about the painting because it's not his business, but I don't believe him. He loves gossip, so he's paying attention to any news about a crime at his workplace."

"You don't think he did it?"

Eliza and her mysterious companion hadn't returned to the garden, which was now empty. This window gave a sliver view of the circular driveway at the front of the house. An older-model black sports car sat behind Ivy's car. It was a sunny fall day, so the driver's window was cracked down.

"Not based on my read," Ivy said. "He's too proud. It would be beneath him to steal from his employer. Did you find the maid?"

I pointed at the black car. "That looks like it belongs to a handsome but shady-looking Afro-Latino who wears a lot of black and looks like he hits the gym every day, right?"

"What?"

"Never mind. Olivia, yeah. I summoned her by breaking a vase."

"You broke—"

"Do you want to hear this or not?"

Ivy shut her mouth.

"She's friendly but focused on her job. She clammed up when I mentioned the painting."

"What was her body language?"

I mimed a robot, sweeping up vase pieces in jerky swipes of a duster.

Ivy sighed. "Use your words, please."

"She was friendly at first, relaxed, conversational. She rushed and took off after I asked."

Ivy raised an eyebrow.

"In her defense, maids are always the first suspects when something is stolen. She could be sensitive to that."

"Fair enough, but we'll keep an eye on her."

I held my hand out. "Give me your car keys."

Ivy blinked, taken aback. "It's a rental. No one else is authorized to drive it."

"You don't trust me."

"I don't know you!"

"I agreed to let you drive us here instead of taking my car, so you can't leave me stranded now." With my other hand, I pointed at my open palm.

"What are you . . . ?" She blinked some more. "I'm not leaving anyone stranded. I'll drive you back to your hotel."

"I checked out of the hotel." I pointed at my palm again.

"I'm not giving you my keys, Rose."

I grinned. "No problem. Can you run an errand for me, and I'll wait here?"

"You want me to—what?" She sputtered, and then realization washed over her face.

I'd backed her into a corner. Between refusing to let me drive and agreeing not to leave me stranded, she'd all but committed to handling any car-requiring duties.

"What do you need?" she asked in a flat voice.

"Run to the nearest drugstore and buy a prepaid phone."

"Don't you have a phone?"

"A prepaid one? No, not on me." I gently turned her around and gave her a light shove toward the front door. Shaking her head, she stomped down the rest of the stairs and went.

Ten minutes later, I was pacing at the top of the circular driveway when Ivy's rental car pulled back up.

She stepped out and shoved the packaged phone into my hands. "Happy?"

"Delighted." I tore off the wrapping and fished my phone out of my handbag. It took less than thirty seconds to scan the QR code from inside the box and get the prepaid device activated online. I handed the package remnants back to her. "Read me the number."

Mechanically, Ivy read the digits, and I punched them into my personal phone. The prepaid in my other hand rang, and I answered it. I strolled over to the black sports car, reached my arm through the cracked-open window, aimed for the space between the seat and the door, and dropped the prepaid.

Ivy's mouth fell open. She ran to my side and pressed her nose against the tinted glass. "What did you do?"

"Is it unclear?"

Her face went so red I thought she'd burst into flames.

I took a large step back before switching my personal phone to speaker. "Now we can hear everything that goes on inside that car."

Her chest rose and fell twice.

I took another step back. I was bound to push her too far eventually.

"Rose," she said, her voice level despite her pink face and

pumping chest, "that is extremely illegal. You can't bug someone's car without a warrant, and we don't even know who this guy is or whether he has anything to do with our case."

"That's the beauty of a burner phone. It can't be traced back to us."

Ivy tried the door, but it didn't budge. She stuck her arm through the window and stretched downward, her fingers waggling inside the car. "It's not about getting caught." She grunted and strained. "It's illegal and unethical, and I don't want any part of it."

"If we get caught, your FBI buddies can help us."

She pulled her hand from the car, still phoneless. "I'm on administrative leave. I can't afford to get in any more trouble."

"Wait, what? Why?" Based on my years of research and days of knowing her, Ivy was the most responsible, capable, rule-following person I knew—granted, the bar wasn't high. The FBI was lucky to have her.

She released a long, eyes-closed sigh.

Footsteps crunched the gravel behind me, and Ivy's eyes popped open. I turned toward the noise.

The mysterious man from the garden sauntered toward us from the side of the house. He glared at us, especially at Ivy, who stood only a few feet from his car.

"Can I help you?" His tone was low and vibrating, dragging out each word.

"Is this your car?" I hit him with a flirtatious smile and batted lashes—anything to distract from the fact that Ivy was in spitting distance of his car.

His attention bounced to me, and Ivy took the opportunity to slide a few more feet away.

"I always liked this look over the newer ones. It's a V8?"

The man gave me an appraising look that started at my feet, lingered around my midsection, and ended at my eyes. There was a silent standoff until, finally, he nodded. He pressed a button on his key fob, stepped around Ivy, and opened the door. Without another glance, he slipped inside and took off.

I watched his taillights glide down the hill away from the manor. "It looks like we have our first suspect."

CHAPTER 12

IVY

Rose and I stood in the driveway of Montgomery Manor as the black-clad man's car sped away.

She waved her phone at me and muted the active call, still connected to the prepaid one inside the vehicle. Through her speaker, the soft hum of the car's engine mixed with strains of mellow jazz. "Nice music."

I backed up. "Get that thing away from me. I want nothing to do with this."

"Don't you want to hear why I did it?"

I eyed her.

"Before you caught up with me, I saw that guy arguing with Eliza in the garden. It got heated, she stalked off to her guesthouse, and he followed."

"Hmm," was all I said because I didn't want to admit it was a reasonable lead, more than anything else we had. It still didn't justify illegal surveillance.

"What do you think it was about?" Rose hopped from foot to foot, too excited to contain herself.

"We could have asked Eliza," I said dryly. "That's normally how investigations work."

"We *could* have. But if the argument was about the painting, she would lie."

Probably true, but not an excuse. "Let's head out." I'd had more of Rose than I could handle for the day.

I slid into the driver's seat of my rented sedan, and Rose climbed in on the passenger side. She slumped into the seat with the phone near her ear. The other end of the line remained silent except for the background noise.

I started the car and headed down the long, private drive that isolated the manor and a few other mansions from town. On Rose's phone, the music ended, and a new piece started, also jazz.

She squirmed in her seat.

"I wouldn't have pegged him for a jazz enthusiast," I said. Even as the words slipped free, I regretted speaking them out loud. I could not afford this kind of trouble. It was better to completely separate myself from what Rose was doing, and that meant *not* making observations and taking advantage of the situation.

Rose glanced at me, her expression as serious as I'd ever seen it. "Sometimes people aren't what you expect."

A phone rang inside the man's car, and Rose sat up so abruptly the seat belt locked. She relaxed and then yanked it until it released so she could sit up straight.

The jazz quieted. "Adrian," the man said by way of introduction. His voice sounded far away and muffled.

Rose mouthed his name to me. I shook my head and put my attention back on the road.

She stared at the phone screen, and Adrian's smooth baritone filled the car. "I got half the money. Eliza is no longer an issue."

I gripped the steering wheel tighter.

"Yeah, I can do math," Adrian said. Agitation slipped into his tone. "I know how much is left."

"This is private," I said. "We shouldn't be listening."

Rose shushed me again.

"Even if it's relevant to our case, we can't use any information obtained illegally. And if it's not relevant, it's none of our business."

"Maybe," she said.

"*Maybe* it's illegal or *maybe* it's not our business?"

"Maybe," she said again in a too-sweet tone that I would bet my left arm was designed to irritate me.

Adrian's voice rose. "No, *you* listen. She promised to have the other half in a week. Whatever you're thinking, it won't be necessary. It's handled, okay?"

My hands clutched the steering wheel tighter with each word. "We shouldn't be listening to this."

Rose rotated her body away from me. "This is good stuff."

My frustration peaked, and my right arm shot out. I tried to snatch the phone from Rose, but she rolled to face the window and tucked it under her.

"Shut that off!" I swiped at her again.

She smacked my hand away.

The car swerved.

Rose screeched. "Watch the road!"

I slapped both hands back on the wheel and righted the car

in the lane. My hands trembled, and my heart pumped like it was on steroids.

I pulled in a long exhale before I spoke. "If Eliza stole the painting, she'd be able to pay Adrian and whoever he works for. Since she can't . . ." I removed one hand from the wheel to gesture at the phone. "This call has nothing to do with us. Can we please stop eavesdropping?"

"Would you be quiet so I can listen?"

"I said I'll take care of it," came Adrian's voice.

"Maybe she hasn't been able to sell it yet," Rose said.

"It's a theory," I said. "But without more information, we're just guessing."

Adrian cursed.

Rose and I shut up, and I willed myself to keep my attention on the road.

"Let me call you later," Adrian said.

There was a sound of fumbling, rustling, and Rose tipped her face closer to the phone as if that would help her figure out what was happening.

"Who the hell is this?" His voice was loud and clear, right next to the speaker.

Rose gasped. Her grip loosened, and she bobbled the phone to keep from dropping it. "Should we say something?" she whispered, even though the call was on mute.

"No way," I said.

Rose extended a finger toward the screen, but I was quicker this time.

I snatched it from her grasp and dropped it in the driver's side door pocket. "You've antagonized him enough." I didn't disconnect the call, though. We were no longer anonymous eavesdroppers. We were just two parties having a conversation, and nothing was illegal about that.

Adrian's voice filled the car, icy and threatening. "That's what you were doing near my car . . . I see you."

Rose pulled her legs into her seat and wrapped her arms around them.

"Stay out of my business," he said, "or you won't like what happens next." The call disconnected.

CHAPTER 13

ROSE

I STOPPED MY CAR IN FRONT OF VERA WATKINS'S COTTAGE. THE yellow paint stood out like a sunflower wrapped in a white picket fence. Two rocking chairs sat in the shade of the porch's extended roof, yelling for folks to come, sit, and rock for a while.

Roller bag in hand, I headed for the door.

Across the street, a gray cottage buzzed with activity. A male couple was moving in, and a large truck hogged that side of the street. Two workers wrestled a couch from its loading door while one of the new neighbors played traffic cop, directing it inside. His husband maneuvered through the chaos with a tray of lemonade, which he set on a side table in the driveway.

My roller bag clunked over the step to Vera's front porch, and I knocked.

Vera swung the door open and hit me with a contagious grin. She looked cozy in leggings and an oversized sweater. An orange tabby stood at her feet, its tail flicking like a metronome.

"Whoa." I made myself big in the doorway to keep the cat inside.

Vera laughed. "Don't worry about him. He comes and goes as he pleases. Blocking the door won't help."

She yanked me into a hug. I left my arms slack, but she squeezed until I gave in and returned it.

"Welcome, welcome." She pulled me inside and closed the door.

"I know this is an imposition, but I promise it's just for a few days. I'll be the perfect tenant."

She pointed to the stairs on the far side of the living room. "I'm happy for the company. Your room is up the stairs, the only one to the left with a bed. I converted the other one to a cardio room." She marched in place, swinging her fists like a soldier. "Got to stay fit for all my gentleman callers."

"I can respect that."

She took in my wide-legged, ripped jeans, fitted graphic T-shirt, and wild curly hair. "Should we expect any gentleman callers for you?"

"Definitely not. I don't date gentlemen. They get attached."

Vera stepped aside and gestured for me to follow her to the stairs.

A camera pointed down at us. I jabbed a finger up at it and fixed Vera with a stern stare. "What is that?"

"Oh, don't worry. There aren't any cameras in your room. I promise I'm not that kind of landlord."

"Home security systems are one of the main ways other people spy on you. They take away more privacy than they provide."

Vera stared at me, her face blank, like I spoke a different language.

"The cameras are on your wireless network, I assume. Anyone on the network can use them to spy on you. The company that manages your security doesn't even need to break into your network. They can peek anytime."

"All the more reason to hit my cardio." She rotated one way and then the other, showing off her assets. "Gotta give them a good show."

I could joke about many things, but cybersecurity was not one of them.

Vera straightened up and matched my seriousness. "It's for my cats." She pointed to her feet, where two felines followed her like baby ducks.

I hadn't even seen the second one show up, all black and looking like an adorable little void. I reached down to pat it, but it bared its teeth.

"He's very protective." Vera reached down, and the black cat purred against her palm.

"It's okay, kitty," I said. "I'm trying to keep your mom from getting raped and robbed in her own home."

Vera gasped.

"Is your wireless network secure, at least?"

"It came fully secured with a password and everything." Vera stood straighter and grinned, pleased with herself.

"You're using the default password?" I screeched. I brought it down several notches before adding, "The one that came with the router? The one that's written on a sticker on the bottom?"

Vera ducked her head.

"No. Absolutely not. Do you have a stepladder?"

She pointed behind me. "In the coat closet."

I set my bag upright on its wheels and opened the closet. I carried the stepladder to the spot below the camera, climbed onto it, and removed the battery.

I returned the stepladder to the closet and dropped the battery into my coat pocket. "You'll get this back after I've secured your network."

Vera looked sufficiently cowed.

I stuck out my hand. "Turn over your phone."

"You can't take my phone away too," she whined.

"I just want to make sure it's locked."

She held out her phone, and I snatched it away. I pressed the side button to wake it, and her home screen lit right up.

"You don't have a password on this."

She tried to grab the phone back, but I dodged out of the way.

"I'm going to give it back." I navigated to her security settings and opened the option to add a fingerprint lock. "Right here. You're going to press here until the phone confirms that it has recorded your fingerprint." I handed the phone back.

She clutched it to her chest as if it were a one-of-a-kind diamond.

I pointed at the screen. "Fingerprint. Go."

The doorbell rang.

Vera flashed me a sly smile before pressing the button to put the phone back to sleep and hurrying to the door.

She opened it to her new neighbors from across the street. One wore salt-and-pepper hair like it was the latest trend, trimmed around the temples and paired with a manicured goatee. Clean-shaven and taller, his partner offered a bright smile with white teeth that had to be veneers or, at least, dedicated visits to the dentist.

The clean-shaven man held out a cheesecake on a colorful ceramic plate. The plate said homemade, but the whipped cream, strawberry jam, and graham cracker crumble artfully arranged on top would make this cake the envy of a high-end bakery.

"For our new neighbor," the other said. "I'm Lawrence Miller-Young, and this is Paul." He pointed to the activities across the street at the gray cottage. "We're the cause of all this trouble."

"Vera Watkins." She lifted the dessert out of Paul's hands. "Isn't the tradition for the old neighbors to bring food to the new neighbors, not the other way around?"

Their laughter harmonized, with Lawrence taking the melody and Paul chiming in with the baritone.

"Most don't bother," Lawrence said, "and that's fine. This way, we meet all our neighbors and start things off deliciously."

Vera stepped aside and opened the door wider. "Please. Have a slice with us."

"We'd love to, but we wouldn't want to leave the movers unsupervised."

"Not that we distrust them," Paul chimed in. "But we'd be devastated if they put our furniture in the wrong places."

Lawrence took his hand. "*Paul* would be devastated. I honestly couldn't care less."

"You care because I care."

They stared into each other's eyes.

Vera cleared her throat. "Then I'll take a rain check."

"We have an ulterior motive for coming over," Lawrence

said. "We were hoping to get your advice on contractors around town. Lawn care, handymen, that kind of thing."

I grabbed my roller bag and retreated from the door. I could check out my room while they chatted. Then I could get back to making sure Vera's home wasn't a target for anyone with a computer and a bad attitude.

As Vera promised, the room was to the left at the top of the stairs. The sage walls matched the earthiness of the handmade quilt on the bed. When I pulled the yellow curtains aside, a large window showed off a view of the garden that wrapped around the whole house.

I set my bag on the floor and unzipped it. I pulled out my lingerie bag, opened it, and dumped my socks and underwear into the dresser's top drawer. My tops and pants found a home in the second drawer. Everything else went into the third. Vera had enough foresight to leave a few hangers in the closet, but I hadn't brought anything worth the trouble.

"Rose!" Vera called from downstairs. "Come try this cheesecake. It's amazing." As an afterthought, she added, "The neighbors are gone."

I closed the dresser, zipped my empty suitcase closed, and headed downstairs.

In the kitchen, my gaze went to the camera installed above the refrigerator. "Absolutely not."

"No one wants to spy on me, Rose," she called to my back as I stomped through the living room to the coat closet to retrieve the stepladder.

I relieved the camera of its battery, just like the last one, and put the stepladder back.

In the kitchen, Vera pushed a fork and a small plate of cake at me. "Eat."

We sat at the kitchen table, and I put a bite in my mouth. It slid across my tongue like sweet, buttery heaven. "Oh my God," I moaned even before swallowing.

"Right!"

"Who bakes like this?" I sliced off another piece and shoved it in my mouth.

"So, what's it like being a private investigator?" she asked.

I forced myself to swallow.

"Is that why you're obsessed with home security? I didn't realize Caleb had a partner—let alone another daughter."

I jammed another forkful of cake in my mouth to stall. "It can be tedious sometimes and exciting sometimes. It depends on the case."

If she asked about specifics, I'd have to lie even more, and Vera was too nice for me to add more fibs to the pile I was growing. But I didn't know her well enough to trust that she wouldn't tell anyone I *wasn't* a private investigator. I was here to find Caleb.

"Thanks so much for letting me rent your room. It's so much cheaper than the inn. More comfortable too."

"It's no problem at all. A pleasure."

My phone vibrated across the kitchen table. I snatched it up and checked the display. "Excuse me." I took the call in the living room. "Hey, Ivy. What's going on?"

"I'm thinking we could meet around nine tomorrow morning to check out the auction house. Should I pick you up, or will you need your car to buy burner phones?"

I ignored her sarcasm. "I'll text you the address."

"What time should I—"

"On second thought, we can cover more ground if we split

up. Why don't I go back to Isabel's and try to catch whoever we missed today?"

There was a pause long enough that I pulled the phone away from my ear to confirm we were still connected. Ivy probably figured I could do less damage if we stuck together.

"Partners, remember?" I said.

"Yeah, right. Let's check in afterward to see where we stand."

Splitting up was the most efficient way to handle this. The faster we wrapped up this case, the faster I could stop lying.

CHAPTER 14

IVY

THE LAKEVIEW LUXE GALLERY HAD NO VIEW OF THE LAKE, BUT IT WAS certainly luxe.

The auction house wore a white stone facade. Its wide oak door spoke of wealth and exclusivity, while the silver-lettered sign promised refinement. Tall tinted windows hid the inside, which only ratcheted up the tension I felt waiting to get in there.

I'd had plenty of time to examine the outside over the last ten minutes as I waited for the auction house to open.

I'd also had plenty of time for research.

For over six decades, the Lakeview Luxe Gallery was the crown jewel of Willow Lake's small but enthusiastic arts and antiquities scene. Founded in 1958 by local entrepreneur Earnest Greenfield, it established itself as one of the preeminent Southern auction houses. Under three generations of Greenfields, the house built a legacy of delivering the finest *objet d'art* and investment pieces to its exclusive clientele.

Finally, my phone's screen flipped from 8:59 to 9:00 a.m. I smoothed the front of my hair, which I'd twisted into a loose chignon for this occasion, and straightened my favorite blazer. I marched to the door.

Inside, the place smelled of polish and old books. Royal blue walls and hardwood floors reflected the soft glow from spotlights highlighting paintings and sculptures throughout the main hall. The ceiling soared high above, and I felt tiny in the grand space.

The place was empty except for a slender Asian woman standing near the front of the building, arms behind her back as if she were a soldier. Her long black hair was tied up, accentuating high cheekbones and deep brown eyes that cut through me.

Mina Lee, assistant to owner Irving Greenfield, had held this role for over two years. The daughter of Irving's good friend, Mina was likely hired due to that relationship. Online articles from that time mentioned a brief stint of chaos in the form of misprinted item lists, missing hors d'oeuvres, and even a public mid-auction argument shortly after her hiring. But eventually, she settled into the job and became Irving's right hand.

I saw none of that disorganization now in her stern, stiff posture and polite expression.

Mina didn't move a fraction as I approached.

"Is Irving Greenfield available?"

"I'm sorry, but Mr. Greenfield is booked for the entire day. I'm Mina, his assistant." The woman's words had sharp points. Crisp, businesslike, wasting no time. She gestured toward her desk in the back of the space. "I can schedule an appointment."

A door behind her desk opened, and a man stepped out. I knew from online photos that it was Irving.

His presence was as distinct as his reputation. The sharp suit matched the refinement of his gallery. His steel-gray hair, combed back neatly, gave an air of authority that was impossible to miss from across the room.

"Never mind," I said. "I see him."

I tried to step around Mina, but she slid in front of me. "Mr. Greenfield is unavailable."

She was smaller and thinner than me, but her sharp expression warned that she would not hesitate to escort me out. I didn't want to make a scene, so I let her block me.

Irving raised a hand and strode toward us.

I straightened my blazer.

"Mina," he said, "did you move Mr. O'Connell's appointment to this morning? I thought it was tomorrow."

"He left a voicemail overnight saying he couldn't make it, so I put him in your first available. It was either that or two weeks out. Should I reschedule him?" She hurried in the direction of her desk without waiting for his answer.

"No, no, you made the right call."

Mina did an about-face and rejoined us.

"Do you have a moment to review his items with me?" he asked.

"Of course."

I cut between them. "I'm here on behalf of Isabel Montgomery."

"Isabel?" Irving looked at my face for the first time. "And you are?"

"Ivy Gray. Mrs. Montgomery has hired Gray Investigations to recover a painting you sold her last year."

His face went grave. "The Monet."

"Then you've heard. It was replaced by a forgery, either at her home or here."

Irving's lips tightened. "No switch happened here. Every item we sell has been authenticated and remains secure until it is transferred to its new owner."

Mina placed her fingertips on his shoulder. "Mr. O'Connell will be here in thirty minutes."

"Right. Of course." He shot another look my way, and irritation deepened his features. To Mina, he added, "I'll see you in my office in two minutes."

She retreated to the back of the hall, but her gaze lingered on me as she went.

I took out my notepad and pen. "Could you walk me through your security process, from when you receive a new piece to when it changes hands to the new owner?"

"Our process is beyond reproach and has been for decades," Irving said.

I waited for him to say more, but he apparently expected me to take his word for it. He had to be outgoing and charismatic for a job like this. A man like that would be prone to finishing my sentences if I gave him a running start. "Of course. When a piece is delivered to you, your people immediately . . ." I waited.

He sighed. "We immediately lock it in our secure holding room."

"An establishment as reputable as yours must have surveillance covering the full path from receiving to the locked room."

"And from the secure room to the auction. Additional cameras cover the front door. Most pickups take place there."

"Most?"

"Larger items can be picked up at the loading bay. There are cameras there as well."

"Conscientious as you are, I imagine you check those videos regularly."

"We can't have even a single mishap if we are to stay in business."

"I completely understand. Authentication occurs *inside* the secure room."

"Exactly." He checked his watch, which looked expensive. "Our authentication process is rigorous. Each artwork, including the Monet, undergoes a thorough examination by our experts."

"Could you walk me through that process? So that I can relay the details to Mrs. Montgomery."

Annoyance flicked across his features and melted away just as quickly. "We verify the provenance, conduct physical inspections, and use the latest technology for age verification and paint analysis. Only after passing all these stages is an item cleared for auction."

I scribbled notes as he talked. "Can you tell me more about this secure holding room?"

"It has a safe-quality door with a fingerprint lock. Cameras watch the door and the room's interior around the clock."

I had more questions, but he'd promised me only two minutes. Time to fast-forward. "What about other regular customers? Have you ever worked with Caleb Gray or Anna Baxter?"

His attention shifted to something behind me, and I turned to see a new customer inside the doorway.

The man's attire blended bohemian and aristocratic—a

black button-up shirt paired with well-worn jeans and leather
boots. Black hair was tied back in a loose knot. He spotted
Irving and came our way.

"Mr. O'Connell." Irving waved him over. "You're early."

"Should I leave and come back?" The man's lips twitched
upward.

"Of course not," Irving practically shouted. In a lower tone,
he added, "Please come to my office."

"Mr. Greenfield," I said. "I have a few more questions."

"Ms. Gray, the likelihood of a switch happening under our
watch is nonexistent. If that's not sufficient assurance for Mrs.
Montgomery, please have Mina schedule you an
appointment."

Irving led Mr. O'Connell to his office. As they entered, Mina
hurried out.

I waved her over. She paused to wipe imaginary dust off
displays along her way to me. When she reached me, she
offered a wan smile.

"I'd like to make an appointment with Mr. Greenfield."

"He has availability in two weeks."

"He has availability tomorrow—the time slot Mr. O'Connell canceled."

She bowed her head as if in apology. "Of course." She wrote
the time on an appointment card and handed it to me. "Please
be on time."

Tomorrow, I would get some answers.

CHAPTER 15
ROSE

Isabel's gardener waved a muddy glove at me and went back to trimming the flowering hedges. Judging by his worn overalls and dirt-caked boots, I took his word that he never went inside the house—not ever. Isabel would have a meltdown if he tracked even a speck across her pristine floors.

We could nix the gardener from our suspect list.

I followed a garden path to the circular driveway. As I approached, Blake Anderson's sleek black sedan glided out of the circle and onto the road leading to the rest of town.

I sprinted, jumped into my car, and gunned the engine.

Besides the gardener, Blake was the only member of Isabel's staff we hadn't grilled yet. Both Olivia and Chef René had been cagey, so Isabel trained her staff well to keep household business private. Blake would be no different.

Right now, stealth might be more valuable than conversation.

The sedan turned into a shopping center and stopped in

front of the Dispatch and Delivery, an ivy-hugged, white-brick building. I tapped a rhythm on the steering wheel as I waited.

Five minutes later, Blake reappeared carrying a stack of four packages. He stopped and balanced the boxes on one knee while the other leg kept him upright. On the edge of the parking lot, he tore open the top box, the smallest of the bunch.

Blake scooped the boxes back into his arms and hustled to his car. He placed the packages inside one by one, then stayed bent over the back seat where I couldn't see what he was up to.

He slammed the door, locked it, and checked the handle. After a glance around, which didn't linger in my direction, he stomped toward the grocery store and disappeared inside. The automatic doors closed behind him.

I scrambled out of my car and hurried across the lot to his. An older model, Blake's sedan gleamed like it had never seen dust in its life.

Three boxes were stacked into a size-ordered pyramid on the floor in front of the passenger seat, like soldiers in formation. The labels were addressed to Isabel Montgomery from a sender with the generic name *Fulfillment*.

Besides the boxes, the interior was immaculate. Not even an empty water bottle or dirty napkin.

I shielded my eyes from the sun and pressed my face against the dark glass of the back seat. There—the fourth box lay open on its side on the floor, with its packing peanuts spilled out onto the mat.

Interesting.

What was so special about that one—so urgent that it needed to be opened this instant?

With a glance at the grocery store to make sure Blake

hadn't emerged, I made my way to the Dispatch and Delivery. A bell chimed as I entered the quiet shop. The air smelled of ink and photocopies. The place was deserted except for a young woman leaning behind the counter.

She straightened up. "Can I help you?"

I summoned my acting chops and pitched my voice high and tense. "Are there any packages here for Isabel Montgomery?" I pulled my phone from my pocket and made a show of checking the time.

The woman blinked at me, caught off guard. "No," she said slowly, "I don't have any packages here for Mrs. Montgomery."

She hadn't needed to check because she'd just given them all to Blake. She knew she didn't have any more.

I feigned agitation. "Can you check? There are supposed to be four. I'm Isabel's new assistant—the last one got fired. I can't afford to mess this up on my first day."

Her eyes widened, and I could see her working out that Blake must have been fired. In a small town like this, Blake had probably picked up mail for Isabel before. I'd bet money she hadn't confirmed he was authorized this time before handing them over.

"Blake . . ." Her gaze flitted to the door and back to me. "Blake Anderson picked them up already. Is he not her assistant anymore?" Her voice ended in a squeak.

"No!" I shouted. "She's going to kill me. I'm new in town, and I'll never be able to get another job here."

"He's not going to steal them, though." She paled. "Right?"

"I don't know. You think so?" I slammed my hands on the counter and cranked my volume up two clicks. "Mrs. Montgomery is going to kill me. One of the boxes was this huge"—I mimed a box almost my height—"magnificent, custom chandelier for the foyer. Someone's coming to install it this afternoon."

She held up both hands, palms out like a stop sign. "It's okay. The packages were all small. Maybe the one with the chandelier hasn't arrived yet."

"So none of them were from . . ." I ransacked my brain for a reasonable name for a high-end lighting company and came up blank. ". . . St. Chapeau's Luxury Lighting? That's where she bought the chandelier."

She turned to her computer. Her fingers clacked across the keyboard. "Look, it's okay! The ones Blake picked up were from Elite Personal Shoppers."

All these theatrics to learn about Isabel's shopping? Time to wind this down. I let relief wash over my face. "All three were from Elite Personal Shoppers?"

As if mirroring me, her shoulders relaxed. "Yes, three from there. There was no fourth package. Do you have the tracking number for the chandelier? Maybe I can give you an updated arrival date."

I rummaged through my purse and pockets. "I must have left it at the house. I'll be back after I sort this out with Mrs. Montgomery."

Before she could offer more help, I hurried from the shop. Blake's car still lingered in front. I crossed the lot and climbed back into my vehicle.

A quick web search showed that Elite Personal Shoppers was a service for curating and selling expensive accessories from overseas. The three boxes on Blake's back seat must be from there, but he'd left Dispatch and Delivery with four.

Where and what was that fourth?

The growl of an engine pulled my attention, and a black

muscle car rolled across the reflection in my rearview mirror. It stopped behind my car and cut the engine, trapping me between it and the parking bumper in front of me.

I'd know that car anywhere—and its driver. Like liquid poison, Adrian slid from the front seat. Black hair in tight curls framed a handsome face with a shadow of facial hair. He walked like he had all day to spare.

I started my ignition and put my car in drive with my foot still on the brake. He was blocking my exit, but I could drive over the parking bumper if I had to.

He rapped on the window.

I pretended not to notice, keeping my gaze glued to my phone. His black T-shirt clung to a well-defined chest, but I pretended not to notice that either.

He tapped again.

I rolled down the window a crack. "Can I help you?"

"You left this in my car." He dropped the prepaid phone through my window.

I glanced up at him with a bored look. "I don't know what you mean."

He leaned closer. "Rose Gray."

My chest tightened.

"What's your game?" He smelled like leather. With those muscles, he could drag me out of this car before I could react.

I lifted my foot a fraction off the brake. "Isabel hired me to investigate her missing painting." Without missing a beat, I added, "Why were you bullying Eliza?"

"Worry about your own business."

"I'm investigating a murd—a missing painting." I swallowed. "My business is *in* everyone else's until this job is done."

Way behind Adrian, Blake opened his own car door and slipped inside. I'd missed his exit from the grocery store. I could follow him, but I'd probably gotten everything I could from him today, and jumping the parking bumper was not exactly a discreet tailing technique.

I looked up at Adrian and batted my lashes. "I've been trying to be a better person lately, but trust me, I'm the dangerous one between the two of us." I paused to let that sink in. "Try me."

He grunted. "Sure." Without another word, he returned to his car and peeled out of the lot. His tires screeched against the pavement.

I memorized his license plate. Adrian was a mystery I looked forward to unraveling.

I PULLED INTO THE DRIVEWAY OF VERA'S COTTAGE, MY HOME FOR THE next who-knew-how-long. A landscaper in a faded blue jumpsuit was using a leaf blower to clear leaves from the front walk. He paused as I passed, and leaves swirled and floated to the ground. He started up again when I hit the porch.

I rang the bell.

Vera's muffled voice called from inside. A moment later, she swung the door open and sighed. "Rose, dear, you pay rent here. Use your key."

"I didn't want to catch you off guard."

"Doing what? Singing in my underwear? No, no, I only do that upstairs." She reached to pull me inside.

"I didn't know you used a landscaper, I could do the leaves

for you, no problem." I pointed at the guy behind me, who once again had leaves swirling in front of him out to the street.

"I don't . . ." Vera nudged me aside and marched off the porch toward the man. His attention was toward the street now, the direction he was pushing the leaves, so she tapped his shoulder.

He turned to her and switched off the blower.

"There's been a mistake. I didn't hire you."

He wiped sweat from his face and pointed at the gray cottage across the street. "No, ma'am. Mr. Miller-Young asked me to clear your yard too."

"You don't have to do that. I don't want them spending their money on me." She gestured for him to leave. "Please."

"I book for a minimum of two hours, and I finished under time. They pay the same whether I do your lawn or not." When she didn't object again, he turned the leaf blower back on.

Vera stomped back to the porch, grabbed my arm, and yanked me inside. "Those two are too much. First the cheese-cake, and now this. Are they trying to win an award?" She scowled, daring me to disagree.

"Maybe they're just really friendly."

"*Too* friendly. Do you think they're doing it on purpose?"

I hesitated. "Being nice?"

"Making me look bad."

"I don't think—"

"Forget it. They want a war, and they'll get one." She looked around the room, and I prayed she wasn't looking for weapons. "And don't ring my bell anymore. You're family."

She was dressed up more than usual in a relaxed, jewel-toned tunic paired with fitted pants. A long pendant necklace and a stack of bangle bracelets accessorized the look.

"You look sharp. What's the occasion?"

"I always look sharp." She twirled. "If I look especially fine today, it's for the Autumn Festival." She narrowed her eyes at my outfit. "Is that what you're wearing?"

"To hang around the house, yes, this is what I'm wearing."

"You should come. Food, music, good company. It's not to be missed."

"I can get those things right here—all without being on display as the new girl in town."

"But you won't meet everyone that way."

I started to tell her exactly how little I wanted that, but she was right. Meeting people was why I pretended to be a PI in the first place. The festival would be swarming with locals, a perfect opportunity to snoop, gather information, and maybe hear some gossip. "I'll go."

She rewarded me with a grin. "It should be in full swing by now, so get changed." She waved me away.

I excused myself to my room and tossed my handbag on the side table.

Back home, I hadn't packed for a festival. I threw open the drawers and my yet-unpacked duffel bag, mostly full of ripped jeans and tops with sayings specifically chosen to keep away strangers.

I dumped the duffel out onto the bed.

A knock on the door jolted me, and Vera's voice floated through the door. "Rose, your sister's here."

I swung the door open, and Ivy stood there with Vera. She waved, but her expression was serious.

"Hey." I pulled her inside.

Vera lingered in the doorway. "Do you need help finding

something to wear? It's the most see-and-be-seen event of the season."

"I can handle it. I assume it's an outdoor event?"

"In the park," Ivy said.

Vera scanned Ivy's polished blazer and wide-legged dress pants and then my graphic tee and holey jeans. "Maybe you'll accept some fashion advice from your sister then."

She retreated down the hallway, and I stuck my tongue out after her before closing the door.

I motioned at the open drawers. "Anything jumping out at you?"

Ivy pushed aside a pair of jeans and a black sweatshirt to reveal more of the same underneath. "Oh, in case I forget." She fished a folded paper from her pocket and handed it to me.

"What's this—besides an obvious attempt to avoid discussing my wardrobe?"

"Found it on your windshield in the driveway."

I unfolded it: *Stay away.*

Simple. Bold. Assertive.

The words were a punch to the boob, knocking out my breath. I flipped it over, but there was no signature.

My hand trembled as I reread the two words. I set the note on the bed and clenched and unclenched my fists, trying to find my control in the moment. My hands stopped their tremors.

"What is it?" Ivy snatched up the paper and read it. Her face paled.

Was this about Isabel's painting, Anna's murder, or Caleb? Maybe all three?

I hadn't been here long enough to piss someone off so that they'd just generally want me to go away. I was good at that, but it took time, and I'd been asking questions for only a day and a half.

This wasn't just a warning, though. It was a confirmation that we were getting closer to uncovering something that someone wanted to keep hidden.

Ivy walked to the edge of the room, spun, and walked back. "This is not okay." She raised the note to her face to read it again as she paced. "We need to rethink this."

I stiffened.

"We might have to drop everything."

"Both cases? Are you kidding?" I needed this case. I needed Willow Lake and everything that came with it . . . I needed Ivy. "We have to find Caleb. He could be fighting for his life right now."

She nodded, but her pacing picked up speed. "If someone's threatening us, Caleb isn't the only one in danger. This is my hometown. I won't put my friends and family at risk too."

I tried to fix my face into something resembling under-standing, but inside, my chest tightened and my stomach roiled. It was too soon to end this. "This could be a bluff. It's not even a threat: *stay away*."

Ivy stopped walking. She tilted her head one way and then the other.

"It's more of a suggestion, really," I added.

"Okay. For now." She rubbed her chin as she spoke. "But if we get even one more whiff of personal danger, we are done."

Another knock came at the door before I could agree.

"Come in." I slipped the note into my pocket.

Vera rushed in with a pile of colorful sundresses over one arm. "These belong to my son's ex. They lived here before she took off with barely a farewell." She laid them across the bed and held one up to me. "This would highlight your assets."

It was a pink dress covered in yellow flowers, with slinky fabric and a low neckline. I cast a desperate look at Ivy.

She looked me in the eye and said, with a straight face, "Oh, I love that for you."

And here I thought we were getting somewhere with our relationship.

She pulled her lips in to hide her laughter, but it bubbled up anyway.

"Fine." Vera pouted. "You can look in the spare closet yourself."

She led us to a guest room decorated with a more masculine sensibility than most of the home. A charcoal-gray and red comforter covered a cherrywood bed, flanked by matching nightstands.

Vera threw open the closet, revealing a full walk-in, eighty percent full of women's clothing. A small corner held several pairs of men's jeans, slacks, shirts, and a coat. Boxes sat in one corner, the top one open as if someone had started packing and given up.

I sifted through the blouses and dresses with my fingertips, careful not to mess them up since they didn't belong to me.

A long, black casual dress caught my attention, and I unhooked the hanger. Vera nodded, and I took it back to my room to change. I applied some lip gloss for flair and rejoined them downstairs.

"I'll drive." Ivy led the way through the front door.

I followed, and Vera closed the door behind us and started down the walkway to Ivy's car.

"Aren't you going to lock up?" I asked.

"We never worry about that here. Everyone knows everyone."

I locked it myself.

"You and your security obsession." She shook her head and followed Ivy to the car.

Until yesterday, she'd had a home full of unsecured cameras, and today, someone was dropping threats on my car. Security was a big deal right now, and no one would hurt us on my watch.

CHAPTER 16

IVY

Set in a park by the lake, the Autumn Festival belonged in a watercolor painting. People laughed and mingled. The lake's surface reflected the reds and golds of festive lights strewn across the space.

Vera, Rose, and I stepped out of my rental car, and the smell of fried dough and barbecue smoke beckoned.

Vera waved at someone across the grass. "I'll catch up with you later." She took off before I could even orient myself.

"I guess we're on our own," I said. "Let's split up and mingle. See what we can pick up." Despite my initial doubts about Rose's ability to get useful information out of people, she'd shown good instincts so far. Dividing our efforts would be more efficient.

Rose rubbed her hands together, evil-villain style. "You mean spy on people."

"I mean tactfully interact and see if they know anything about Dad, Anna, or the painting."

"Tactfully spy. Got it."

I pointed to a secluded bench near the lake, away from the activity. "Let's meet there in twenty minutes to check in and swap info."

"You got it." Rose headed off for the carnival games.

I melted into the crowd, a hive of activity with children weaving through, couples hand in hand, and clusters of laughing friends.

My first targets would be Felicity Davis and Taylor Bennett. If nothing had changed in the last decade—and nothing ever did here—those two gossips would know everything that happened in public and most of what happened in private.

I spent the next fifteen minutes exploring the festival, making small talk with a hundred people who remembered me from when I was a baby, as I searched for Felicity's distinctive red hair. Everyone wanted the scoop on Anna—how I'd found her and what she looked like. I wanted to be a scoop recipient, not the other way around.

I finally spotted Felicity's head bent low, its owner whispering with dark-haired Taylor. Their faces leaned close together.

Taylor raised a hand to call someone over, and I followed her look . . . to Jay Matthews. *Deputy* Jay Matthews now, although he still had that Hollywood chin he'd had during our high school dating days.

I was not prepared for that meetup right now.

I pivoted—and collided with a massive chest. Farther up was the face of Sheriff Foster. Despite his gray sheriff uniform, he took advantage of his off-duty hours with a giant, unidentifiable fried thing clutched in one hand.

He waved it at me. "Ivy Gray!"

In his late forties, Dan Foster had the same killer grin that had swooned all the young ladies when I was a kid. A home-grown boy-next-door type, Dan loved the stereotypical man's man activities: hunting, fishing, hitting the gym. Despite his jock appearance, though, Dan was a shrewd politician who knew how to schmooze when it benefitted him. His charisma, smooth tongue, and dedication to justice had won him multiple sheriff elections over the last decade.

"Sheriff Foster, good to see you. You look well."

"Do I?" He rubbed his belly, which did nothing to make him look soft.

I laughed. "You do."

"I hear you're in the FBI now. Big time." His voice boomed.

I ducked, as if that could save me from all the public eyes pointed this way.

"We're proud to claim you as one of ours." He bear-hugged me.

His fried thing would probably leave a grease spot on my blazer.

"I understand you're working for Isabel Montgomery. Do you have your PI license too? They let you moonlight on your own time?"

I licked my lips while I thought of a way to explain the situation without lying. "I'm assisting Rose while I'm in town."

Sheriff Foster tore off a piece of the fried thing, stuffed it in his mouth, and swallowed after one chew. "Let me know if I can assist. I've never had the pleasure of working with the Bureau."

"I'm not technically here on business."

"Tomato, to-*mah*-to. I'm here if you need me."

"I appreciate that, Sheriff Fos—"

"Dan."

"Dan . . . I appreciate that. If you'll excuse me, I see someone I need to talk to."

He waved his fried thing as I went.

Rose beat me to our bench by the lake and made a show of staring at her smartwatch while I joined her.

"So?" She leaned forward like it was Christmas Day. "What's the juicy news?"

I caught her up on my small talk with the locals and the sheriff.

"So you've got nothing," she said when I finished.

"Investigations take time. Speaking of which, what's the status of your private investigator license?" I had no idea how long it took to get one or whether she was even qualified. There was probably a test involved.

She smirked. "I've got one. I'm just waiting for the paper copy to arrive." Her tone was nonchalant, too much so.

"You asked someone nicely to make you a PI, and they approved you in two days?"

"It's better if you don't ask questions."

I stared at her.

"I wouldn't want to involve you in anything . . ."

A headache was building near my temples. "Tell me right now."

"Rose Gray obtained a PI license in Nevada. With a bit of ID showing, I got a reciprocity license here in Georgia."

I squinted as I tried to interpret her words in the context of the ones she *wasn't* saying. "You're using some other Rose Gray's license?"

"It was either that or break into the state license database and create one from scratch. This seemed easier and less illegal."

I squeezed my eyes shut to stave off the headache.

"You shouldn't have asked if you didn't want to know."

"Next time, please refuse to tell, okay? I can't be implicated in your shit."

She threw her arms in the air. "I tried. You insisted."

"We never had this conversation."

"What conversation?" She shifted subjects before I could recover. "Do you know George Baxter?"

"Anna's husband?" I asked. "Not personally. They got married after I left for college."

Rose leaned close. "Supposedly, she was having an affair with Caleb, *and* George was the jealous type. That's according to one of Vera's friends."

I ground my teeth—not this same rumor again. I couldn't imagine Anna would cheat on her husband with my dad—of all people—after the guilt she felt for her years of covering for him. "Is George here?" I scanned the crowd.

"They say he hasn't left his home since the murder."

"That's understandable. Guilty or not, I doubt he's in the mood for a party."

Rose popped to her feet. "I'm going to grab some funnel cake. Meet back here in twenty minutes?"

"We're here to work," I called after her as she barreled toward the food stalls.

"I can work while inhaling funnel cake," she tossed over her shoulder.

She didn't get far before a woman blocked her. "Rose, darling!" The woman clasped Rose's wrist and tried to pull her back toward the bench.

Rose locked her feet. "Can I help you, strange woman in my personal space?"

"Rose, this is—" I started.

"I'm Faye." The woman gestured at me. "Ivy's mom."

Rose squealed and threw her arms around her. My mother returned the embrace, and they squeezed each other like old friends separated for too long.

"Ms. Donovan, it's so nice to meet you! I've heard such good things."

Mom thumbed in my direction and said, with skepticism, "From this one?"

"From everyone else."

"Mom, I haven't had a chance to—"

"Shush." She glared as if it were my fault that she hadn't met Rose after five whole days of her being in town. To Rose, she said, "None of this formal stuff. It's Faye. You're Ivy's sister, which makes you a daughter to me."

"Technically," I said, "she wouldn't be your stepdaughter unless you and Dad were married."

Mom sniffed but restrained herself from a rant about what a cheating jerk my dad was—which was progress from a few years ago. I had to give her credit. Many women would resent Rose just for being conceived while my parents were still married, but my mom was all smiles.

She clasped Rose's shoulders. "Why haven't you come to see me?"

"I . . . didn't realize I was invited."

"That's because Ivy is a terrible host."

"Mom!"

She gestured in the direction of the festival. "Go on. Leave us to get acquainted."

I stared at them, and they stared back like I was interrupting the most important conversation on the planet.

"I'll be back," I muttered and stomped off.

I went to the art booths, where local artists sold paintings, ceramics, metalwork, and sculptures. Shoppers bent over each piece, all while avoiding eye contact with the artists themselves.

A black-gray ponytail and linen shirt caught my eye—the man from the auction house who'd caused Irving Greenfield and Mina Lee to fawn all over him. He stood in front of a work of painted paper expertly draped into a Minotaur sculpture. The paper was a whirl of crimson and amber hues blended together like a fiery dance across the folds, making the Minotaur look like it had emerged from hell.

The man held his hands in his pockets, his head tilted to one side. Next to him stood an elegantly dressed woman with straight black hair and a bored expression.

I stood beside him. "That's a beautiful piece."

"It's Eliza Thompson."

"Really?" The way Isabel spoke of her niece's art, I had expected something more mundane, less enthralling. "The use of color and form is striking."

"It has a certain depth." He turned to me with the same discriminating look he'd given the sculpture. "You have an eye for art."

"I know when something is valuable."

He squinted. "Have we met?"

I held out my hand. "Ivy Gray. We crossed paths at the auction house this morning."

"Liam O'Connell." He shook. "And this is my wife, Mayling."

Mayling gave a curt nod in my direction before her gaze drifted away into space. She raised her wrist in a weak attempt at a wave and wandered off.

"This is not her scene," Liam said.

Despite the appearance of being a kept woman, Mayling O'Connell was the brains of their duo. She'd graduated with honors from a prestigious university, built an online investment startup at the beginning of the dot-com boom, and sold before the bubble burst. She walked away with millions and married her high school sweetheart, Liam.

"Art isn't for everyone," I said.

"True enough. But still a shame."

"We have a common acquaintance, Isabel Montgomery. She hired Gray Investigations to return a painting that was swapped with a forgery."

"The Monet." His face showed no signs of nervousness. But if he'd stolen the painting, he was too cool to give himself away. A man who made other rich men trip over themselves to please him wouldn't shake easily.

"That's right. What else have you heard about it?"

"Is this an interrogation?" He turned back to the Minotaur sculpture but didn't shy away.

"An interview. I could tell by your interaction with Irving that you're a regular in the local art scene. I'm sure you have useful information to contribute."

"Mm-hmm. I suppose you're wondering if I bid on the Monet."

"The question crossed my mind."

Liam O'Connell had only a small online footprint, but I'd noted his presence in media photographs taken during a past auction at the Lakeview Luxe Gallery. I hadn't been able to pinpoint his net worth, but judging by how Irving Greenfield had fawned over him, I guessed Liam was stinking rich. A man like that was used to getting his way. He might have taken action after losing a prize like Isabel's Monet.

"Very well, I'll oblige. I did indeed. Isabel valued it higher in the end, so I let her have it."

"You mean she outbid you."

He raised one eyebrow. "Is that not what I said?"

I bowed my head in apology. "Go on."

"She took the painting home, and that's the last I saw of it."

"You never saw it at the manor?"

"If you want to ask me if I'm ever at her house, where she kept the painting, feel free."

I mocked his words from a moment ago. "Is that not what I said?"

He chuckled. "Touché. I do visit Isabel from time to time, but I never saw the painting at her house. My guess is she kept it squirreled away in some private spot where she could view it exclusively."

"In her office," I confirmed. "It sounds like you know her well."

An amused smile twitched his lips. "Is that a question?"

I laughed. "Do you know her well?"

"As well as anyone in a town of three thousand."

Cagey answer. I'd give it fifty-fifty odds he was sleeping with her, especially since his wife didn't share his love of art while Isabel did.

"As someone who frequents the auction house," I asked, "do you think it's possible that the paintings were switched there?"

"In Irving's house? Extremely unlikely."

"Is it possible the painting was never authentic, and there was never any swap?"

He let out a delighted yelp. "That would be interesting. But no, the auction house has a certified expert examine every piece. Their reputation is on the line with each sale, and Irving does not take chances with that. Then the pieces are under lock and key in a secure room before and after auction."

"Do you happen to know who has access to the keys for that lock? For the secure room, I mean."

"Irving. Probably also his head of security. It's a tight circle." He shrugged. "His assistant Mina too, I'd guess. He trusts her like his right hand."

I filed the information away.

Mayling reappeared and tapped her long fingernails on Liam's shoulder. Two chunky gold bracelets clacked together on her wrist. "Let's go look at the jewelry." She gave him a hard stare that might have cut him if it were any sharper.

"Not her scene," Liam whispered to me before taking the woman's hand and wrapping it around his elbow. "As you wish."

"Thank you, Liam. If you think of anything else, please reach out to us." I gave him the number to Gray Investigations and moved aside, allowing Mayling to lead him away.

Liam O'Connell was an interesting character. Despite his claim that he made peace with losing the painting, he had both motive and opportunity. That made him a suspect.

CHAPTER 17
ROSE

"What did you find out?" I asked when Ivy joined me on the bench after our second round of mingling-slash-snooping at the Autumn Festival.

She slumped beside me, out of breath and red-faced. "You first."

"The funnel cake here is legendary."

"That explains this." Ivy pointed at my nose.

I wiped the spot, looked at the powdered sugar on my fingertips, and licked it. I needed another funnel cake. "Second of all, I'm supposed to meet your mom back here in a minute. She saw someone she needed to chat with but promised to come back and tell me all about little Ivy's childhood traumas."

Ivy's face morphed through a range of emotions that landed in a flat look. "Skip it."

"Excuse me?"

"You don't need to know me." The words growled out, leaving even Ivy looking surprised.

"Why is it a problem for your sister to meet your mom?" I picked my words carefully. Unlike me, Ivy was straight-laced, a rule-follower. People like that hid who they were in favor of who they were supposed to be. I pushed her boundaries, but only because I wanted to know the *real* her.

"I'm not your sister."

Ouch.

"Not in any way that counts, I mean. We don't know each other." Her words were whispers that cut like screams. She stared into empty space through narrow, slitted eyes. "Family isn't about blood. It's about trust, loyalty, having someone's back. Anna taught me that."

The knife twisted in my gut, rummaging for vital organs. "You're right." I paused to steady my voice. "Blood and family aren't the same. We don't know each other."

After a minute, Ivy cleared her throat. "Can we get back to your report?" Her voice was all business.

I straightened up and matched her tone. "I saw Deputies Marks and Ramirez near the food stalls, whispering about something. When they spotted me, they took off in different directions."

"That could have been cop business."

"In a town of three thousand, how much cop business can there be?"

"Lots. Petty theft, illegal fishing, illegal burning, vandalism, trespassing, public intoxication, loitering, noise complaints—"

I touched her hand. "I got it." When she looked down, I yanked my fingers back.

"What else?" she asked.

"Some creeper dude watching people. He started talking to

a vendor when he caught me looking, but before that, he was standing around like he was searching for someone."

Ivy leaned closer. "What did he look like?"

"Average build. Dark hair. Too far away to get an eye color."

"So . . . thirty percent of the country's male population." She leaned back, interest lost.

"I tried to talk to him, but he ran away like he was on fire. If I see him again, I'll know." I jerked my thumb at her. "You go. Who did you talk to?"

"Liam O'Connell. He was at the auction house earlier, and the owner treated him like royalty."

"He's rich?"

"Ridiculously, mostly from marrying up. Liam has a lot of faith in Lakeview Luxe. All the art is authenticated and locked up. He thinks the painting swap must have happened at Isabel's."

"Or *he* swapped it at the auction house and is trying to throw you off the scent."

"The *scent*? I'm not a dog, Rose, and this is not a detective novel. We committed to finding this painting. If we screw up, it'll be that much harder to figure out why Anna died." Ivy was touchy today.

"Are you okay?"

She pulled a long inhale. "Sorry. It's not you."

"Of course not. I'm delightful."

She cracked a smile, but it melted. "I just really need to get justice for Anna. She . . . my last words to her weren't kind, and she deserved better."

I hesitated, then put my hand over hers. Instead of shaking me off, she glanced down and squeezed my fingers before pulling back.

"Who has access to the auction house's lockup?" I asked softly.

"Irving Greenfield, his assistant Mina Lee, and the head of security—according to Liam."

"They should all be suspects then. Speaking of which, we should put together a list."

"What do you think I've been doing?"

"I didn't mean to suggest otherwise. Who else is on it?"

"The folks you'd expect. Blake, Eliza, Olivia, Chef René. Also Liam—he bid on the Monet too and has auction house connections. He may or may not be sleeping with Isabel."

I raised my brows. "What's our next move?"

"Dig up dirt." Ivy shuffled her feet in the grass. "I spotted two of Willow Lake's biggest gossips. They'll know everything being said about Isabel, Anna, and Dad. It's a good place to get ideas."

"What do they look like?" I bounced up and stood on my tiptoes to scan the crowd.

"Look for red hair," Ivy said. "That's Felicity. She's in a red dress too formal for the occasion. Taylor has pixie-cut dark hair. She's more casual but just as vicious with her rumors. Felicity will be easier to find. She loves to stand out."

I spotted a flash of red. "Got her." I grabbed Ivy's wrist and dragged her into the throng of the festival.

The pair were exactly as described. Felicity had bright skin, delicate features, and over-lined burgundy lips. She rocked a vibrant red maxi dress, and her hair fell in big curls. Taylor was plainer in styling but had cheekbones that didn't need help. Her look was lower key with a silky button-down and tailored slacks—a sharp look to match her sharp haircut.

They stood at a ring toss booth. Felicity closed one eye,

aiming a ring at a collection of glass bottles on the other side of the counter.

Next to the bottles stood a young man in his early twenties, still battling acne. He wore a baseball cap over reddish-brown hair.

"I think she's going to flunk out," the guy said. "She can't focus, and the good meds make her heartrate wonky, so she can't take them anymore."

"Do you think she'll go back to the diner," Taylor asked, leaning in, "if she can't hack it? Not that there's anything wrong with working at the diner."

"Who knows," he said.

Taylor returned her attention to Felicity, who was still aiming the ring. "A little to the left. You want to catch that green bottle for the bonus prize."

Felicity shushed her.

"Actually," the guy said, "the best strategy is to aim for the clear ones first. Since the green bottle is in the corner, if you miss it, you won't get anything. If you miss a clear one, you'll probably still get something." He raised a finger like he was about to deliver wisdom. "Go for the green after you've already locked in a prize."

Felicity tossed the ring. It glanced off the green bottle and clattered to the dirt.

She jumped, cursed, and scowled at Taylor like it was Taylor's fault she had done what the booth attendant warned against. Felicity snatched another ring from Taylor's grasp.

Ivy nudged me forward. "This is Rose."

I held out a hand to Taylor.

She looked at it like it might sting her, so I took it back. A beat later, she gasped, "Wait, is this the sister?"

Felicity leaned close to her friend and said, in a too-loud whisper, "You can't call her *sister* just because she's Black."

Ivy coughed down a laugh. "My father is her father."

Felicity stared at Ivy, then at me. Her gaze bounced back and forth before her eyes widened. "Oh!" She was seeing two women apparently the same age, one white, one Black. If Felicity could sniff out a scandal, this one was ripe. Her expression went bored, not to give away her excitement at this morsel.

Taylor stepped away from the ring toss to give me her full attention. "Where are you from?" She looked at me like I was a fat pastry and she hadn't eaten sugar in weeks.

"Atlanta. I'm in town at least until Anna's funeral. She and Daddy were so close, you know." I hadn't called Caleb *Daddy*, or even *Dad*, since my preteens. That was about the time I realized he wasn't coming back, and the best I could hope for were Christmas and birthday cards, which, to his credit, came like clockwork.

Taylor's hand flew to her mouth. "It's so horrible."

Felicity nodded gravely.

Ivy looked like she might throw up from all the fake sympathy.

"Did the FBI send you to investigate your father for murdering his mistress?" Felicity's too-sweet tone was in danger of giving me a cavity.

"The FBI doesn't handle state crimes," Ivy said with just as much sugar. "I'm here for my family."

The two ladies stared at me with wide, curious eyes. I inched backward.

Ivy cleared her throat. "I'd like to help the sheriff by pitching some theories, and you two know everything happening in town. Do you know if Anna had enemies? Anyone who might be angry with her?"

Felicity preened at the flattery.

"Are you going to throw or not?" The booth attendant pointed behind us to a man and a small boy awaiting their turn.

Felicity yanked the ring from Taylor and chucked it toward the booth without looking. It zoomed toward the attendant. He shouted and ducked, but it clipped him above the eye. He cursed so loudly that the man behind us glared and dragged his son away.

Taylor snort-laughed, followed by a mock gasp.

The attendant slapped a hand to his eyebrow. When he brought it away, blood spotted it. He slapped his hand back over the spot and used the other arm to vault over the counter.

"I'm taking a break." To the attendant in the next booth, he added, "Watch my stuff?"

The woman nodded. "First aid's over by the parking lot."

With a grunt, he headed that way.

"What about my last throw?" Felicity called after him. "I get another ring."

He muttered something indecipherable. I would bet everything in my checking account it was a curse.

Felicity returned her attention to Ivy. "Caleb and Anna were having an affair. Obviously, he killed her when she tried to break it off and go back to her husband, or—"

"Anna's husband, George, killed her when he found out," Taylor finished.

"Why are you so sure there was an affair?" Ivy asked.

Felicity fluffed her hair and leaned closer. "They worked long hours together in that tiny office."

Gray Investigations wasn't that small, but the story played better if it was. I kept my mouth shut.

"They're the only PI outfit in town," Ivy said. "They get a lot of cases . . . hence, long hours."

"Caleb's wife practically lives at the bar," Felicity said. "Put a few drinks in her, and she wails about how her husband comes home freshly showered."

"My cousin works with George," Taylor added. "He doesn't trust Caleb—never has. And why should he, since he's having an affair with his wife?"

"Do you see how that logic is circular?" Ivy asked.

Taylor blinked at her.

"George doesn't trust my dad because he's allegedly having an affair with George's wife, and George knows about the affair because he doesn't trust my dad."

Taylor stared for another second before concluding, "It is what it is."

"What if they weren't having an affair?" Ivy asked. "Any other theories?"

"What if they weren't? Are you serious?" Felicity's voice went high-pitched, and she jerked her head toward me. "Has the man ever been faithful?"

It was a fair argument.

"Hypothetically," Ivy said.

"We know you have other theories," I chimed in.

Ivy gave an almost imperceptible nod of approval. These two didn't like being doubted, but they wanted to share what they knew. Better to frame this as giving them an opportunity.

"If it wasn't the affair," Felicity said, "it definitely has to do with one of their cases."

"Drugs!" Taylor volunteered.

Felicity cocked her head.

"Maybe Anna got involved with drugs but became a liability, and the dealer . . ." Taylor mimed shooting a gun.

"Oh, oh, I know!" Felicity added. "Mrs. Montgomery's prized Monet was stolen. What if Anna took it, and Isabel killed her for it?"

Wouldn't that be nice—Anna's murder and the missing painting both wrapped up into a neat bow? Mystery solved. We could all go home.

Taylor raised her brows, and I couldn't keep the skepticism off my face.

"What?" Felicity pouted. "That painting is worth millions, totally a motive for murder."

"And prim-and-proper socialite Montgomery shot her in the face for it?" Taylor asked.

"I mean," she mumbled, "she probably hired an assassin."

"You ladies have been enjoying your night?" A new voice sliced through our conversation.

I jumped.

Felicity spun around so fast she had to grab Taylor to keep from stumbling. Her face went as red as her hair.

Isabel stood behind us with perfect posture, looking like she'd just left a lavish party in powder-blue slacks and an ivory silk blouse. Her hair was looped into a loose bun that she probably considered casual. She sipped from a wine glass—everyone else here had to settle for plastic cups.

Blake and Eliza flanked Isabel on either side. Eliza fidgeted with her shawl, pulling it tighter around her shoulders. Blake's eyes looked glazed, not the sharp-eyed alertness from our first meeting.

Isabel squinted at me and then at Ivy. "Any progress on the case?"

I pasted on a sticky-sweet smile. "Mrs. Montgomery. We're actually here primarily to work on your case."

"Then why am I hearing that you're asking about your father instead? You're still new in town. Don't forget that everyone is talking about you and what *you* are talking about. I hope you're not splitting your focus."

Ivy stepped forward, mirroring Isabel's posture with her chin raised a notch too high and her back stiff. "Mrs. Montgomery, we are fully invested in your case. We are not, however, obligated to spend all of our time on it."

It wasn't like Isabel was *paying* us anyway. We'd waived our fee—technically, our dad's fee—so we could spend our time how we wanted.

Felicity grabbed Taylor and scurried away.

Isabel angled her face away as if slapped. "Of course not." She thrust her wine glass at Blake.

He stared at it until she pushed it toward him again. He lifted it from her fingers. His hand trembled, and wine sloshed over the rim.

Isabel glared at him.

Blake gripped the glass with both hands and dipped his head.

"We're here to enjoy the festival," Ivy continued, her voice steady. "We understand the importance of your case, and it is our top priority during work hours."

"I just want to make sure you understand the stakes."

I stepped toward Isabel.

Ivy stuck a foot out to stop me. "You are our VIP client, Mrs. Montgomery. Please be assured of that."

"I should hope so."

Ivy launched into a string of reassurances full of official-sounding words about the investigation's progress. Isabel ate it up.

Eliza looked off to the side and shifted her weight.

I moved to stand beside her. "Everything okay?" I whispered.

"I just don't like it when she gets like this," Eliza said. "Demanding. Like she owns everything."

"She owns a lot of things." I tossed her a grin.

Eliza returned a shaky smile before glancing back at her aunt. Ivy kept talking to Isabel with a soothing tone, and Isabel's tension slipped away with each word.

"Investigations take time," Ivy was assuring Isabel. "We'll have an intermediate report for you shortly. For now, we have a list of suspects and a plan of action."

I touched Eliza's arm and urged her several feet away. "Who do you think took the painting?"

"I have no idea." Her smile wavered and fell. "Everyone loves my aunt. I can't imagine who would steal from her."

Lie. Isabel was horrible, and I counted at least two people in this huddle who didn't love her. I squinted at Eliza . . . Maybe three.

"Yesterday, I saw you talking with Adrian," I said casually, like I knew the guy personally. "You looked upset. Is everything okay?"

Eliza took a step back. "I'm sorry, I can't—I have to go." She turned, paused long enough to lift her aunt's wine glass from Blake's unsteady hands, and scampered away.

"Blake," Isabel snapped, "we're leaving." She stomped after her niece.

He trailed behind them at a slower pace.

"Well, that was a disaster," Ivy said.

Isabel caught up with Eliza, who pulled the shawl even tighter around her shoulders. Eliza slowed and let her aunt pass her so that she could trail behind like a loyal puppy.

"Maybe not entirely," I said.

CHAPTER 18
ROSE

I reached Lakeview Luxe Gallery out of breath but five minutes early. Ivy was the punctual type, and I needed her to count on me.

Her car was already parked. I steered mine into the spot beside it, popped the door open, and hurried to the entrance.

The building was an elegant mix of white stone and modern design. A heavy oak door marked the entrance, and its polished brass handle gleamed. In the mirror-tinted windows, I straightened my longline blazer and hole-free jeans and picked stray green stuff from my teeth.

Inside, the high ceiling made the room feel like it deserved a throne. Silver-framed artwork glinted against royal blue walls, and sculptures dotted the space. An Asian woman stood ten feet from the entrance, arms behind her back like a soldier at attention.

I turned to look behind me. Sure enough, the windows that

were mirrored outside were transparent inside. She'd just watched me pick my teeth.

I was not off to the best start.

"I have an appointment with Mr. Greenfield." I squared my shoulders and raised my chin. "Rose Gray. My sister, Ivy Gray, is already here."

The woman's gaze shifted to a spot above my head.

I turned again, and a clock over the doorway put the time at three minutes before the hour.

"Mr. Greenfield is already in with his nine forty-five," she said in a cool tone. She didn't move an inch. Her arms stayed hooked behind her as if molded from cement.

"Great. I'll talk to him when he's done."

"You misunderstand. Ms. Gray is his nine forty-five. He's with her now."

My body went numb, and I stared slack-faced at the woman.

"Would you like a bottle of water while you wait?"

"I'm not . . . No, I'm not waiting. I'll join them."

"I have no record of a third for that appointment."

"She invited me after—" Why was I arguing with this person?

I stormed past her toward the glass-walled office in the back. Inside, Irving sat at his desk in a plum suit that fit him like it was built on him. Ivy sat with her back to me. Her dark ponytail bobbed as she spoke words I couldn't hear.

The woman stepped around me, blocking my path. A vein stood out on her forehead. "Mr. Greenfield doesn't tolerate late additions." She hovered a hand above my shoulder, and the other open palm pointed toward the exit.

Hadn't Ivy told me ten o'clock, or had I screwed it up?

Probably the latter. Ivy would already be pissed that I was late. Better not make it worse by scuffling in the middle of a fancy auction house.

I raised my hands. "I'm leaving."

I stomped back the way I came and banged the main entrance open. The hydraulic damper slowed it to a soft close, robbing me of the dramatic exit I wanted.

The parking lot held several cars but was empty of people. I checked around to make sure no one was watching—except probably the tight-faced woman on the other side of the tinted windows—and headed for the side of the building, head bent low.

If I couldn't be in the meeting, I could still make myself useful.

Behind the building, a loading dock with a garage-style door stood wide open. An unmarked truck sat at the end, its back facing the open dock.

After another peek around, I circled the truck and squeezed between it and the edge of the door into the loading bay. Inside was mostly empty except for a few dollies, handcarts, and lifting equipment.

I climbed into the back of the truck. The inside dropped my jaw.

Paintings wrapped in brown paper leaned against the walls, secured by bungee cords. Two sculptures stood in the corner, one in striking bronze. Boxes took up the rest of the space. A couple sat open, and vases and other treasures peeked out from inside.

I turned a full circle to confirm that—yes—I was alone in this truck full of loot I would never be able to afford.

"So much for security," I said.

My fingers itched to grab something. If this were two years ago, I would have done it already and been halfway back to Vera's place.

But I was a better person now.

I shoved my hands in my jacket pockets where they couldn't do any harm.

If the shipping area was lax, I could only guess what else was amiss. I jumped down from the truck and took a chance on the back door. The knob turned. I pushed the door open and stepped into a dimly lit corridor.

Laughter burst from down the hall. I froze, but no one appeared. Two muffled voices followed, and I let them lead me down the hall.

As I crept forward, I passed a door secured with a fingerprint lock. That must be where they kept the valuable auction items before they went under the hammer.

I tracked the voices to a closed metal door with a small window. Inside was a break room. Three people huddled around a table stacked with shoeboxes. One, a Black man with bleached hair, wore a black suit. The other two wore khakis, matching black polos, and lifting belts.

These were the missing security and delivery guys who— I'd bet money—were supposed to be unpacking that truck.

One of the delivery people lifted sneakers from a box and held them to the floor by the suited man's feet. "What did I tell you? They've got your name on them."

The security guard folded his arms. "How much?" He played it cool, but the way he stared at the shoes told the whole story.

"For you? One-fifty."

The guy shook his head. "Can't do it. Make it a hundred, and you've got a deal."

The two delivery people exchanged a look, and the first one nodded. The second, a tall woman with slicked hair, held out a hand.

The security guard slapped a stack of cash into it.

The customer took a moment to admire his purchase before tucking it under his arm. "Rigsby is going to kill me if we don't finish this delivery soon." He moved to the door.

I darted down the hall and ducked into an alcove just as the door opened.

The three of them laughed and chatted as they walked to the loading dock.

According to Ivy, both Liam and Irving insisted security here was unbreakable. I'd just proven otherwise. Meanwhile, Isabel claimed no one in her household would steal from her. Her story looked stronger now.

With a click that made me jump, a door opened two feet away from me.

The man who walked through froze as he spotted me. He stood north of six feet, with closely cropped white hair and dark-brown skin that creased at the forehead and around a pair of glaring dark eyes. This could only be the infamous Rigsby that the suited man had worried about.

We stared at each other.

"Oh, good," I said, more dramatically than I intended. "Thank God you're here. I got lost."

His lips turned down, but he said nothing.

I pointed at the door he'd come through, still propped open by his sizeable form. "I was in the gallery, and I thought there was more art this way." I gestured down the empty corridor.

"This door requires a key card." He flashed a card and slipped it into his pocket. "It locks automatically."

"Whoever used it last should have made sure it was closed." I held my breath.

He didn't call me on my lie. Instead, he gripped my shoulder and led me through the door, his fingers pressing so hard I'd have bruises.

But at least he wasn't calling the police—yet.

The door to Irving's office opened, and Irving and Ivy stepped out. Her eyes narrowed as she spotted me.

"Hi, Ivy!" I said way too cheerfully.

"Hi . . ." Her gaze shifted to Rigsby, whose fingers still dug into my shoulder.

"This is my sister," I babbled. "She and I had a meeting with Irv—Mr. Greenfield. I was late, so I figured I'd look around until they finished. I didn't want to interrupt. So when I saw the door was open . . ."

Rigsby's face showed no emotion.

Ivy glanced the way we'd come and saw the door at the back of the space. She immediately brightened. "Rose, I was wondering what happened to you." I had to give her credit—she was quick, and a better actress than I was.

I held a hand out to Irving. "I'm Rose Gray. Ivy's sister."

Rigsby released his grip to allow me to shake hands.

"Thanks again for your time," Ivy said to Irving. "I'll call if I have any more questions." She grabbed my wrist and yanked me toward the exit.

"Nice to meet you," I called over my shoulder.

"What was that about?" she whispered as we banged out the front door.

"I have a theory," I said.

CHAPTER 19

IVY

THE JUKEBOX BLARED '90s MUSIC AS I HESITATED IN THE DOORWAY OF the local bar just before 11:00 a.m. The scent of stale beer hung in the air, and the heat blasted too high considering the mild weather outside.

"Maybe we should go somewhere else," I said.

Rose squeezed past me through the door. "I heard this was a cool spot, and I want to see more of Willow Lake."

"It's too early for drinks."

She raised one eyebrow. "Is that what your rulebook says?" Without a glance to confirm I was following, she led the way to the high-top bar counter.

The place was mostly empty except for a few loners and a pair of men at a table, one with a beer and one with a pink drink. As we passed, Rose slowed and shifted to my left, putting me between her and them. I gave her a look but let her keep her secrets.

A dark head of wavy hair had its back to us as its owner sat on a barstool. As we reached the high top, I gripped Rose's shoulders and switched places with her again. I pulled out her stool, pointed to it, and grabbed the one to her left.

We slid into our seats.

"Are you going to tell me why I have to sit on your right?"

"Are you going to tell me why you're avoiding that nice couple?" I jabbed a thumb over my shoulder.

"Those are Vera's neighbors, the Miller-Youngs." Rose emphasized their last name. "They are extremely . . . nice."

"How awful!" I flew a hand to my chest.

"It's a lot. I'll introduce you after a couple drinks. Your turn."

I nodded to our right without looking. "That's Dad's wife, Pearl."

Rose's head swung like a pendulum.

"Don't look," I said, even though she was already staring.

"That's Caleb's wife," she said with a healthy dose of awe. "Our stepmother."

"That's literally what I just said."

She released her target lock on Pearl and faced me. "That might not mean anything to you because you've known both your parents forever. For me, this is another piece of Caleb."

Pearl Gray had been married to my dad for nine years. When I first met her, she was sitting in his office with one tan leg draped over the other in a silky skirt with a slit up the thigh. Dad told me she was a client, and Anna backed that story. Maybe that had started true, but with her luxurious black hair, large eyes, and all-day curves, Pearl had claimed the title of Dad's ten millionth mistress. My parents divorced, and she upgraded to wife shortly after I left for college.

According to town gossip, this bar was her second home.

Rose got to her feet. "I should say hi."

I pushed her shoulder down. "Trust me. This is not the place to get to know her."

"She might know where Caleb is."

"She doesn't know where he is when he *isn't* missing." When she looked unconvinced, I added, "We'll talk to her, but she's drinking now. Probably best to catch her sober."

Rose pouted.

"Fine. I'll introduce you . . . after a couple drinks," I said, echoing her earlier words.

The bartender, a burly man with a thick mustache, came over. He gave Rose a once-over and raised his bushy eyebrows. "What can I get for you?"

I peered around him at the rows of bottles. "What do you usually serve at this hour?"

"Absolutely anything that I have in stock. Would you like me to recommend something?"

"How about red wine. Cabernet?"

"You got it." He turned to Rose. "What about you?"

Rose scanned the bar and shrugged. "Same."

He grabbed two glasses, popped the cork, poured our drinks, and the rest of the bottle disappeared under the bar.

I sipped as I waited for him to get out of earshot. "Tell me what you found at the auction house," I said, more into my drink than to Rose. "It has to be better than what I got."

Rose hesitated, rubbing her glass between her palms. "About that . . . Didn't you tell me the meeting was at ten o'clock?" Her words tumbled forward. "Don't get me wrong. Sometimes, I'm late, but I'm good with numbers and time, and I think you said ten." She sucked in a breath and waited.

"Uh-huh." I raised my glass to stall while I figured out the best approach. I went with the truth. "I told you the wrong time."

"On purpose?" Her brows rose, and expectation was written all over her face.

I sipped. "The auction house is a formal place, and I felt I could make a better impression alone."

Hurt flickered across Rose's face before she schooled her expression back to neutral. I had expected anger, not this quiet disappointment that twisted my stomach.

"Look," I started, "It's not like—"

"Forget it. Tell me about the meeting. Did you learn anything useful?"

Grateful for the pass, I set down my glass. "Irving showed me the security manual. It uses the exact wording he does. Authentication, locked room, limited personnel, yada, yada, yada. Word for word. We could have skipped the meeting if he just sent us the manual."

She narrowed her eyes. "Did it sound too practiced?"

"It sounded like he believed it. He wouldn't let me near the security footage, though. He said there was nothing suspicious around the time the painting was in residence."

"You don't think he's guilty, though."

"He was nervous," I said. "Fidgety. Closed body language. Stared me in the eyes a little too much. But no, I think he feels like he's under attack. He's not necessarily lying."

She grinned like she had a secret.

"Now spill."

She gulped down half her wine and slammed the glass on the bar. "Whether Irving believes it or not, his security is a tragedy."

"Do tell."

"I snuck around back. The loading dock was wide open, and a truck was half unloaded. The other half was just sitting there like a yard sale."

"Shit."

"I snuck inside and watched a security guard buy bootleg sneakers from the delivery people."

I cringed. "Not a good look."

"If they're always that secure with their security, anyone could have swapped that painting."

I pointed at her with one finger of the hand holding my glass. "Anyone with access to a forger. Do *you* know how to find one of those?"

Rose whipped out her phone and scrolled her contacts.

"That was rhetorical." I pushed her hands back to the bar top. "So what's your theory?"

"Isabel might have been right about the switch happening at the auction house."

I frowned into my drink. "Except that wouldn't explain why this is the only theft reported. If someone at Lakeview Luxe is forging and swapping art, why stop at one piece?"

"Maybe it's personal," Rose said, "or this is a special case because it's a Monet, and someone was willing to risk everything for it."

Investigating the auction house had been about covering our bases, but now it was a legitimate possibility. "Special case or not, once you get a taste and are in the clear, you try again with a new target. I'm betting it's personal, which doesn't leave the auction house in the clear. I—"

Pearl shot to her feet, almost toppling her chair, and hurried to our side of the bar on dagger-thin heels that clicked against the floor.

The bartender was shaking a drink several feet away, and she pointed at his back. "Whiskey sour! Don't pretend you can't hear me when I'm right here. I've been down there waving my arms for an hour."

Rose and I went quiet and sipped our drinks, watching Pearl make a scene in our peripheral vision.

Pearl had raised a finger to get his attention exactly once, from what I'd seen.

He turned to her with a mild scold. "Wouldn't dream of it, darling." He paused in shaking the other customer's drink to offer his palm up. "Give me one minute."

He poured clear liquid from his shaker into a glass, placed a lime on the rim, and set it in front of an older gentleman at the end of the bar.

He turned back to Pearl. "Double whiskey sour."

She grinned.

The bartender added whiskey, sour mix, and ice to a shaker and started again.

Pearl slumped onto the stool beside me. Either she was oblivious or ignoring me. I shifted my chair more toward Rose, just in case.

"But do you really know a forger?" I asked.

"I know where to look. I could find a kidney if I search the right corner of the web."

"I'm guessing most people don't have those connections."

"They're probably better off. So why wouldn't Irving let you watch the security footage?"

It was almost definitely a desperate attempt at a subject change, and I let her have it. "He was offended at the suggestion that something was off with his security team. He claimed they watched the videos, and he didn't need me or anyone else prying further. He's confident the switch happened at Isabel's."

"I could probably sneak back in and find the room where they keep the footage." Rose chuckled into her drink.

The bartender poured a yellow mixture from his shaker into a glass and passed it to Pearl.

"Thank you!" she said too loudly while spinning back toward her seat.

Her foot hooked the leg of my chair. She flailed, and her drink splashed over Rose's chest.

"What the hell?" Rose screeched and jumped to her feet.

"It's her fault." Pearl spun back to me. "Ivy tripped me."

I cursed under my breath.

"You tripped me," she said, her alcohol-tinged breath inches from my nose. "You owe me a drink."

Rose grabbed a handful of bar napkins and pressed them to her chest. "This is my favorite shirt."

It was actually a nice black blouse, a step up from her usual graphic tees.

"Don't blame me." Pearl wobbled on her feet, and the rest of her drink sloshed in my direction.

I dodged it. "It's okay," I said. "It was just an accident."

"Accidents happen when you're too drunk to stand," Rose said, dabbing at her shirt.

The bartender nodded at someone across the room. Before I could look that way, Pearl threw her glass at the floor. It shattered as she lunged at Rose.

Her open palm nailed Rose right under the eye.

I jumped in front of Rose, but she sidestepped around me and reeled her fist back.

This was so bad.

Out of nowhere, Deputy Leila Ramirez stood between Rose and Pearl, and Rose's fist kept coming.

"Rose!" I shouted.

Wide-eyed, she tried to pull her punch, but momentum won. Her fist glanced off the deputy's cheek.

Ramirez staggered back. She straightened up fast, and five seconds later, she was twisting Rose's arms behind her back and slapping cuffs on her.

"It was an accident." I reached for Ramirez, thought better of it, and raised both hands. "She was defending herself."

Ramirez's face was bright red where Rose had hit her.

"She assaulted a deputy." Ramirez pulled Rose's bound wrists toward the door. "You can pick her up at the substation."

Rose's shoulders slumped as, head dipped, she allowed Ramirez to lead her out the door.

CHAPTER 20
ROSE

I swung Ivy's car door open and stepped onto the curb outside Vera's house. "Again, I'm really sorry you spent your evening at the jail."

Ivy offered a tight-lipped smile that could be either concern or irritation—probably both. "I'm just glad you weren't charged."

They'd tossed me in the drunk tank—with Pearl—until she sobered up. My guess was the deputies thought an afternoon and evening with her was fitting punishment for clocking a deputy. Pearl slept the whole time, so I didn't even get a chance to ask her about Caleb.

"Thanks for the ride," I said. "I'm really sorry. I promise to be on my best behavior from now on."

The edge of her mouth quirked upward. "Was this not that?"

I closed the door—too hard—and mouthed an apology for *that* through the closed window.

Always graceful, Ivy waved her fingers.

The front porch light glowed a warm yellow, and more lights sparkled in the garden. Vera's house made a good substitute for home after a long day.

The smell of apple pie greeted me in the foyer, and the sound of Ivy's car faded as she turned off the street. I shut the door, shrugged out of my jacket, and reached for the coat rack.

I froze.

Speared by an otherwise empty hook was a photo on plain printer paper. The print lines of the inkjet were visible on the page, but I recognized myself front and center.

I lifted it off the hook and leaned closer. It showed Ivy and me leaving the auction house this morning, just ten hours ago.

My heart banged a parade in my chest, and I swung a half circle in one direction and then the other. No one was watching me.

I yanked the door open and stuck my head out to find an empty street, except for Lawrence and Paul Miller-Young waving from a porch swing across the way. I closed the door.

"Vera!" I called, hurrying through the living room. "Are you here?"

The kitchen was empty. A pan sat in the sink, filled with soapy water. The backsplash behind the stovetop showed grease spatter from recent cooking.

An apple pie with golden-brown crust sat on the breakfast table. Despite my growing panic, my mouth watered. A note beside it told me the leftover chicken and green beans were in the fridge, but the pie was for the neighbors.

I scowled at it.

"Vera!" My shouts reached a panicked pitch. "Are you here? Make a noise."

I stilled and listened. Someone had been in the house, someone who'd followed me earlier. If she was hurt, maybe she could bang something, knock something over. If she was dead . . .

Nothing.

I ran to the stairs and bolted up them two at a time.

"What's wrong?" Vera's voice hooked me from behind before I reached the top.

I spun toward her, almost toppling backward. "You're okay!"

Vera's hair was flat on one side, and her eyes looked dazed. "Is everything okay?"

"Where were you?" My voice came out sharper than intended.

"Sleeping." She yawned. Her two cats wound around her legs and stretched against her. "What's wrong?"

Vera put her foot on the first step, but I hurried down to save her the trouble. She looked barely conscious, and the last thing I needed was her toppling backward down the stairs. I pulled her into a hug.

"You're worrying me," she said. "Tell me what's going on."

I stepped back, tucking the photo into my back pocket. I didn't want to scare her. "Did you have any visitors while I was gone?" I kept my tone casual.

"No, I went out. Why?"

"What time? When did you get back?"

"I left not long after you and got back before five. What's this about?"

The photo was taken around ten thirty this morning. That gave the stalker from then until five to sneak in and leave it.

"Rose?"

I forced a smile. "It's nothing. I heard about a break-in when I was at the coffee shop earlier. It's got me on edge."

Vera's eyes widened. "How far from here?"

"I'm overreacting. I stress too much about privacy and security." I tried to look nonchalant. "Speaking of which, I promise I'll reinstall your indoor cameras tomorrow and get you an outdoor one too. Sorry for disabling them." I was probably up to ten apologies for the day.

"As long as I can check on my babies when I go out, I'm good." She scratched the orange cat's head, and he leaned into her hand.

"I'll take care of it."

She squeezed my hand. "Did you see the chicken in the fridge?"

"Yes, thank you. It smells amazing." I gave her a nudge toward the sunroom. "Go relax."

Vera led the way, her black cat trailing behind. The tabby gave me a last, suspicious look before following.

I waited until the sounds of her movement stopped and peeked into the room to see her curled in an armchair with a book, one cat on her lap and the other on the windowsill. Then I locked the front and back doors and checked all the windows on the main floor.

No one was getting in here tonight—I hoped.

CHAPTER 21

IVY

Blake answered the door of Montgomery Manor wearing a crisp suit, black glasses, and a scowl. "Is Mrs. Montgomery expecting you?"

"She's expecting our report." Rose squeezed between him and the doorframe. "She asked for regular updates."

"I'm sure she meant via phone or email." Since Rose was already inside, he stepped aside to let me in too.

"Since you're here . . ." He straightened his already impeccable jacket. "I'll take that report. Proceed."

Rose grinned. Dread twisted in my gut as I braced myself for the inevitable train wreck that was Rose Gray.

"How long have you been sleeping with Liam O'Connell?" she blurted out.

I slapped my hand over my face.

Blake stumbled a step backward. "I'm not—what! I'm not even . . ."

Rose clasped my blazer and opened it to pull my notepad from the inner pocket. She flipped to a page in the middle. "I'm sorry. It says here I was supposed to ask that to Mrs. Montgomery." She peered at him over the top of the notebook. "You're not her."

"Rose," I warned.

"My mistake," she continued. "We should probably talk to Mrs. Montgomery directly."

Blake continued to stare at her like a shocked deer.

"If you prefer," I said, "we can provide this theory in our formal, written report of the case status."

Rose nodded. "Very official. We're required by law to retain those records for years. Just to be safe, Gray Investigations keeps all records indefinitely. We can do that with digital files."

Blake typed a quick message on his phone and turned toward the stairs. He made no gesture for us to follow, but he hadn't thrown us out either. We filed up the long, curved staircase with Rose humming an upbeat tune from the rear.

"Give me my notepad," I whispered.

She handed it over, and I slipped it into my pocket.

We turned into the hall outside the office, and I checked the ceiling. Like last time, the camera still looked down on us, probably getting a view of the entire long hallway.

Blake rapped on the French doors of Isabel's office, waited a second, and opened them.

"I have Ivy and Rose Gray." He placed both doors wide open.

Isabel sat behind her desk. A red shawl draped over her shoulders highlighted a sleek black suit-dress. A long necklace that twinkled in the overhead lights hung down to almost waist length. The rings on her fingers cost more than my wardrobe—twice as much as Rose's.

The fake Monet still held a place of honor on the wall behind her.

Rose pointed at it with an upturned, open hand. "Why do you keep the forgery up?"

"To remind myself what I'm owed." She spun her chair to look at it. "When the authentic piece is back, I'll replace it. Until then, I know I can't trust the people in my circle."

"We will find your painting," I said.

"In the meantime," Isabel added more brightly, "even the forgery is more valuable than what most have."

Blake positioned himself at Isabel's right, and I took the seat across from her. Rose stood behind the other chair.

"Are you seeing Liam romantically?" I asked.

Isabel set her hands face down on the desk. "How would that be relevant to the investigation?"

"Romantic relationships are always relevant. People do for love what they would never do otherwise."

Isabel's lips tightened. "I understand you have a report for me."

Rose launched into a summary of our work so far, starting with our interviews with the staff and ending with our visit to the auction house. Since he was in the room, she left out the part about following Blake to the shipping store.

"You have nothing," Isabel concluded when she finished.

"We have a theory," Rose said.

"The paintings could have been switched here or at the auction house, but we believe someone from your household was involved," Rose said. "If you were a random target, there would have been others."

"And there have been no other reports of inauthentic art

from the Lakeview Luxe Gallery," I added, "even though it's been a year."

Isabel cringed. It pained her that it took so long for her to discover the forgery—especially if one of her people betrayed her.

"How did you discover the switch?" I asked.

"I don't take enough time to admire what I have," she said. "One day, I did. I took a moment to stand behind my desk." She gestured behind her without looking.

"You didn't do that when you first brought it home?" Rose asked. The disapproval in her voice wasn't well hidden.

I shot her a look.

"I admire it every day." She paused and then, "I don't often stand in front of it and stare enough to notice that Monet's signature is missing. That's my error."

Her shoulders slumped, and for a few seconds, Isabel was a sad person who had lost something important to her. The moment slipped away, and the haughty, better-than-everyone woman returned.

"It doesn't sound as though you've narrowed the suspects," she said.

"Can you think of anyone in your household, or anyone who visits, who might have a connection to the auction house? For instance, who goes there or knows someone who works there?"

Rose left her post behind the chair and wandered toward a gold-framed painting on one wall.

"Eliza," Isabel said. "She enjoys art, and examining the new pieces gives her something useful to do."

I didn't interrupt to tell her that her niece was an artist herself, and that was useful.

Rose pushed her face close to the painting until her nose was less than an inch from it.

"Blake sometimes accompanies her because he has a better sense of what I like. Eliza can be distractible. If I want something done right..."

She gestured at Blake, who still stood at her right hand like a statue.

Rose sauntered to a corner of the room behind Isabel, where a human-sized glass sculpture stood. Although its jewel tones reflected a stunning pattern on the wall, its mouth hung open in an inhuman, grotesque roar.

"Aside from Eliza and Blake," I asked, "is there anyone else who frequents the auction house or has a particular interest in art?"

Rose stood beside the sculpture, mirrored its body position, and dropped her mouth open in a silent scream.

I closed my eyes for a second to keep from snapping at her —or cracking up.

Blake stiffened but said nothing.

Isabel turned to see what had my attention, but Rose snapped into a soldier stance, her expression all empathy and concern.

"Could you not stand behind me?" Isabel said. "It makes me nervous. I prefer to keep my employees in plain sight."

"You'd have to pay us if we were employees," Rose cracked as she circled the desk and finally dropped into the empty chair.

I glared at her.

"Some things are more valuable than money." Isabel's tone was thick with privilege. "Even my accountant knows that."

Her face crumpled, and she looked down at her hands, which she twisted together on her desktop.

"Anna," I said. "She was your accountant."

Rose sat straighter. "Any thoughts on who killed her?"

I rammed my heel into her toes. "Let's focus on the case at hand." The last thing we needed was for Isabel to return to thinking we cared more about that case than her painting.

"I need a diazepam." Isabel reached into her desk and extracted a pill bottle. She popped the childproof cap like a professional and tossed the pill in her mouth before swallowing it dry.

We *did* care more about Anna and our father than the painting, but no need to throw that in her face.

"What about Liam?" I asked. "He's a close friend of yours who has an interest in art."

"Liam is not a member of my household."

"But he's here often," Rose said.

Isabel waved her off. "He's knowledgeable about paintings. That's the extent of it."

We'd gotten all we would get from this conversation, so I stood. Rose popped to her feet too.

"Oh," I said as if it were an afterthought, "you said you'd think about getting us a copy of that camera footage for the last year, or as much of it as you have?"

"That shouldn't be necessary if the painting was stolen from the auction house."

"We want to be thorough."

"If you like, but I'll warn you that I've already had my security expert review it."

"You have a security expert?" Rose asked.

"On retainer. He is not an investigator—more of a consultant who stays fit and travels with me for protection."

"Sounds like a boy toy," Rose muttered, low enough for only me.

"The footage?" I pressed.

"Of course." She waved a hand. "Blake will send it over when I give him the okay. I'm still unsure whether I'm prepared to give you that level of access to my personal life."

"It's important."

She flicked her hand by way of a dismissal.

Blake led us back down the stairs and to the front door. In silence, he opened it and stood aside.

I tightened my blazer around me, and Rose and I stepped out into the fall air.

"It's going to take us forever to get through that video," Rose said after the manor's door closed behind us. "We don't have time for that, and we don't have the money to hire help."

"We'll cross that bridge when we come to it. For now, let's dig deeper into Eliza, Blake, and Liam."

LIAM O'CONNELL'S RESIDENCE WAS AS CHARMING AS THE MAN HIMSELF. Its exterior melded modern and rustic, with dark wood panels blending seamlessly into expansive black-framed windows.

I trailed Rose up the path to the porch. The door swung open before we reached it, and Liam flew out.

He stopped inches from slamming into her. "I'm sorry." He straightened his red-stitched charcoal vest.

Rose stepped back out of his personal space. "No problem."

"On your way out?" I asked.

"Yes, can I help you ladies another time?" He stepped onto the porch and reached to close the door. "Ivy and . . . Rose, is it?"

"We can tag along," I said. "We don't mind."

He froze, the door still open behind him, then he stepped back through it. "I can chat for a few minutes." He motioned us inside.

The foyer enveloped us in a blend of sophistication and bohemian charm, with soft lighting showing off the art on the walls. The paintings had a cohesive style and mood, with thick brushstrokes in earthy tones. It gave the space warmth.

Liam held out an arm to the left, and I followed it into a sitting room. Leather sofas beckoned near a grand fireplace, and cloth-spined books and curios lined the shelves.

"I'd love to sit and chat at leisure," Liam said, his words tripping over one another in a race, "but I have only a moment."

I settled into the sofa, and the leather sighed as it accepted my weight. "You've been so helpful. We have just a few follow-up questions so we can exclude certain suspects. We're trying to narrow our list."

"I'll try." His gaze darted toward the door.

I looked at Rose and patted the spot beside me. When she didn't sit right away, I left my hand there and stared at her.

She sat.

I pulled out my notepad and pen, readied myself to take notes.

Rose got straight to the point. "We were at the auction house yesterday, and the security was crap. I went in through the loading dock because no one was watching it. There was even a delivery truck with its door open and art inside."

"That doesn't sound like Irving. Are you sure?"

"Am I sure I climbed in through the loading bay and saw unsecured art? Yeah."

Liam paused and squinted at her. It took people a moment to get used to her sarcasm—I was still working on that myself.

"Based on your experience with the auction house," I said, "would items in that truck have been authenticated already?"

"No." He recovered his composure, and the lines on his face smoothed. "Irving authenticates every item after it comes under his care, and those were still in the care of the delivery company."

I wrote that down. "So let's assume the real painting made it off that truck and into Irving's lockup. It was authenticated and then, hypothetically, stolen before the handoff to Isabel."

"That could have been before or after the auction," Rose added.

"Before is extremely unlikely," Liam said. "The authenticator would have done her work right in the lockup. Once in there, it would stay until the auction. That makes the thief's work harder."

I scribbled a note. "The transfer is the weak point."

"In my experience," Rose said, "the best time to steal something is when people think it's impossible. Then they're off their guard."

Liam and I stared. His expression said confusion while mine said *Why would you say that?*

"So I've heard," Rose added. "What about the authenticator? Is he reliable?"

"*She.* And very." Still standing in the doorway of the foyer,

Liam shot a look at the exit. "I can give you her card if you like, but then I really have to go."

"No need," I said. "I got it from Irving a couple days ago." To Rose, I added, "The authenticator was in town for less than eight hours. She specializes in impressionist works, so Irving hired her specifically for the Monet. Outside of that short span, she has zero connection to Isabel or Willow Lake."

"I'll also add to that," Liam said, "she and I have mutual acquaintances. From what I hear, her credentials and trust-worthiness are above reproach."

Rose leaned over to me. "An authenticator would probably make a good forger."

I shushed her.

Liam's eyes ping-ponged between us like he was watching a match. He checked his watch. "But I can't help you exclude Irving." He was back to speaking too quickly. "If the switch happened at the auction house, Irving was in on it. He's a micromanager. Nothing gets past him."

"Is there a chance he let his guard down?" I asked.

Liam pointed at the corners of the ceiling. "You might have noticed the cameras."

I looked up, but there was nothing there.

"In the auction house," he added. "Everywhere. Irving has those reviewed every day."

"So if he didn't know about it at the time," I said, "it didn't stay secret for long."

A quick nod and then, "I can't help you exclude Mina either. In the past year, she's become more competent, the only one he trusts and delegates to. If he did something, she's in it with him."

I tapped my pen against the notebook. "Do you know how well Isabel pays her staff?"

Liam's eyebrows shot up. "You suspect one of her people?"

"We're considering all possibilities."

He thought for a moment. "Isabel isn't big on giving raises or praise—I know that much. I'm sure that doesn't go over well."

"Anything else that might cause them to be disgruntled?"

Liam chuckled. "She can be overbearing, but the staff knows they signed on for that. She's not all bad, though. She pulled strings to get her maid, Olivia, her apartment despite Olivia's bad credit. Olivia probably doesn't even know. She also gave Eliza an allowance to help her get back on her feet after her divorce."

"Eliza's been divorced two years?" I asked.

"That's when she moved in with Isabel. It was meant to be short-term. Last year, Isabel mentioned being fed up with the arrangement and that she might stop the payments."

Rose clutched my hand, and my pulse hurried forward. We were on the same page.

"Did she?" I asked. "Stop the allowance?"

Eliza had all the trademarks of someone who would have a personal grudge against Isabel. Her aunt treated her poorly, and she'd stopped giving her money. That would leave Eliza resentful and in a position to refill her funds by stealing the painting. Plus, she was an artist. She could have done the forgery herself.

Liam shrugged. "I'm sorry I can't say for sure. Do you think it's pertinent?"

"I didn't realize she was so generous," I said, my tone casual despite the excitement throwing a party in my head.

"Tax write-offs, suggested by her accountant."

I wrote that down, and Rose and I exchanged a glance.

Rose inched to the edge of her seat. "Was Anna Baxter Isabel's accountant?"

Liam closed his eyes for a second. "I assume so. I was devastated to hear of her passing." He checked the time on his phone. "Are we almost done? I'm meeting my wife for lunch, and she hates me to be late."

"Just about," I said. "You seem to know Isabel well."

"It's a small town." He walked to the archway that led back into the foyer. "That's all I have time for."

We'd caught him off guard and pushed him enough. Any more, and he would get hostile.

I got to my feet and snapped my notepad closed. "Thanks for your time. We really appreciate it."

He led us to the door, ushered us out, and followed us onto the porch.

As he locked it, he added, "I wish I could give you more time, but I don't know what else I could tell you. If there are shady dealings at the auction house, Irving knows about them, and there's a reason he hasn't acted on that knowledge."

"What reason?" Rose asked.

"Excuse me?"

"For what reason might Irving allow shady dealings to go on under his roof?" Rose asked.

Liam stared at her and then at me. "It's your job to find that out."

CHAPTER 22

IVY

ROSE WAS OUT OF THE CAR BEFORE I PUT IT IN PARK. I KILLED THE engine and shot after her toward the building that housed Gray Investigations. I took the stairs two at a time.

When I caught up, Rose was rattling the doorknob. "Tell me you can open it."

"Who do you think locked it?" I fished the key from my purse and opened the door.

We stormed into the waiting room and headed straight for Caleb's inner office. Rose's hand hitched on the doorknob, and tension tightened her shoulders.

"The cleaning crew is done, and we were going to have to go in there eventually," I said quietly. "Follow the money. This case was always about money."

Rose pushed the door open.

The two filing cabinets stood against the side wall. We hovered in the doorway.

"We'll have to break them open," Rose said.

"You don't pick locks?" It was half a joke and half a hope.

She shook her head.

I marched to my dad's desk, ducked, and searched the drawers. A screwdriver or something else long and metal might work to pry the cabinets open. Nothing. The bloody letter opener that had been here when we first found Anna was long gone too.

Movement above caught my attention, and I glanced up to find Rose standing closer than before. The desk calendar that had been squared up perfectly with the desktop was now skewed.

I cocked my head at her.

Rose shuffled backward. "Personal space, right?"

I sat back on my heels. "We'll have to go find some—" My gaze landed on a metal stapler on the desktop. I swept it up and bounced it in one hand to measure its heft. "This will do."

Rose slid aside, and I banged the metal stapler into the lock of the left cabinet's top drawer. It didn't budge.

I slammed it again, and the heavy metal stapler clanged against the lock. The entire cabinet rocked.

"Again," Rose said. "Break the lock!"

I grunted. "What do you think I'm doing?" I swung again, putting my whole back into it.

The metal drawer bounced open, the lock still fully intact.

She and I stood still, staring at it.

I pointed. "That was locked before, right?"

Rose grabbed the top drawer of the other cabinet and slid it right open. "The sheriff's people must have searched it."

"Works for me." I walked my fingers across the files in my

drawer, peeking into every other one. "These are all Dad's cases."

Rose pulled a sheet of paper from hers and angled it toward me. "Financial reports." She tapped the top of the filing cabinet. "These are for Anna's accounting business. They're arranged by date."

"Look for Montgomery." I closed my drawer and squatted next to Rose. I pulled open the third drawer of her filing cabinet while she riffled through the first.

"I know that," she snapped.

Rose closed the top drawer and moved to the second one. I closed the third and started on the bottom one.

After a minute, I waved Isabel's file in the air. "Found it!"

We closed our drawers with unison bangs, and I opened the file folder on Anna's desk. Rose read over my shoulder, her face so close I could feel her breath.

The first page was no help, so I flipped to the second.

After a moment, Rose reached over me for the stack of remaining paper to flip another page.

"Don't mind me," I said with all the sarcasm I could push into the words.

She flipped another page.

I grabbed her wrist.

She froze. "Look." She pointed at a line item. "Isabel stopped Eliza's allowance twelve months ago."

"And less than three weeks later . . ." I flipped the page and pointed to a much larger amount. "She bought the Monet."

Rose perched on the edge of the desk. "Eliza divorces her rich husband on Isabel's encouragement and moves in, expecting the financial support her aunt promised."

"Isabel reneges after a year, but she still has Eliza running errands to the auction house." I raised a finger in the air. "Which presents the perfect opportunity."

"Eliza's pissed and resentful about her situation. Discovering the Monet must have felt serendipitous—a way to get money and get back at her aunt. She was familiar with Lakeview Luxe, so she probably knew about its security issues. All she had to do was paint the forgery and swap it."

"Eliza stole the painting," I finished.

ROSE CUT THE ENGINE AS WE PULLED UP OUTSIDE ISABEL'S GRAND mansion. The imposing white stone structure loomed over the landscaped grounds.

I snatched my car keys from her. "You're not authorized to drive my rental."

"You didn't have to go along for the ride."

"You stole my keys!"

"Then call your FBI buddies and report it."

"The FBI doesn't usually do car theft, and you know that. Second, if I didn't get in, there'd be no one to talk you out of this terrible idea. Confronting Eliza right now—"

"You talk a lot." Rose was out of the car before I could finish.

I hurried after her but paused to press the lock button on my key fob. The car's horn honked to confirm.

"Rose," I called after her, "it's too soon to confront her. We need to question her just like we did with everyone else. We need more evidence."

"Confronting her will get us that evidence."

"No, confronting her will put her on guard and give her the opportunity to destroy anything before we find it."

Isabel emerged from the house with her hair in a high bun and a tan peacoat slung over one arm. Blake followed and closed and locked the door behind them.

"Ms. Gray, two reports in one day?" he asked me. He glanced at Isabel as if waiting for instructions.

Isabel's brow scrunched as her gaze landed on Rose, who had almost reached the path around the house. "Ms. Gray," she called.

"Rose," I said.

"Ms. *Rose* Gray!" she shouted.

Rose stopped and turned in our direction.

"What's going on?" Isabel's voice was higher-pitched than usual, so she must have been thoroughly annoyed to find us here unannounced.

"We're here for Eliza," Rose said. "She—"

"We didn't have an opportunity to question her along with the rest of your household," I said. "She might have information, especially since she frequents the auction house."

"Ms. Gray, both of you, come here." Isabel waved us over, and Rose and I exchanged a look before meeting her at the bottom of the white stone porch.

Blake came down to our level while Isabel stopped one stone step above the ground.

"Eliza stole the painting," Rose blurted out. "The real one is probably still in her guesthouse, waiting to meet its buyer."

"That's not helping," I muttered low enough for only her ears.

When I'd told her not to confront Eliza, I had not meant we should confront Isabel instead. If we wanted our client's continued cooperation, accusing her niece was not the way to get there.

"She's an artist," Rose went on, "and we know you were giving her money on a monthly basis until twelve months ago, shortly before you bought the Monet. I'm guessing she helped you pick it out."

Isabel licked her lips rather than answer.

That was a yes.

I shifted in front of Rose. "What my sister means is that Eliza is on our list of suspects, but we are still in the midst of fact-finding."

"In the midst of fact-finding?" Rose whispered from behind me. "Who talks like that?"

"Since Eliza was familiar with the auction house," I continued, "she might also have insight into whether any employees there might have a reason to conspire to steal it."

"She's a painter," Rose said, "so she could have forged it herself."

I squeezed my eyes shut for a second because Rose was determined to dig us deeper into this hole that I was trying desperately to fill.

Isabel spread her feet to shoulder width as if readying for a fight. "Eliza would never . . . She could never. She's never been that talented of an artist, and you're telling me she forged a Monet."

"As I said, we're just—"

"Don't." Isabel cut me off with one raised hand. "It was a mistake to bring you on this case with no proof of your experience."

"She's in the FBI," Rose said.

I stepped backward and pressed my heel into her toes.

"Eliza's work is mostly fantasy creatures for a reason. She never could get the hang of painting real people and places."

I tried to keep the irritation off my face at this insult to Eliza. I'd seen her work firsthand and, abstract or not, it was brilliant.

I pulled Rose farther away from Isabel. "We're sorry to have upset you, Mrs. Montgomery. We are more than capable of handling this investigation."

From her perch on the porch step, she had a great angle to peer down her nose at us.

"Rose." I tugged her arm. "Let's go. We can call Eliza to set up a conversation later."

"There is no later," Isabel snapped.

Blake's eyes widened, and he took a step back.

He knew her well, so I cringed for whatever was incoming.

"You're fired. Both of you. I'll confer with the police to find my Monet."

"The local police aren't equipped to investigate a forger," I said. "It's not exactly common in small towns. Plus, they have their hands full with the murder."

Isabel paled but stood firm, still staring down at us.

Rose spun toward the guesthouse. "In that case, there's nothing to stop me from seeing her now."

"Trespassing!" Isabel called after her.

I ran after Rose. With a huff, Isabel came too, and Blake's long-legged stride took up the rear.

The cottage exterior was a picturesque display of off-white stone and blue shutters. A garden of vibrant flowers flanked the path to the entrance.

Rose got there first and banged on the door.

By the time Isabel caught up, her bun had fallen loose, and

her red face looked as if it might catch fire. "I really must insist you—"

Rose banged again. "Eliza, are you in there?"

"Should I call the sheriff?" Blake asked in a tone almost too low for my ears.

Isabel waved him away as if he were a gnat. "She's home. She usually answers."

"She may be sleeping," I said.

"No, she usually paints at this hour," Louder, she called, "Eliza, would you answer the door, please?"

"Eliza!" Rose rattled the doorknob. When that failed, she tried the window next to the door. "Locked."

"Eliza," Isabel called, her voice now tinged with high-pitched worry.

Rose was staring in through the window, her jaw slack.

"What?" I came up beside her.

She moved aside and pulled me into her spot.

Inside, an end table and lamp lay on the floor, the lamp shade askew. The coffee table was on its side, pushed up against the sofa.

"We need to get in there," I said.

Rose searched the ground and lifted a rock from the side of the path. She hoisted it to her shoulder as if checking its weight.

"That's Plan B." I held up my hands for her to wait. To Isabel, I added, "Do you have a key?"

She rummaged through her oversized purse with shaking hands. She pulled out a key ring and fumbled to flip through it until she landed on a brass-colored one.

She fit the key in the lock and pushed the door open.

The three of us filed into the cozy, colorful living room. The walls were adorned with vibrant abstract paintings, staring down at a cramped, disheveled space.

"Eliza!" Isabel emitted a strangled roar.

Rose pulled her back to the doorway as if to shield her from what was inside.

Eliza lay on her back with her reddened eyes wide and her mouth open in a forever scream. Red marks circled her throat.

CHAPTER 23
ROSE

Ivy, Blake, and I stood aside while Isabel wailed over Eliza's body.

The guesthouse looked like a tornado ripped through it. The low coffee table was flipped on its side, tangled with the cord of a lamp smashed beside a toppled side table. Farther in, an armchair had been shoved out of the way, leaving a deep scrape in the hardwood.

At the end of the wreckage was Eliza, her neck red, blue, and bruised and her head lolling to one side. She lay with legs stretched straight and her arms flopped near her head. A cracked phone, the same model as mine, lay inches from one hand.

Isabel slumped to the floor and pulled her niece's lifeless form onto her lap.

Hot saliva filled my mouth, and I swallowed hard to keep from vomiting. "Guess Eliza wasn't guilty after all," I mumbled, mostly to myself.

Pale-faced, Ivy grunted but didn't respond. She hugged her arms around her waist.

Beside her, Blake glared at me through red-rimmed eyes. His hands trembled, and he pressed them to his legs as if to steady them.

"Please," Isabel mumbled between sobs, "just leave. The painting isn't here. If Eliza had it, whoever killed her took it." She smoothed Eliza's hair away from her face and let out a trembling breath. "She was all I had left of my sister. I just wanted her to live up to her potential."

Blake took out his phone and stepped to the corner of the room—I assumed to call the sheriff's office.

"Mrs. Montgomery," I said. "I'm so sorry for your loss. If there's anything we can do to help..." I opened my hands at my sides.

"There's nothing . . . There's nothing . . ." Isabel rocked back and forth, her arms clasped around Eliza's body.

With unfocused eyes, her gaze skipped over Eliza's paintings, the mismatched furniture, and the dim fairy lights draped around the ceiling. Her attention kept going back to the door like she was looking for an escape from her grief.

I wasn't an FBI agent, but even I knew this was not the way to treat evidence.

"Mrs. Montgomery." Ivy stepped forward, but I held out a hand to stop her.

"She's already touched the body," I whispered. "Let her grieve."

Ivy stepped back and bent her head.

Isabel scanned the room. Unfocused, her gaze skittered left to right before returning to the open door. She squinted at a small geometric statue beside the doorframe.

She stopped rocking.

"Mrs. Montgomery?" I said.

Isabel laid Eliza's head on the floor and crawled to the sculpture. Ivy and I exchanged a look, her face mirroring my concern for Isabel's state of mind.

The woman gripped the statue like a bat. She dug her nails into it and ripped away the outer paper that had been draped to look solid. Painted and molded on the outside, the paper was dull brown on the inside. Tearing it away revealed a plain rectangular block standing on . . .

Isabel revealed the Monet that had been used as the statue's base, hidden only by skillfully wrapped paper.

"The painting," Ivy whispered.

Blake ended his call and slipped the phone away with shaking hands. He stepped forward to reach for the Monet, thought better of it, and stepped back.

Isabel crawled back to Eliza and clutched both her niece and the painting to her body. Sobs wracked her chest.

"How did you know it was there?" I asked.

Isabel gasped, and her sobs quieted to a whimper. "We used to play this game when she was a child. Eliza would hide things inside her art." She rubbed her hand across her face to wipe the tears. "The sculpture was just the right size."

Blake cleared his throat. "The sheriff is on his way."

Isabel sniffed and wiped her nose.

"We should all wait outside," Ivy said, "to preserve the crime scene."

Isabel tightened her arms around her niece and the painting. "I'm not leaving her."

I looked around for a seat farther away from the body,

found a chair in the corner of the room, and settled into it. "I'll stay with her."

Isabel glanced at me with red eyes and nodded.

Ivy looked around for a spot to stand. Finding none that suited her, she stayed put and crossed her arms over her chest. "I guess I'll stay too."

Blake moved to the still-open door. "I'll meet them at the main house." He left and pulled the door shut behind him.

Ivy flinched as it clicked closed.

The three of us waited in silence, except for Isabel's occasional whimpers, until Blake returned maybe five minutes later.

Deputies Marks and Ramirez followed him inside.

I didn't know what those two had done to get on someone's shit list, but they seemed to catch all the murders in town.

Marks's face was ghost pale. A sheen of sweat covered his forehead. But he kept his shoulders square and head high.

Beside him, Ramirez glared at me. Her straight black hair was tied back, and her sharp features looked even more severe with the scowl she leveled. To be fair, I probably looked like a jinx to her by now.

"I need everyone to wait outside." Ramirez kept it crisp and professional.

"Not yet," Isabel said in a tone hoarse from crying.

"Mrs. Montgomery, please. We need to clear the crime scene to give us the best chance of finding who did this."

"Give me a minute!" Isabel wailed.

After a second's hesitation, Ramirez collected everyone else in the room except Marks and guided us through the door.

"Don't touch anything else," she told Isabel before stepping outside.

She left the door open and pointed at Blake. "Wait at the house. I'll get your version there in a moment."

He nodded and hurried away.

"You two know the drill by now." She pointed at Ivy. "You, stay here." She pointed at Deputy Marks and then me before gesturing away somewhere into the distance.

Marks motioned for me to follow him. We walked the garden path in the direction opposite the way Blake went. It wound around to the back of the guesthouse and off to the side. Soon, the entrance was out of view.

Marks pointed an open hand at a bench. Before I could sit, movement caught my attention, and my head jerked up. I squinted into the shrubbery.

Olivia peeked up over a flowering bush. Black hair and brown skin made her hard to spot in the dusk, but I was on high alert after what I'd just witnessed.

I opened my mouth to call out to her, but she shook her head like it was on fire. I clamped it shut.

"You okay?" Marks asked. He followed my gaze, but Olivia ducked lower. "Do you see something?"

"No." I waved to draw his attention back to me. "Just a little shaken up."

I sat on the bench.

He took the spot beside me and turned to face me in a posture that couldn't be comfortable on this hard metal seat. "Take me through it, starting from what brought you to the manor today."

I took a deep breath and launched into my story about

Isabel's painting, how we had worked the case, how I suspected Eliza, and how we ended up here standing over her body. He asked questions, and I answered as truthfully as possible. Luckily, he didn't ask about my PI license, so I didn't have to lie at all.

He scribbled it all down on his notepad.

We went over it twice before he snapped the notebook closed.

"We're done for now, but I may need to follow up at a later date."

"Do you think this is connected to Anna's murder?" I asked. "I don't imagine you get a lot of homicides here."

"I couldn't say." He stood, and I took my cue to do the same.

When we reached the front of the guesthouse, crime scene tape had been erected in an arc protecting the entrance. Marks ducked under it. I peeked around him as he opened the door, but he slipped inside and closed it before I could see anything.

Ivy sat on a bench just outside the tape, her hands folded in her lap like she was at a tea party.

I took a seat beside her.

"Ramirez questioned Blake, and Isabel is waiting at the main house," she said, still looking down at her lap. "Ramirez is inside working the crime scene."

"Efficient," I said.

Ivy nodded. "Isabel's back in the main house resting."

The conversation lulled. The quiet of the garden pressed in too hard. "Finding dead bodies really puts a damper on private investigations," I said.

Ivy's face twitched, and she barked a laugh. She went somber again a few seconds later. "Thanks. I needed that."

Ramirez marched out the door and stood over us. "Marks

said something about a painting." She eyed me. "Where is the painting?"

"It's not inside?"

"I wouldn't be asking if it was." To Ivy, she added, "You didn't mention anything about a painting."

She raised her hands, palm up. "You haven't questioned me yet. You keep telling me to wait."

"Let's do that right now." Ramirez pointed at me. "You can go."

I stood. "The painting's not in there? Isabel had it right next to Eliza's . . ." I gestured at the guesthouse. *Body* was the word I didn't say.

She scowled but kept her attention on Ivy.

I headed back to the house. Ivy should be safe. She was capable and accompanied by two armed deputies.

The case of the missing painting—the innocuous case we'd picked up to allow us to be nosy all over town—was now a murder investigation.

CHAPTER 24
ROSE

THE NEXT MORNING, I SQUATTED ON THE PORCH, DRILL IN HAND, TO install the doorbell camera I'd just picked up. The instructions were short, and the only part left was to wire it to power.

The front door opened, and I scrambled out of its path.

"Sorry." Vera stepped through with last night's pie in one hand and a tub of fried chicken in the other.

"No problem. I'm almost finished here."

She squinted at the packaging for the new doorbell and the remains of her old one on the porch along with her drill. "I know you're good with computers, but shouldn't we hire someone to do this?"

"This is a problem I created." I squinted at the skeleton of the new bell, its cover off and wires exposed. "I'm going to finish it."

"Maybe hiring an electrician is the best way to do that."

I gave her a flat look until she raised her food in the air in surrender.

"Have it your way." She set the pie and tub on one of the rocking chairs on the other side of the door. "Can I help?"

"I've got this. I already put the batteries back in your other cameras and connected them to your newly secure Wi-Fi. It's got a new password now."

"Great. What is it?"

I rattled it off.

She gave me a blank look.

"Don't worry. I saw your laptop in the sunroom and put the new credentials in there. It's connected to the network."

"That computer is locked."

"With a terrible password. You should really change that."

She gaped, shaking her head. "Give me the Wi-Fi password again."

I said it more slowly this time.

"I'm never going to remember that."

"I can teach you how. There's an art to it."

"Why don't you just write it down for me?"

I gave her a flat look.

"Okay, okay, I'll try to remember it." She swept up the food and stepped off the porch. "I'll deliver this offering to Paul and Lawrence."

"You could give them a *half* pie, you know. They sell halves at the grocery store. It's a perfectly normal amount to gift." Even at room temperature, it still smelled amazing.

She shifted the pie farther away from me. "They brought a whole cheesecake. I will bring them a whole pie."

She lifted the chicken tub in a wave and headed across the street to the gray cottage.

I turned back to the new doorbell and connected the wires

just like they'd been on the old one. I pressed the button and held my breath for the familiar chime.

Silence.

I hissed, but the bell didn't look intimidated.

Ivy's sedan pulled up to the curb and stopped. She said nothing as she got out and strolled to the porch. By the time she reached me, she had my full attention.

"What's up?" I asked.

She sat in one rocking chair and waved at the other.

I dropped into it and steeled myself. I didn't like the tension in her face. Usually, people knew me for at least a month before breaking up with me, but we could do this now if she wanted.

"I'm sorry about that thing at the bar," she said.

I raised my brows.

"I could have handled it better."

"In what way? By *not* warning me to leave Pearl alone, or by *not* trying to break up our scuffle? Because you did both those things."

She placed her hands palm up on her knees. "There must have been a way to handle that without you ending up in jail for hours. I'm sure that wasn't pleasant."

I shifted in my seat. Seconds of silence followed.

She folded her hands.

"See," I said, "it's awkward because you don't know if I've ever been in jail before."

"I know you don't have a criminal record. Possibly, that means you're a very *good* criminal."

I pointed at her. "Innocent until proven guilty. No record equals no crimes."

"Fair enough."

"About the bar, though. I make my own choices. I'm the one who swung at Pearl. I'm the one who hit Deputy Ramirez. I got what was coming to me. Not your fault."

She shook her head.

"Not everything's on you," I said.

She unfolded her hands and clasped them in the other direction.

"This isn't on you at all. You can't control everything."

"That's not what I'm doing," she snapped. "I'm not a control freak."

Whoa, soft spot. "Control *enthusiast*, then? Control expert. Connoisseur of control."

She laughed, and her hands relaxed. "Those are all okay. Thank you."

I would win her over yet. "You came all the way here to apologize that I got into a fight?"

"And to talk about the case."

I nodded for her to continue. "The one we're fired from."

For the first time, her gaze landed on the naked doorbell. Its wires still hung loose. "What's this?"

I made a point not to look at it or the drill lying beneath. "Just installing a doorbell camera."

Ivy's eyes narrowed, but she said nothing.

"Security is kind of my thing." Against my will, my pitch rose at the end like I was asking a question instead of answering one.

"Is this about the note?"

I tensed.

"The person who left it on your car probably didn't do it here. It could have been there for hours. Besides, there have been no more threats. It was clearly a bluff, and we called it."

My tension loosened, and I slumped back into the hard wooden seat. Ivy didn't know anything about the stalkerish photo, and I wasn't going to tell her. She'd made it clear she wouldn't investigate anything in Willow Lake if we were threatened.

"I figured the camera couldn't hurt," I said.

She nodded. "Isabel fired us, but she was pissed at the time. We still need the information she has about Dad. I say we go back with a new plan, ready to impress her into rehiring us. We've split our focus between Dad's case and Isabel's. I think we need to focus on Isabel's for now—which is officially a murder investigation."

I drew a long breath that was shakier than I wanted to admit. I'd signed on to this case for a front-row seat to find my deadbeat dad. Now, that came with not one but two murders. Anna's and Eliza's.

"Eliza's death is connected to the painting theft," Ivy continued like I wasn't two whole inhales from a panic attack. "The best way to solve both crimes is to create a timeline for her murder and identify her killer."

"Do we know what time she died?"

Ivy closed her eyes in a long, irritated blink. "The coroner and the sheriff's office refused to tell me. We'll pay Isabel another visit to get that information since they'll have filled her in on the details."

"After we get the time of death?" I asked.

"We'll use that to exclude people from our suspect list."

After a few seconds of silence, I asked, "Is this how you investigate in the FBI?"

"Yes and no. I identify suspects and narrow them down. Press them until the truth falls out." Her face scrunched.

"People think the FBI is all asking permission to ask permission. To some degree it is, but I have autonomy to follow my cases as I see fit as long as I stick to procedure."

"Yes *and* no. What's the *no* part?"

"Normally, I have more resources. I could run checks on our suspects. That sort of thing."

"You don't have access to all that because you're on leave?"

She scrunched her lips. "I'm not on the best terms with my squad at the moment."

I gave her time to expand on that.

Instead, she refolded her hands in her lap.

I changed the subject. "Next time we have a team meeting, we should have it at Gray Investigations."

Her hands tightened their grip around each other for a second and then loosened. "The cleaners did a good job, and we *are* investigating . . ."

"And our name is Gray," I finished for her.

Across the street, a door slammed, and Vera marched back toward us. She stomped up the porch, fuming like a chimney.

"Problem?" I asked.

"They're so *nice*," she said in short bursts. "I bring them food, and they insist I eat with them. Then they invite me to dinner next week." Her voice had gone maniacally high. "Apparently, Paul is a chef."

"I don't see the problem," Ivy said.

The door across the street opened again, and Lawrence hurried over, carrying the same plastic tub Vera had brought him.

"Vera," he said when he reached us, "you forgot your container."

She reached for it but stopped when he lifted the lid, revealing a collection of lemon squares.

"What's this?" she squeaked.

"Paul baked yesterday and couldn't let you leave without a parting gift." He lifted the tub toward me. "Enough for everyone, of course."

She snatched the tub from him and clapped the lid back on. "Thank you." She stomped into the house. Through the open door, the sound of her heavy footfalls continued until she disappeared into the sunroom.

Lawrence pointed to the drill and the two doorbells. "What's going on?"

"We had a security scare a couple days ago," I said, "so I'm installing a doorbell camera. I think it's a dud, though."

He leaned close to inspect my wiring, then grunted approval. But when he pushed the button, nothing happened. "Did you install the jumper cable into your chime box?"

"Excuse me?"

"Where's the packaging?"

I pointed at the box the new bell came in, tossed off to the side.

He laughed and bent toward it. "Do you mind?"

"Go for it."

Lawrence opened it and extracted a short cable with a connector on each end. I swiped the instructions page off the porch and offered it to him, but he declined with a smile and a hand wave. He paused in the doorway until I waved him through.

"Where's your chime box—the thing that makes noise when someone presses the bell?"

I pointed. It was above his head, so I pulled the stepladder from the closet. He grabbed it from me before I could set it up. In thirty seconds, he'd opened the chime box and installed the jumper cable.

"Try it now," he said as he returned the stepladder to its place.

I stepped outside and rang the bell. It chimed, and I clapped. "Awesome."

"I'm an electrician." He gestured across the street. "I've done a thousand of these, including my own."

"So you would have footage from two days ago?" I asked.

He stepped back, his brow crinkling.

"The security scare I mentioned . . ." If I told him someone had actually come inside and left a vague-but-not-subtle stalkerish threat, he'd probably spill it to Vera. A half-truth would have to do. "Someone was hanging around outside our front door, and I want a closer look."

"Oh my God! Did they steal anything? Break anything?"

I waved my hand. "Nothing like that, but it would be great if I could see your footage from ten thirty in the morning to five."

"Sure, no problem. I'll grab it from the cloud for you and send it over the first chance I get."

"Fantastic."

Soon, I'd know who was stalking me and whether it was related to Eliza's murder or Anna's.

CHAPTER 25

ROSE

Ivy rang the doorbell of Montgomery Manor while I hopped from foot to foot behind her on the porch. The chill gnawed through my sweater like it was made of wet tissue paper.

"Ring it again," I said after a minute.

"You should have brought a jacket."

"My sweater is fine. Ring it again." I stamped my foot to keep my toes from going numb.

My home city of Atlanta wasn't far from here and had a similar climate, so I should have known better. In my defense, it was entirely too cold for fall in the South.

"We should have called ahead," Ivy said.

I was rubbing off on her. The Ivy I'd met a week ago would not have come here without an appointment. This new version of my sister needed only a little convincing and a promise to wait until the afternoon—which we had. Now, it was two o'clock, and the household should be wide awake, although still reeling from last night.

I shoved past her and rang the bell three times in quick succession. We had an investigation to finish and couldn't do that from this freezing porch.

First, close the painting case. Second, close Eliza's murder. Then, and only then, could we gain the townspeople's trust and dig into our father and Anna.

The door swung open, and Olivia stood there with a smile that cracked and crumbled as soon as she spotted me. The door reversed course, but I stuck my foot in the way and shoved through.

"Rose," Ivy said. "You can't—"

"I need to talk to you," I said to Olivia.

She backed up.

I pointed at her. "She was in the garden last night, sneaking around like a criminal."

Ivy raised a brow.

"I don't know what you mean." Two more steps back, and Olivia's knees bent like she was ready to bolt.

"Drop the act," I said. "We can report what I saw to Isabel, or you can tell us what's going on."

Olivia glanced around the empty grand entrance. "Not here."

She led us up the grand staircase to the sitting room where we first met when I knocked over the vase. It had been replaced with a larger, more ornate one.

Olivia ushered Ivy and me inside. "Mrs. Montgomery never comes in here."

As far as I could tell, the only purpose of a second-floor sitting room was to prove you were rich enough to have rooms you didn't need.

"Why were you in the garden last night?" I shot as soon as I verified we were alone.

Olivia stood stiff as a plank, eyes wide as if a truck beared down on her.

Ivy put a hand on my shoulder and gently moved me aside. "Easy," she whispered. At speaking volume, she added, "Where is Blake? He normally answers the door."

"In class. He's dedicated to his studies." Olivia leaned forward as if taking us into her confidence. "His office is spotless, and I never clean it. He's very particular about the things he does."

Ivy grinned. Olivia was impossible not to like. Even under stress, she put other people at ease and made me root for her. None of that changed the fact that she was our best lead right now.

Ivy led Olivia to a seating cluster in the corner of the room, opposite the massive fireplace and mantle. Olivia dropped into a seat. Ivy took the chair across from her, and I stood to the side, hands on hips, itching to jump into the real questions.

"When was the last time you saw Eliza alive?" Ivy asked in a soothing voice designed to put the other woman at ease.

Olivia pulled in a deep breath and sighed it out. "Monday morning around ten thirty. She was sitting on the bench outside the guesthouse."

A chill skittered down my spine, and I gripped the back of Ivy's chair to keep from shuddering. She and I had sat in that same place after finding the body. Just hours earlier, Eliza had spent her final peaceful moments on that bench.

"What was she doing?" My voice came out quiet, so I cleared my throat and repeated, "What was she doing?"

"She sometimes sat in the garden for inspiration," Olivia continued. "Meditation, thinking . . . living."

"What did she do after that?" Ivy pressed.

"I don't know. I didn't want to disturb her, so I let her be." Olivia's voice shook and fell apart. She pulled a small water bottle from under her apron, uncapped it, and gulped it down like she'd crossed a desert.

I saw an opening and pounced. "Later that night, why did you go back to the garden and hide from the deputies?"

"I had nothing to do with Eliza's death, if that's what you're thinking."

"Murder," I corrected.

"Excuse me?"

"Eliza's murder."

"I had nothing to do with it," she repeated firmly.

"Convince me."

Ivy glared a warning my way. "I believe you." She leaned forward. "So why were you there?"

"To see Eliza. But . . ." Olivia gestured but couldn't summon the words.

"You didn't kill her. I believe you," Ivy said in a voice so smooth it made melted butter jealous. "But it looks bad. The sheriff's office could get suspicious. Isabel has cameras. They'll know you were there."

I rolled my eyes at this obvious trap. They did this on cop shows all the time—get the witness-slash-suspect to think they were on her side, show empathy to put her at ease enough to spill the truth. Olivia was too rattled to notice.

"We need to know everything so we can help you," Ivy continued.

Olivia shot a look over Ivy's head at the doorway. I moved to block her escape route.

Ivy changed tack. "You were friends with Eliza, weren't you?"

Olivia nodded, opened her mouth, clamped it shut, and nodded some more like a bobblehead.

"What does friendship mean to you, Olivia?"

"Loyalty, kindness," Olivia whispered. "Love."

"Shouldn't a loyal and kind friend want to help find her friend's killer?"

With a sob, Olivia dropped her face into her hands and made muffled sounds that might have been words.

Ivy reached over and lifted her chin. "Could you repeat that, please?"

"I . . . I did something terrible."

CHAPTER 26

IVY

"What did you do, Olivia?" I asked the sobbing woman across from me in Montgomery Manor.

My pulse pounded in my ears, excitement dragging it forward. This feeling of chasing a suspect and getting them to confess—this was what led me to the FBI. Knowing I played a role in bringing justice to the world kept me moving forward.

Despite her soft spot for Olivia, Rose stood nearby like a sentry ready to jump into action if she bolted.

"I stole Mrs. Montgomery's jewelry," Olivia blurted before dropping her face back into her already damp palms.

"Oh." I fought to keep my disappointment from showing.

"Did you steal from Eliza?" Rose asked.

"No!" Olivia's back straightened, and her hands fell into her lap. "I would never."

Rose circled my chair and sat beside Olivia. "And the painting?"

"No, no, no. I could never." She looked up at Rose and then

me with wet, pleading eyes. "Mrs. Montgomery—she leaves her things lying around like she doesn't even care about them. Careless with such expensive things!" Spittle sprayed from her lips, and she brought a hand up to cover her mouth.

"It's okay," Rose said. "Go on."

"She does not deserve such things, and I only took what *I* deserve."

"What you—" Rose started.

My glare cut the words right out of her mouth. This was still my interview, and sometimes the best option was to shut up and let the interviewee speak once their lips were loosened.

After a few seconds, Olivia continued, "She cuts my wages when something breaks or goes missing. She says either I stole it or I allowed it to be stolen." Venom flashed across her features. "As if my job is security!"

The room went silent except for Olivia's ragged breathing.

"In the past, I've been able to sell her jewelry online, no problem."

"How many things have you taken?" I kept my tone judgment free.

"This was the third time, and definitely the last."

"What happened *this* time?"

"The necklace was lovely and plain. I figured I could keep it, and no one would guess it was stolen."

Olivia pulled from her pocket a thin gold chain with a circular pendant. I reached out, and she dropped it into my palm. The chain fell over the back of my hand as I examined it.

I passed it back. "What's the problem?"

Olivia held up the narrow edge of the pendant. A tiny inscription read, "With Love, from Liam."

"Bummer," Rose said.

I shot her a glare. "What does Eliza have to do with the necklace?" I asked.

"She saw me wearing it at the Autumn Festival," Olivia said, her voice steadier now. "Kept staring at it. She must have recognized it. I just wanted to explain. I thought she could understand because . . . Mrs. Montgomery was cruel to her sometimes too."

"Cruel, how?" Rose asked.

"Putting her down all the time. Giving her money and then justifying the constant verbal jabs by saying Eliza should be grateful."

"Did you talk to her about the necklace?" I asked.

"That's why I was in the garden yesterday," Olivia said, her voice shaky again, "that night and in the morning too. I lost my nerve in the morning." She turned to me. "That's the real reason I didn't talk to her. We were friends . . . It was a lie—what I said before about not wanting to disturb her."

Rose squeezed her shoulder, and Olivia squeezed her hand right back.

"And last night?" I asked. "Did you see her again?"

She shook her head hard and blinked out tears. "She was already dead. I'm sorry. That's all I know."

I patted her hand and stood. "We believe you." I looked at Rose for confirmation.

"We believe you," she echoed.

Olivia wiped her eyes. "Please don't tell Mrs. Montgomery. I know she'll press charges."

Rose got up from her chair, pulled Olivia up, and hugged her. "Don't worry. We won't sell you out."

I cut another glare her way. We couldn't guarantee our silence. If Olivia's theft played any role, directly or indirectly, in the swapped painting, Eliza's murder, or our investigation of either, we couldn't stay quiet. If we needed to disclose her theft to make our case, we would.

I didn't like making promises I couldn't keep.

"We won't tell," Rose said.

"We promise not to tell," I added, "unless we need the information to complete our case report. Can you take us to Mrs. Montgomery? We have more questions, and only she can answer them."

Olivia inhaled an audible breath, wiped her face, and led us from the room. When we reached the hallway, Rose took the lead, storming down the corridor to Isabel's office.

I grabbed her arm. "Don't upset her. She just lost a niece."

All I got in return was a dismissive wave before she flung the French doors open.

"Blake, I—" Isabel halted mid-sentence. She squinted past us. "Did he let you in?"

"He's in class," I said.

"Very well. It's a waste of time for that boy. He'll never move up in the world without the proper connections." She shook her head. "So you barged in here to . . ."

"We need to talk about Eli—" Rose began. She stopped as her gaze lingered on something below her eyeline, something she was blocking from my view.

I stepped around her. On Isabel's glass desktop sat two identical miniature Monets. A void on the wall behind her marked where the authentic piece should've hung.

"Quite the pair, aren't they?" Isabel drummed her fingers on the glass.

"There are two," I said.

"Both belong to me, and I'll not have the true painting

wasting away in an evidence locker. It's mine to do with what I wish."

"Monet died a hundred years ago," Rose said. "If the painting hasn't wasted away already, it's not going to start now."

I gave her an elbow to the flank.

Isabel flipped one painting upside down, reached for the second one, and retracted her hand to her lap. I'd bet everything in my bank account the second painting was the real one.

She leaned back in her seat. "Why are you two still here? Eliza stole the painting. The case is over. I fired you."

"Eliza is dead," I said.

She held her chin up, but her eyelids fluttered over red eyes.

I spaced out my next words and softened my tone. "That, and the fact that the painting was hidden in her ransacked home, means there's more to this. Someone was looking for it."

"Nonetheless, you are still fired." She crossed one long leg over the other, showing off a pair of heels too thin for most people to walk in and too expensive for most to afford. "Tread carefully. Willow Lake can be quite unforgiving to those who stir its waters."

She could ruin us if she wanted to. With her influence and money, if Isabel told people not to patronize Gray Investigations, they would go two towns over to the next PI. No one would talk to us about their cases—let alone what happened to my father and Anna. More importantly, though, we needed the information Isabel had about our father.

And we needed justice for Eliza.

Even under her icy facade, Isabel couldn't hide the tremor in her hand as she brushed a stray strand of hair from her face.

I sat to put our eyes on the same level. "Isabel, let us help you find out what happened to Eliza."

"The sheriff can handle it." Her words were clipped.

Rose plopped into one of the high-backed chairs across from Isabel and gave it a spin. "About Liam . . ."

Isabel stiffened.

I shot Rose a glare, which she ignored.

Rose gave her chair another spin. "You wouldn't want rumors of an affair getting out."

Isabel widened her eyes at me, as if it was my job to keep Rose in line—as if anyone could keep Rose in line. "Excuse me?" Her voice was ice over steel.

"Client confidentiality is a cornerstone of our business." Rose stopped spinning and jerked her chair forward. "But that only applies to clients."

"I assure you, Liam and I are not involved."

Her voice was too high-pitched, and her hands fidgeted in her lap.

"He is married," she spat.

"I know." Rose grinned. "I understand Liam's wife is the source of his money. She's almost as big a deal as you are."

Isabel's mouth fell open, but she snapped it closed. She was more appalled at being compared to someone else than she was at being accused of an affair. "Who gave you this ridiculous idea?"

Rose's grin almost fell, but she managed to lock it in place. She didn't want to squeal on Olivia.

I picked up the slack. "If he's bought you jewelry, one of the shops in town will have a record of it. It's better to be honest with us now."

"He has not," she sputtered. "I buy all my own pieces."

"What's your Wi-Fi password?" Rose asked suddenly. "I've got no bars in here. Must be these thick, expensive walls."

Isabel glared but reached for a pen and a small notepad. She printed a string of letters and numbers before sliding it across the desk toward Rose.

Rose swiped up the notepad and examined the Montgomery letterhead at the top. "Fancy." She typed it into her phone.

Isabel blinked at her and then shifted her attention back to me. "Jewelry stores wouldn't disclose—"

"Look," Rose cut in, flashing us her phone screen. "There are only two places in town that have jewelry expensive enough for your tastes. I can call them right now to confirm that Liam bought you something from one of them. I can be pretty persuasive." She batted her eyelashes.

Isabel paled. "That won't be necessary. Liam and I are friends. He may have bought me earrings for a birthday at some point. But that's all."

"You were in a romantic relationship," I said. "Don't deny it. The truth is all over your face."

Isabel's face morphed through a series of expressions that ended in resignation. "You are rehired." She opened the top drawer of her desk and withdrew a small pill bottle. She wrenched off the top and popped a pill before returning the bottle to the drawer.

"You need to cover expenses for this case," Rose said. "Gas, surveillance, all of that. Or else we can't accept you back. We're already not getting paid."

I resisted the urge to grab her chair and shake her.

"You can't be serious?" Isabel screeched.

"Client confidentiality," Rose said.

"Plus," I added, "this is now a murder investigation. Murder is more expensive than theft."

After a pause, Isabel said, "The relationship ended over a year ago, well before I bought the painting."

"Irving treats him like a king at the auction house," I said, "so I assume everyone else there does as well. He had the connections to pull off the swap before the painting even got here. Easy peasy."

Rose turned to mouth my words back at me. *Easy peasy?*

I scowled. "He has motive too. He wanted that painting. Plus, he could have resented you for breaking things off."

"It was mutual."

"It's never mutual," Rose said.

"In either case, Liam would never steal from me. We have been friends for decades."

"You don't think he might have teamed with Eliza to steal the painting, and when she hid it instead of cashing in, he . . ." Rose touched her neck with her fingertips.

Isabel shuddered. "Absolutely not."

"Who else might have been connected to Eliza then?" I asked, redirecting the conversation before Rose could offend our client even more. "Whoever killed her was looking for the painting, which means they probably worked with her to steal it."

Isabel uncrossed her legs and fell back into the seat. "I . . . I don't know. Eliza was such a free spirit, such a sweet girl. I can't imagine she would be friends with someone who would . . ." She sat up straight. "Her ex-husband, Jake Thompson."

I reached for my notepad. "Do you have his number?"

Isabel rattled it off from memory, and I wrote it down.

"Let's talk timeline." I softened my voice because this would be a difficult conversation for an aunt who, despite all her flaws, loved her niece. "Did the sheriff's office give you a time of death?"

"Between one and five in the afternoon."

"When was the last time you saw Eliza alive?"

"Just before one o'clock," she said without hesitating. "We left for brunch around ten. When we got back, it was almost one." She pressed her lips together. "I'm afraid I drank one too many mimosas and went right in for a nap. The next time I saw her was with you when we found her."

So Isabel had been with Eliza during the murder window. Interesting. A Monet was valuable enough to kill for, so if Isabel had discovered Eliza had it . . .

Footsteps pounded down the hall, and a man appeared in the doorway, his expression dark and eyes red. His flushed face looked only seconds from bursting into flames. A gray T-shirt and jeans fit as if tailored for his lean frame. Disheveled dark hair stuck up in thick pieces where he'd been worrying it with his hands.

This was a man in distress, and people in distress could be dangerous.

I shot to my feet and shifted to put myself between him and Rose. She and Isabel were up from their seats too.

"Jake." Isabel backed up until she hit the wall.

"The ex?" I asked, swiveling back in his direction. In a murder investigation, the significant other was always the first suspect—especially if they were on the outs with the deceased.

"What happened?" Jake demanded in a voice that broke and shattered. "Isabel, what happened to my wife?"

"She's not your wife anymore!" Isabel screamed. "Did you do this? Did you do this to her?"

"What? No, no." Color washed from his face, leaving him drawn and tired. He dropped into the chair Rose had occupied just seconds before. "How could you think that? I would never hurt Eliza. I would take every bullet for her. I loved her."

Rose stared at him, not with fear and anger like Isabel, but with curiosity.

"Get out," Isabel said, "before I call the sheriff."

"I just want to know what happened. How did she die?"

"Get out!" Isabel screeched.

Jake locked his feet on the floor in front of him. "Just tell me. Please."

"She was strangled," I said quietly. "In the guesthouse, likely related to a stolen painting that was found in her possession."

"She's not a thief," he said. "Did she suffer?"

"I honestly don't know."

He stared straight forward for a moment, then nodded and stood. "Thank you." His manner had changed. Instead of the hurricane that tore in here, he was a quiet rain after the storm energy had died.

"Get out of my home," Isabel said with venom.

"Take care of yourself." Jake stood and left.

I moved to the door after him.

"One more thing, ladies." Isabel took a few calming breaths and flopped into her chair without her usual poise.

Jake's shoulders slumped as he trudged back the way he

came. At that pace, it would take him a minute to reach the driveway, but this could be my only opportunity to talk to him.

"I'd like to question him before he leaves," I said.

Rose squinted at Jake's back, her head tilted at an angle.

I elbowed her and whispered, "What?"

She shook her head. "Not sure."

"I'll just be a moment." Isabel cleared her throat, but her voice still trembled. "I'm selling the Monet at an auction in two days."

"So soon?" I asked. "Could you delay it? It might come in handy as we investigate."

"Eliza loved this Monet. But you have convinced me that it"—she stole a look at the painting—"played a key role in my niece's murder. I need to put this mess behind me. I can't stand to look at it anymore." She flipped the painting face down on her desk beside the fake.

"Maybe you could push it back just for a week?" I asked.

"There's already an auction scheduled. Irving said he could squeeze me in, and I intend to take him up on that." She gestured toward the door.

Rose nodded and darted down the hall after Jake.

I hesitated in the doorway for only a second longer. Isabel had her mind made up. We weren't going to change it, so we might as well catch up to Jake before he disappeared. He might head right out of town again, and we would lose him as a lead in this investigation.

"We'll be in touch," I called to Isabel over my shoulder as I took off after Rose and Jake.

We caught up with him in the circular driveway, where an open-top blue convertible sat behind my rental sedan.

"When was the last time you spoke to Eliza?" I called out.

Jake turned, only feet from his car. "Last week. Why?"

"We're investigating her murder. Did she mention a Monet at all?"

"She didn't steal any painting."

The evidence said otherwise, but now wasn't the time to tell him he hadn't known his ex-wife as well as he thought. "How about friends—did she mention anyone she connected with in town?"

He raised his hands and dropped them back to his sides. "I don't know. We don't chitchat anymore. We haven't been close for some time."

"When did you get to town?" Rose asked. It was the first time she'd spoken to him directly.

Jake ignored the question. "Look, I'm not up for an interrogation. The love of my life is dead." He got into the convertible, which looked freshly detailed.

He closed the car door.

Since the top was down, I didn't let that end the conversation. "How did you know Eliza was dead?"

Jake sighed. "Eliza and I are still . . . *were* still legally married—although Isabel likes to pretend otherwise. The authorities notified me. Now, please, I need to get my head together. My wife just died." He started the engine, and it flipped into a low purr.

"How long will you be in town?" Rose asked.

"I'll get a room at the Willow Inn until the funeral." Jake inched the car around us and sped off.

I watched its taillights recede down the hill. "No bags in that shiny convertible. He didn't come straight here when he arrived in town, or his bags would be with him. He wouldn't be able to fit much in that tiny trunk."

Rose's eyes widened, and she pointed at me. "That's it! I remember now. I saw him at the Autumn Festival last weekend, skulking around alone."

"Before Eliza's murder. There's no telling how long he's been here."

"We could check with the hotel."

"They probably won't tell us."

Rose grinned. "We could ask nicely."

"Whatever we do," I said, "we better do it fast. The auction is in two days. We have that long to catch a killer."

CHAPTER 27

ROSE

I NEEDED A BREAK. MY HEAD WAS SPINNING FROM TOO MUCH deception and not enough solid information.

"Hey, Vera," I called as I unlocked the door to her home and stepped inside. She emerged from the sunroom, her expression bright and welcoming. Her two cats slinked behind her, eyeing me warily like I might snatch their favorite human away.

"I wasn't expecting you home until tonight." Vera sipped from her coffee mug.

"I needed a break." I headed straight for the kitchen, with Vera trailing behind.

The fridge was packed with groceries, plus a bunch of leftovers. I started pulling out plastic tubs of food that didn't require work.

Vera set her coffee on the breakfast table and slid into a seat. "I noticed you went grocery shopping. You don't have to do that."

"I'm paying you for the roof." I pointed at the ceiling and grabbed a plate from the cabinet. "Not the food."

"I like feeding you. That's what you do for guests."

"I'm a tenant."

She shrugged. "Call it what you like."

"If you're going to cook, the least I can do is buy." I loaded up my plate, stuffed the containers back into the fridge, and joined her at the table.

"Speaking of someone else paying for food . . ." Vera started.

I stopped stuffing my mouth to catch the build-up.

"I won't be home this evening. I have a date."

I dropped my fork, my mouth still full of half-chewed mac and cheese.

Vera's eyes narrowed. "Am I that repulsive?"

"No!" I swallowed. "No, of course not. It's just . . . I didn't realize you dated."

"All the time I spend in my cardio room, someone was bound to notice." She turned her cheek to show me her profile and struck a model pose.

"You're a hottie." I meant it. The years had done nothing to dull her large eyes and prominent cheekbones. It had been almost a year since my last date, so it was good one of us would be getting some. "I won't wait up."

"What about you? What's your plan for dinner?"

I gestured at my plate and dramatically put a forkful of chicken in my mouth.

"It's one thirty in the afternoon, dear. This can't be it."

I covered my mouth as I chewed. "There's more in there, or I'll order delivery."

She squinted. "Say again."

I shoved more food in my mouth. "Ivy is attending a family dinner." The words came out muffled by mac and cheese.

"Why are you mumbling? Swallow and say that again." The look on her face was as severe as any my own mother had ever given me.

I obeyed. "Ivy is going to a family dinner at her mom's."

She set her coffee cup down with a clatter. "How do you feel about that?"

"What are you—my therapist?"

"Do you have one?" She leaned closer. "I can refer you."

I raised my fork to my mouth again.

She reached out and pushed it back to the plate. "Speak, child."

I shrugged. "I wasn't invited."

"By Faye? Don't take it personally. She may need time to warm up to you."

"I met Faye at the Autumn Festival, and she was plenty warm. It's Ivy who didn't offer to bring me along."

"I'm sure it's just an oversight. She's not used to having a sister."

"It doesn't take years of experience to know you invite your sister to family dinners."

Vera picked up her mug again and sipped.

I stuffed more food in my mouth.

"The video!" Vera slammed her drink back down. "Lawrence sent over a link to his doorbell cam footage in the cloud. He said you asked for it." She rolled her eyes. "I hope he knows there's no nicest-neighbor award."

"Lucky for you," I said, "because he's kicking your ass."

She glared. "We're not talking about that right now. I'm very competitive."

"Maybe you can buy him a pony. But in the meantime, can I see the video?"

She huffed and stood. A moment later, she returned with her phone.

"Did you put a password on it?" I asked.

Ignoring the question, she texted the link to me. "What exactly are you looking for? Lawrence didn't say why you asked for it."

"I'm just being overcautious because of that break-in across town. I want to make sure no one suspicious has been lurking around, casing the joint or something like that." Guilt stabbed at me, but I shoved it away. I didn't need Vera to freak out about someone having been in the house when she was out. I'd already taken care of the problem by installing the new doorbell cam.

I pulled up the footage on my phone. An empty street appeared, with only the edge of Vera's yellow cottage in view. I set it to play on fast-forward and laid the phone on the table.

Eventually, a car zipped across the view. I stopped the video, reversed it, and played it at normal speed. The car came back across the screen. A blue sedan, not brand new but not old either. Only a vague shape of the driver was visible.

Vera pointed. "That's Malcolm. He comes home from work at lunch every day. Stays for two hours before going back. Lucky he still has that job."

"What does he do?"

"Something with computers." She shrugged. "Sales? Marketing?"

I wouldn't describe that as something with computers, but I guessed he used one in his job. As far as Vera was concerned, that was the same thing.

"He's nothing to worry about," she said.

"How do you know?"

"This is the normal time for his long lunch." She pointed at the timestamp. "What exactly are we looking for?"

"Anything suspicious. I want to make sure we're safe and there's not going to be a break-in here too."

I put the video back on fast-forward and leaned closer. Again, I stopped it when a shape zipped across the display. I backed it up and watched a woman jog down the street past the house.

"That's Priscilla," Vera said. "Fitness fanatic. She's not breaking in anywhere. She wouldn't risk chipping a nail."

I started the video again and stopped it when a small, shaggy dog trotted up the street. It bounded up the steps to Lawrence's porch. The dog sniffed around the door just under the camera lens, then hopped off the porch and ran away.

"Sweet thing," Vera said. "Next, his owner comes after him and gives him a treat. Then another neighbor—"

I stopped the video. "You watched this already."

"I'm retired. Spying on my neighbors is good entertainment."

"Why am I looking at it if you've already done this?"

"It seemed like you needed a boost. Spying always cheers *me* up."

"What did you see?" I asked. "Cheer me up by saving me the trouble of watching this whole thing."

"Just people I know from the neighborhood. No one suspicious."

My phone dinged, and I checked the new message. It was from Ivy. She wanted to catch Liam and question him about the missing painting. He was now a suspect instead of an informant.

Now *this* cheered me up. I'd been a PI for less than two weeks, but I already knew questioning suspects was my favorite part.

A second text came through, also from Ivy. I grinned at it.

"Gotta go." I swept up my plate and set it in the sink.

"Don't touch that. I'll do the dishes later."

"Like all the other times you did the dishes?" Vera asked in a sarcastic singsong.

"A broken clock is right twice per day," I said. "Maybe it's that time."

"Why are you grinning like a jackal about doing the dishes?"

"Texts from Ivy. She's not attending that dinner. She was just helping her mother cook."

"So she didn't not invite you."

"Exactly. Also, I get to interrogate a suspect."

Her mouth made an O-shape. "Who's the suspect?"

"Liam O'Connell. Very rich. Very artsy. Kind of handsome."

"*Very* handsome," Vera corrected.

"He and Isabel were having an affair."

She sniffed. "I never liked him."

"And that's completely confidential because she's my client."

Vera put one finger to her lips.

"Thank you."

"Hold on. I'll get my bag." She hurried from the room.

I called after her, "You aren't coming with me."

She stomped back into the room with a pout. "I cook for you and everything."

"I'll see you later." I gave her a quick hug and took off out the door.

I was new to this PI stuff, but even I knew you didn't take an audience with you for interrogations. More importantly, if Liam worked with Eliza to steal the painting, he was also a murderer.

CHAPTER 28
IVY

THE FRONT DOOR TO LIAM'S HOUSE OPENED BEFORE WE REACHED IT, and Thomas Rigsby stepped out. A piece fell into place. We were looking for connections between visitors to Isabel's household and the auction house, and here was the Lakeview Luxe Gallery's head of security leaving the home of Isabel's lover.

Rigsby just skyrocketed to the top of my interest list.

Like the first time I'd seen him, his gray hair was short with an edged hairline. Though soft when the door first opened, his expression locked into the stern look he'd worn when he ushered Rose from the employees-only section of the auction house.

He stood in the doorway like a statue. "Ivy and Rose Gray."

The look on Rose's face matched the shock I felt. She didn't hesitate, though. Rose ducked under Rigsby's arm into the house before he could blink.

"Hey!" he shouted. "You can't do that."

She barged through the foyer and into a great room. I followed. The kitchen to my right featured white marble countertops over warm brown cabinetry. The living space to my left was arranged around a fireplace instead of a television. Just like in the foyer, the walls held paintings in a consistent style of thick brush strokes and warm tones.

Rigsby caught up with Rose and gripped her arm. "Ma'am, you can't be here." His tone was all business. The chief of security was back on duty.

My protective instincts flared. "Take your hands off her."

"Liam!" Rose tipped back her head and hollered. "Liam O'Connell, get your ass out here."

Rigsby's grip on her arm tightened, and she flinched.

"Get your hands off my sister, or I will have you charged with assault." I would be damned if a man was going to grab her without her consent on my watch.

The grip loosened. Rose cast an impressed nod in my direction. I gave her a subtle one back, keeping my gaze locked on Rigsby. He put both hands up and took a large slide back.

Liam appeared in a dark doorway to our left. Behind him, a set of stairs led down to a basement. He rubbed paint-stained hands on the front of a smock that he wore over a plain T-shirt and dark jeans. Green and brown paint smeared from his fingers.

Liam was a painter? Just like that, we could wrap up this case and tie it with a bow.

Rose leveled an accusing finger. "You're the forger." She swung her pointer toward Rigsby. "You helped him get around security to swap out the Monet."

I held up a hand toward my eager sister. "Let's not jump to conclusions." My voice was steady, in control, just like I aimed to be. But inside, disappointment churned in my gut. I had assumed Liam was a useful witness, but now I had to question my own judgment—something I seemed to be doing a lot lately.

"I . . . I . . ." Liam stuttered, his eyes wide.

Rigsby moved until he stood partly in front of Liam like a bodyguard. "He did no such thing. Neither of us did."

I fixed Liam with a hard stare. "Why wouldn't you mention to us that you're friends with the security chief of the auction house? His name came up in our conversation, and you failed to mention you were friends."

Liam's gaze slid away from my face and searched the room as if looking for an exit. "It never came up."

"You mean it made you look guilty. We specifically asked you about connections between Isabel's household and the auction house." I gestured towards him and Rigsby.

"I'm not part of Isabel's household."

"But you were," Rose cut in. "You and Isabel were a thing."

Rigsby rotated from Rose to Liam, and one eyebrow went up. This was news to him.

"What are you talking about?" Liam's voice had gone thin, panicked. His gaze cut toward the staircase that led up to the second floor, presumably where his wife was. "Could you keep it down?"

Rose lowered her voice. "We're talking about a necklace inscribed from you." She made air quotes. "With love."

"How do you know about that?"

"We're investigators," she said. "We investigated."

Liam's chest rose and fell, and his shoulders sagged. "We did have an affair." He held up both hands. "But it was a mistake, and it's over."

"You didn't think to mention that?" I couldn't keep the accusation out of my voice. Betrayal was a sore spot with me.

He gestured to the stairway. "I love my wife."

People who loved their wives were faithful to them. Trust was too valuable a commodity to tuck it away when it caused inconvenience. I'd seen for myself that trust could be so often misplaced, and the result could be devastating. "Because she's filthy-stinking rich?"

He scowled, and disgust curled his top lip. "I don't care about her money."

That was what they all said. "Is she ignorant of the affair?"

Rose gave me a questioning look, and I fought to return my expression to neutral.

"One hundred percent. As of this morning, she still considers Isabel a friend. She mentioned visiting to give her condolences, and she was sincere."

"But you cheated on her. You betrayed her trust."

Liam's face crumpled, and he pressed a hand over his eyes. "I know. God, I know. I got caught up in having so much in common with Isabel—the art, the lifestyle. But I've loved Mayling since we were teenagers. I'll love her forever. She's my world." His voice broke on the last word.

I studied him, trying to gauge his sincerity. The devastation on his face seemed genuine, but I had been fooled before.

"Isabel broke it off with you," Rose said, still giving me that questioning look. "To pour salt in the wound, she outbid you on the Monet. You weren't about to be suckered twice. You painted the forgery." She gestured toward Rigsby. "And you had your buddy pull off the swap."

Rigsby straightened up to his full height. "That's about enough. You can't come into his house and sling accusations at him." He slapped his own chest. "*Or* at me. My work for Irving has been impeccable, above reproach."

Rose guffawed. "I got through the back door of the auction house because the loading dock was wide open. A truck was sitting there, also open, with valuable items inside completely unattended."

His eyes narrowed to slits under thick eyebrows. "What are you talking about?"

Rose took a step back. I moved in front of her.

"Don't back down now," he said in a low rumble. "Explain."

I crossed my arms. "You heard her. She came through the back door and found what she found. She also saw one of your security personnel buying shoes from the delivery guys in the break room."

Rigsby glared at Rose. "You said you got lost."

"You didn't believe that," she said. "So now I'm thinking you know that the security is lacking at the auction house, and you do nothing about it. You look the other way, like you did when you caught me."

"Why is that?" I asked. "You seem like a person who takes pride in his work."

Rigsby's jaw tightened and untightened a few times before he spoke. He pressed his fingertips to his forehead and sighed. "Describe the person you saw buying shoes."

"Just over six feet. Black. Short bleached hair."

He closed his eyes in an over-long blink. "My wife's nephew."

"So, *your* nephew," I pressed.

He waved a hand. "The boy is terrible at everything. Fired from job after job. She damn near threatened to divorce me if I couldn't make this work."

"You look the other way," Rose said.

"As long as nothing terrible happens, yeah. It's either that or divorce. I don't love a lot of things, but I love my wife."

And unlike Liam, Rigsby displayed that love through his actions, even at the expense of his work. I walked over and stood face-to-face with him. I wanted to see his eyes when he answered this question. "So you weren't involved with the painting swap?"

"Not directly. But corners have been cut since Lamar came on board." He threw his hands up in the air, and they landed with a slap on his thighs. "I can't say for sure. If this happened on my watch, it's on me—but only indirectly."

He seemed honest—if my instincts were to be trusted.

"What about the forgery?" Rose asked Liam.

"It's not a forgery," Liam said. "It's a copy. It has my signature on it."

He pointed to the bottom right corner of a nearby painting. Rose and I moved closer to examine it. Though hard to read, a tiny name camouflaged within swirls of paint could indeed have said Liam O'Connell.

"Why create a copy at all?" I asked.

Rose mouthed the word *copy* and rolled her eyes. It was a convenient term in this context, lacking the legal ramifications and assumed intention behind a forgery.

"It was a gift," Liam said. "It could be displayed anywhere, and Isabel could keep the original for her own exclusive viewing." One side of his mouth twitched, but there was no humor in it. "She enjoyed things that were exclusive."

"Like married men," Rose muttered.

Liam nodded slowly, pain revealing deeper lines on his

face. "Tom would never help me steal from the auction house. We're friends, but he's the sort I expect to keep me on the straight and narrow. When I want advice, Tom is the man."

"Hence why you never told me about Isabel," Rigsby said, his tone scolding.

Liam glanced down at his feet for a second and then back up at his friend. "I'm fine here. Go on home."

With one last discriminating look at Rose and me, Rigsby headed toward the entrance. "Call if you need me." He pulled the door shut behind him.

Liam straightened his shoulders, but I could see the cracks in his composure. "Anything else, ladies?"

"Did you see Eliza yesterday?" I asked.

He shook his head. "The last time I saw or heard from her was at the Autumn Festival, and we didn't get a chance to chat."

"How did she seem?"

"Normal. She was stuck under Isabel's thumb, but finding her happiness the best she could. We waved to each other from across the grass."

"Where were you from one to five yesterday afternoon?"

His eyes widened. "You don't think that I . . ."

"We have to consider every possibility," Rose said. "Where were you?"

"Mayling and I went up north to a winery and stayed overnight. I'm sure you can confirm that we checked into the North Ridge Resort and Winery around four thirty. It's a three-hour drive in each direction."

If that was true, it would *almost* clear Liam. Unlike most of our suspects, he had two possible motives—retaining the

Monet and keeping his affair a secret. Living in that manor with Isabel, Eliza might have known about the relationship.

"I'll call the resort to confirm," I said.

"Of course." He sat on the sofa, pressed his fingers against his eyelids, and rubbed. "What can I do to convince you I had nothing to do with this painting mess?"

"But you did," I said. "You created the copy that made it possible."

"And Eliza died for it." His chest seemed to cave inward, and he stared straight forward into space.

Until this moment, he hadn't thought of his own actions as the impetus for Eliza's murder. They'd probably gotten close, had conversations while he and Isabel were dating.

Now she was dead—maybe because of him.

CHAPTER 29

ROSE

"Liam could have killed Eliza," I said as we hurried up the steps to Gray Investigations, "based on his partial alibi. Even Isabel could have—we only have her word for it that she went straight to bed after their brunch."

Ivy's phone pinged, and she slowed to check the notification. "It's a voicemail from Liam's hotel." She pressed a button and raised the phone to her ear.

I reached the top of the stairs and froze. My chest tightened. "Ivy."

She stopped walking in the middle of the staircase as she listened to the recording. "The manager at Liam's hotel confirms he checked in at just after four thirty."

"Ivy," I said again, this time with more force.

She looked up and saw the expression on my face. She ran up the rest of the way.

The frosted glass door was shattered, and the remains of

the words *Gray Investigations* littered the floor in shards. Ivy's hand went to her waist as if to find a gun, but came up empty.

"Stay behind me." She stepped through the doorframe, and glass crunched beneath her toes.

I slipped in after her to stand at her side.

Case files were strewn across the floor, mixed with torn pages of the magazines that had probably sat on that coffee table for a decade. The coffee table leaned at an angle, one leg snapped off. A toppled chair had its arm torn open, spilling stuffing. The photo of Caleb and the mayor lay face down, the frame cracked.

Anna's desk had been swiped clean, her monitor, keyboard, and mouse now on the floor next to a pile of pens and the mug they used to occupy.

Ivy stepped deeper into the room. "This is bad. This is really bad."

I followed her. "It's not great."

The door to Caleb's office stood wide open, and files spread across the threshold led back to the filing cabinets. One cabinet had all its drawers hanging open. The other lay on its side.

Everything had been swept off Caleb's desk onto the floor. His large desk calendar. His mail tray. A *World's Best PI* mug lay shattered on the floor.

The room still smelled of Anna's blood, like it had crawled into the walls and set up camp. Or maybe that was just my imagination now. I couldn't shake it.

Ivy was trembling.

"Hey," I said, "It's okay."

She nodded again and again, like rapid fire. If Ivy was losing it, we were in trouble.

"You've dealt with stuff like this before, right?"

She pulled in a long breath. "Usually, the targets don't go after the investigators. That's movie and book stuff. The FBI is off-limits. No one messes with us . . . usually."

And now, someone may or may not be following us, someone broke into my place, and our office got trashed. We were definitely targets.

"You're a problem solver," I said. "What would you tell a witness if they were on edge?"

"Get it together. We have work to do." She straightened her spine and pulled out her phone to dial 9-1-1.

While she spoke to dispatch, we moved to the hall and settled on the bench, steering clear of the shattered glass.

It wasn't long before Deputies Marks and Ramirez stomped up the steps of the building. Marks looked grim. I couldn't blame him. He'd caught two dead bodies with us in less than two weeks.

Ramirez glared at me. If looks were bullets, I'd be toast. The shiner I'd given her had faded to a faint yellow.

When they reached us, Ramirez stationed herself in front of Ivy. "What have we got?"

"The office is ransacked," Ivy said.

"No dead bodies?" Marks asked, one hand near his belt, near the comfort of his gun.

Ramirez shot him a dirty look.

"Not today," I said.

He dropped his arms.

Ramirez glared at him until he wiped the relief off his face too.

Over the next hour, Marks and Ramirez inspected the office, snapped photos, and peppered us with questions.

As they were wrapping up, a phone rang. For a few

seconds, the four of us stared at one another, trying to figure out whose it was.

"Are you going to get that?" Ramirez finally asked, waving toward the landline on Anna's desk.

I dove for it. It was our first call at Gray Investigations.

Ivy beat me to it. "Hello."

I pressed my ear right next to hers and cranked up the volume button.

"Is this Gray Investigations?" a man's voice asked.

Ivy put on her best receptionist act. "Yes. Gray Investigations."

"This is Irving Greenfield from—"

"From Lakeview Luxe, yes. This is Ivy Gray. What can I do for you?"

"I'm calling as a courtesy because, despite my hesitance to speak with you, I do want this painting thing solved. It's a stain on my business."

"Of course." Ivy moved the phone from her ear and elbowed me away. "Personal space," she hissed before putting the receiver back to her face.

I moved my ear back close to hers.

"You may or may not be aware that Isabel's Monet will be back on the auction block in two days."

"We're aware," Ivy said.

"Then I've wasted your time. I wanted to make sure you understood that any further investigation involving the painting would likely come to a halt at that time. We expect a global pool of buyers for the item."

"If you want to help," Ivy said, "I'd still be happy to review your security footage."

"Nice try, Ms. Gray. Good luck." He disconnected.

I snatched the phone from Ivy and slammed it into its cradle. "Well, that was a colossal waste of time."

"We're about done here," Ramirez said. "Now that you've had more of a chance to look around, have you noticed anything missing?"

"No," Ivy said, "still nothing."

"It looks like vandalism," Marks said. "There's nothing more we can do here, but if we come up with anything, we'll be in touch."

"You mean you're never going to find who did this," I said.

Ivy closed her eyes and shook her head.

"What? That's what they mean." To Marks, I added, "Isn't it?"

Ramirez crossed her arms over her chest, showing off the muscles in her biceps. "We're working two murders out of a tiny substation, so no, your vandal is not our highest priority."

Ivy hustled them out. "Thank you for your time." She shut what was left of the door behind them.

"I guess we better get that cleaning crew back in here," I said.

"I don't think they do glass."

I patted her on the back. "I'm sure you can handle it. You're resourceful."

"Right now, my resources are these"—she waved her hands in the air and then pointed at mine—"and those. Get to work. I'll find a glass person later."

We went quiet, surveying the mess that was our father's office. It was clear we'd become a target.

CHAPTER 30

IVY

Glass crunched under my feet as I knelt to gather the files scattered across the floor of Gray Investigations.

In the waiting room, I stacked them so their edges aligned. During the vandalism—if that was indeed what it was, and I doubted it—most of the loose pages had stayed near the original files they belonged to, but a few were now homeless. I'd have to match them with their folders later.

For now, I set the loose papers aside. Maybe we could hire someone to handle them.

"Anna must have been a fan of the paper-and-pencil method," Rose said as she picked up pens and highlighters.

Previously, the files had been ordered by date, a terrible method for anyone not already familiar with the cases. Since Anna wouldn't be managing them anymore, it was time for a new system.

I opened each folder and rearranged them in two stacks

based on the client's name in alphabetical order. The pile on the floor was the end of the alphabet, and the one on Anna's desk was the beginning. Eventually, they'd reach the center, and my work would be done.

As I flipped through one folder, a ripped piece of paper fluttered to the floor. I set the file aside and picked up the torn note. The top half was missing.

The bottom half said, *I told you to stay away. This will not end well.*

Normally, I'd chuckle at this. Bad guys were usually big on threats and small on follow-through. But given my recent experience with the FBI, Anna's murder, and Caleb's disappearance, this could be important.

I scanned the floor for the other piece but didn't see it. I stood and peered under Anna's desk. "Have you seen the other half of this note?" I flapped the paper at Rose.

Rose glanced up from the pens in her hands and stared at me with wide, blank eyes. "Excuse me?"

"This note." I waved it at her again. "It's torn. Have you seen the other half?"

"I'll look for it. Let me handle the filing. That's below your pay grade." She stepped over to my stack of folders, reaching for the paper in my hand.

I stepped back, holding it out of her reach. "I've already started a new system. I'm just looking for the rest of this note."

She sidled closer and tried again to snatch the ripped page.

I jerked my hand away. "What's your problem?"

"Ivy, come on," she said, her voice saccharine sweet. "Just give me the files, and you can sweep up the glass. You wouldn't want me to miss a piece, and one of us gets cut a week from now." She laughed, but it came out like more of a screeching wheeze.

I squinted at her.

She lunged for the note, but I leaned back and to the side. Basic self-defense. Rose's momentum kept her moving forward, and she tripped over my folder pile.

She yelped as the files tipped, and she landed in a heap on top of them.

"Nice," I snapped.

As I bent to gather the folders and papers, a torn page caught my eye. A few feet away, a piece of paper had a tear that matched the note in my hand. I crawled toward it and snatched it up.

"To the Grays." I stood, holding the two pieces together. "I told you to stay away. This will not end well for you."

I froze. Rose kept giving that wide-eyed look that made her irises look tiny, but she made a show of restacking the files.

"Stop," I said, using my best commanding tone. "Put the folders down."

She slowly set the files back and rose to her feet.

"When were you going to tell me about this?"

She licked her lips. "It was mixed in with the rest of these files. It must have been Anna's, not for us."

"It says *to the Grays*. Anna is not a Gray." I pointed between us emphatically. "As far as I know, this is the first time more than one Gray has worked here. Cut the crap."

"Do you think the vandal left it?"

"Stop playing dumb. The vandal didn't tear up their own threat." I shook the two pages in her face. "So again, when were you going to tell me about this?"

"Yesterday," she mumbled.

I stared at her.

"I found it when we were looking through the accounting records."

"You hid it."

"I didn't—" She stopped herself and let out a long breath. "Not exactly. I just hadn't decided how to present it to you yet, so I put it under Caleb's desk calendar when you were searching for something to break open the filing cabinets. And then Eliza died, and there was everything going on . . ."

My chest tightened. Rose didn't care about rules or the law. All she cared about was getting what she wanted, and it was impossible to trust someone like that. "We said we'd quit this if it got intense."

"No." Her brows lowered and nostrils flared. "*You* agreed to quit and expected me to obey. You never asked me what I wanted."

"It doesn't matter what you want!" I shouted. My hand flew and hit the remaining pile of files on Anna's desk. They crashed to the floor. I cursed.

Rose pointed at the disarrayed mess of folders and loose pages. "That one's not my fault."

"I don't care about the fucking papers, Rose. You lied to me."

"I omitted."

My chest tightened like it was on fire, and the room spun. "You *omitted* an essential fact that you *knew* I'd want to know. That's worse than lying. It's a betrayal." My breaths came in short bursts.

Rose touched my shoulder. "Are you okay?"

I shook her off. "For whatever reason," I said, my voice

strained, "you're obsessed with finding Dad, and you don't care whether my family gets hurt along the way."

Rose flinched at the words *my family*. "No one is going to hurt us."

"Why? Because you say so? People get hurt during investigations, Rose. People die." My voice cracked. Tears welled behind my lower lids.

She stepped back. "What—"

"You can't make decisions like this without involving me. I can't trust you if you . . . I can't." My voice lodged in my throat, and my skin was on fire.

"Are you having a panic attack?"

"I'm fine," I snapped. I *would be* fine as long as I got as far away from Rose as possible.

"I wasn't keeping it from you," she whispered. "I just needed a moment to think. I was scared that you would cut me out of your life if we weren't working together. You don't talk to Caleb anymore, or Anna . . . or Pearl."

"Pearl is no one."

"That's what I mean." Rose pointed at me. "I couldn't risk having you throw me away."

"Don't turn this around on me. You are reckless and impulsive." I was shouting now, and each word drove a tear down my face. My body shook like all the fault lines had shifted. "You put both of our lives in danger by withholding crucial information."

Rose stood there with shock painted across her face like I had slapped her.

My throat tightened, but I forced the words out. "I don't need you to make decisions for me. I don't need *you*."

"You're my sister," she whispered.

I wiped my face and locked my voice in a steady tone. "We are nothing to each other except shared DNA."

Rose's lips quivered, but she sucked them in.

"We are done as partners. We are done with this investigation. We are *done*." I turned and strode from the room. The door was already busted, so I didn't have to slam it behind me.

CHAPTER 31

IVY

FIRST THING IN THE MORNING, I BURST INTO MUGGED WITH A LARGE notebook tucked under one arm. I found a booth, set the notebook down, and shrugged out of my jacket, all while keeping my phone pressed to one ear. I was on hold.

I'd been on hold for going on eight minutes.

Tourist season had officially hit Willow Lake. Although I'd beaten most of the crowd, a buzz of conversation blended with the low, acoustic sounds playing in the background of the coffee shop.

"He's unavailable," the receptionist said when she returned to the line. "Can I take a message?"

"No, I'll try him—wait, yes." This was my third call to him this week. If I couldn't catch him directly, leaving a message was the next best thing.

I flipped the notebook open to the speech I'd scrawled last night. I would have preferred to say this to him directly, but my options were limited.

"Do you have a pen?" I asked. "You might want to write this down."

"Go ahead." Her voice was flat.

"I'm calling to express my deepest regret for any embarrassment or inconvenience my recent actions caused. I understand the seriousness of the situation and take full responsibility for the lapses in my judgment." I paused.

"Is that all?" she asked.

"No, but I want to make sure you make it clear to him that I take full responsibility. Did you get all that so far?"

"I type one hundred words per minute."

I flipped to the next page. "I'm eager for a resolution on this matter so that I can return to work as soon as possible. I look forward to an update on the status of the investigation and an estimate on when I might expect to be reinstated. In the meantime, I remain available to answer questions."

"Mm-hmm," she murmured.

"Got all that?"

"I got it," she said, her voice tight.

I closed the notebook. "Do you know when you might expect to hear back from him?"

"I do not."

Corina approached with a mug of coffee that had steam curling up from the brim. When she set it down, the smell of mocha made my mouth water. She patted my free hand and retreated.

"Did you let him know about my call from yesterday?"

"It is literally in my job description to take messages for him and pass them along."

"I know. I'm sorry. You're very good at what you do. It's just that this is really important to me. I need to get back to work."

"Agent Gray." Her tone softened. "I will put your message in his inbox right now, and when he arrives, I will double-check that he received it."

"Thank you."

"Take care of yourself." She disconnected.

I held the phone to my ear for another few seconds, as if my supervisor would suddenly appear. Finally, I set it down and wrapped both hands around the mug.

Its warmth felt good, comforting.

Corina slid into the booth across from me. "How's the FBI's finest this morning?"

"Don't," I said.

She reached across the table and patted my hand. "I know you're made of steel, but if you need to talk . . ."

I didn't feel like steel right now. I felt like a puddle—maybe *melted* steel. "How high do you have to heat steel to melt it?"

She squeezed my hand.

"I blew up at Rose yesterday."

Corina said nothing, just nodded.

"She hid a note that threatened us off the case."

"Your dad? Or the painting?"

I shrugged. "It was vague."

"Did she deny it?"

"Not for long."

Corina raised an eyebrow. Even in her silence, I sensed her judgment and skepticism.

"I can't trust her, Rina. She has no qualms about invading people's privacy with her computer, and she obviously doesn't care about hiding things or lying to me."

"It's a new relationship. It'll take time to feel out each other's boundaries."

I considered that but shook my head. "I don't think so."

Corina's eyes widened. "You can't mean that. She's your sis—"

I held up a hand. "Don't make this about DNA. Sometimes, people just aren't compatible. She's too different . . ."

"Different from what you expected?"

I didn't answer.

"Different from *you*?"

I chewed the inside of my mouth.

"Give it time," Corina said. "You're both adults now. It'll take more than a week to figure out your relationship."

"I don't have that time. I need to get back to LA." I lifted my phone off the table. "I have more calls to make."

She released my hand and slid out of the booth.

Before I could dial, I spotted a missed call. It must have come through while I was leaving the message for the supervisor. I checked the display: Derek. My stomach used to flutter when I saw his name. Now, calling him back was just something to add to the to-do list.

I called my FBI partner instead. The line rang four times. My finger hovered over the button to disconnect just as he answered.

"Ivy," Clint said. He sounded tired, like he'd been up all night and was exhausted with the red tape—or just exhausted with *me*.

"Sorry to bother you."

"It's fine. I'm just . . . Can we make this quick?"

"Of course." I straightened in my seat. He couldn't see me, but body language has a way of showing in your voice. "Have you heard anything about my administrative leave?"

"Can't talk about it."

"Excuse me?"

"Look, I may not be on leave because I wasn't there when it happened, but I'm under investigation too."

"I didn't know that."

"Of course you didn't." He left it unspoken, but what he meant was I hadn't bothered to find out.

"I'm really sorry to hear that."

"Yeah well, I can't discuss personnel matters while I'm under investigation." He said that last part as if reading from a script, stilted and monotone.

I opened my mouth, but no words came out.

"Gray," he added in a lower, urgent voice, "I'm serious. Do not call me about this again. I can't help you. I can barely help myself."

"I'm sorry. I didn't know." The apology sounded lame, even to me.

"Good luck." The line went dead.

I stared at my phone for a moment before clearing the screen and calling Derek. Might as well take all my hits in one sitting.

He answered on the second ring. "When are you coming home so we can finalize things?"

"Soon."

"Great," he said, and there was no mistaking the irritation in his voice. "Another vague answer. That's new."

I closed my eyes and took a deep breath. "I'll let you know soon."

As soon as the words were out, I regretted them. I had no intention of being vague with him because I knew how much he hated it. But right now, I didn't have the energy to deal with this.

"It's always something."

"My dad is still missing."

"He's not exactly known for being reliable."

I pulled the phone from my ear long enough to glare at it. "I'll call you later. I have to go."

"Yeah, later."

We disconnected, and I switched my phone to silent. That was about as much conversation as I could take. Three calls and three strikes. I was officially out.

I gulped down half my coffee and swept up my notepad and pen. I grabbed my jacket, tossed it over my arm, and headed for the door.

"Watch it," said a familiar voice.

I slammed directly into Deputy Jay Matthews.

He caught me around the waist to keep me from falling. I yelped as my things kept moving from momentum, but he held me firmly as my notepad and jacket tumbled to the floor.

Jay clasped me against him a second longer than needed, long enough for me to feel the warmth coming off his chest. He released me and bent to grab my things. "Ivy," was all he said.

Hearing him say my name sent my heart fluttering into my feet. With that smile and those kind eyes, he couldn't possibly be having the dirty thoughts I was.

Or maybe he was better at hiding it.

"Jay." I reached out for my belongings.

"Sorry," he said. "I should have given you a warning."

"You should have warned me before *I* barreled into *you*?"

His mouth curled into a slow smile. "Something like that."

"Always a gentleman."

He steered me back toward my booth. "Stay for a minute.

Collect yourself before you run off and leave me . . ." *Again* was the word he didn't say. Before I ran off and left him *again*.

"I really have to go," I said. I didn't, though. I had nowhere to be.

He still clutched my jacket close to his chest as if holding it hostage.

Jay hadn't changed. I looked up into concerned blue eyes, blocked partially by a piece of stray dark blond. He could never keep it in place, even in his long-retired hair gel phase. The gray deputy uniform fit him in more ways than one, showing off his trim waist and his helpful heart.

His bicep tensed as I tried to yank the jacket from him, and on second thought, he had changed. Those muscles hadn't been around in high school.

I collapsed into the seat I'd just vacated.

"That's more like it. What's going on with you?" He paused, then licked his lips. "How long are you in town?"

"Not long."

"I could buy you a coffee?"

Moments like this made me wish Derek and I wore wedding rings. We used to, but mine irritated my finger, so I stopped. Then he stopped. I didn't believe in signs, but if I did, I might have read something into that.

Jay probably didn't even know I was married—not that it mattered at this point, but a ring might get me out of this conversation with minimal awkwardness.

This wasn't a conversation I wanted to have.

I snatched my jacket and popped back to my feet. "I have to go. Let's catch up later."

Or not. Catching up with Jay would serve no purpose. In a

few days, I'd find my father, and I'd be home picking up my life where I left it.

I shot toward the exit and ducked out before I changed my mind. My car was at the edge of the small parking lot, where I'd parked it thinking the short walk would lift my mood.

Corina's hand landed on my shoulder before I could open the door.

I turned. "Sorry to leave in such a hurry. I would have said goodbye—"

"But you are training for Olympic sprinting and wanted to practice?"

I ducked my head.

"Maybe be less obvious next time you need to escape a guy because that"—she pointed toward the coffee shop entrance—"was not an exit that says you're over him."

"I have to go." I reached for the car door.

She put her hand back on my arm. "I know this is none of my business, but maybe there's more for you in Willow Lake than you think."

"I have to go." This time, I opened the door and slipped behind the wheel.

She didn't stop me as I slammed it shut and raced away from Mugged. It wasn't so easy to escape the rest of Willow Lake.

CHAPTER 32
ROSE

My head was pounding like a British dollar, and the sun assaulted me through the sheer curtains. My mouth tasted like a brewery, which was odd since my stomach was on a roller coaster—a place where beer was definitely not allowed.

Last night, I'd attempted to drown out all thoughts of Ivy, but my sister's presence was stronger than beer.

I rolled over to escape the sun, and my phone screen said it was 10:55 a.m. It also showed a text from Vera fifteen minutes earlier: *Please come downstairs.* Vera was more of a caller than a texter, so it must have been important.

When this headache subsided, I'd get right on that.

I called my mom—because that's what I always did when my world was collapsing. After five rings, her phone dumped me to voicemail. I disconnected.

A new email waited in my inbox, inviting me to access cloud-stored video footage from Montgomery Manor. I clicked through.

My web browser opened a folder with twenty subfolders, each for a specific camera on the property. Ivy had asked for videos from just the camera outside Isabel's office, but Isabel had been reluctant. Probably, Eliza's death had changed everything.

I now had access to videos of Isabel's entire property for the last year, almost two hundred thousand hours of footage by my quick math. This could be a gold mine or a time sink.

Maybe I could write a program to filter it, but I'd still need to come up with appropriate filtering parameters . . . It would take some thought.

Another text from Vera popped onto my screen: *Get your butt downstairs!*

I scrambled out of bed, tangled my foot in the cover, and sprawled onto the floor. The break-in here, the ransack of Gray Investigations, and now Vera texting me *twice.*

This was bad.

Someone could be down there with her, holding her hostage, and she had to sneak to text me.

She was probably fine, but I couldn't risk it.

Probably. Fine. Just in case, though, I needed a weapon. The worst-case scenario would be to get down there unarmed and end up a hostage right beside her.

Nothing in here would do. I ran into the bathroom and scanned the counter. I snatched up a can of deodorant. The can was metal, but I could do better.

I dashed into the hallway, grabbing the doorway to spin my momentum left and down the hall. Vera's cardio room had a stationary bike, a treadmill, some resistance bands, and several light barbells.

I ditched the deodorant and swapped it for a five-pound

weight. Oh yeah, I could bash someone's head in with this. I gave it a few practice swings for good measure before shooting down the hall toward the staircase.

I skidded at the top of the steps and tiptoed down with the weight tucked behind my back. I hit the bottom as quiet as a graveyard in my socked feet.

No one noticed me.

Lawrence Miller-Young and his husband Paul sat on the sofa with mugs and empty saucers on the coffee table in front of them. Vera sat in an armchair across the room. Her eyes widened and then thinned, on and off, like she was sending a message in Morse code.

Paul was mid-monologue. "When I go to the farmers market, I look for leafy greens that are really fresh, you know?" He raised a finger to acknowledge my entrance.

Vera jumped out of her chair so fast that it shuddered and almost tipped over. She rushed to my side.

Paul kept talking. "The ones with taut leaves and vibrant color. Those are the best for my salads. The other produce isn't always—"

"Rose!" Vera said too loudly. "So lovely of you to join us." She pointed at me. "You two remember Rose."

"Why are you shouting?" I murmured, the weight still hidden behind me. "Are you under duress?"

"Oh, I forgot to tell you about the napkins," Paul droned on. "We picked out these gorgeous cloth coverings and matching napkins. You'd think these kinds of details would be boring, but we pored over catalogs. There are so many shades of white. Ivory, eggshell, alabaster, vanilla, oyster, dove, pearl—"

"Lawrence and Paul came over to make sure we had everything we needed from their doorbell video," Vera said, her voice climbing into panic territory.

I covered my ear. "Please stop shouting."

Lawrence stood and swept up Vera's empty plate, followed by his own and his husband's. "Does anyone want more pie?"

"Pie!" Vera shouted.

I flinched.

She hurried over and snatched the plates from his hand. "It's my house and my pie," she snapped in short, clipped words. "I'll get the refills."

He stared after her, mouth open, as she stomped away. I followed.

"Remind me to tell you about the silverware when you come back," Paul called after us.

The two-way kitchen door swung shut behind us.

Vera slammed the plates next to the sink. She reached into the narrow space between the refrigerator and the counters and pulled out a small, collapsible step stool. She snapped it open, set it on the floor, and climbed up to open a top cabinet.

"Vera," I said, "is everything okay?"

"It will be." She leaned forward to thrust her arm to the back of the cupboard.

"You texted me twice."

"I needed the distraction." She grunted. "Got it!" She pulled out her hand, fingers clutching the neck of a whiskey bottle.

Vera hopped down from the step stool and sat on it. Her face scrunched as she twisted the cap until it gave way. She grinned before taking a long swig and swallowing. "Good stuff."

"Vera, do you want me to call the sheriff?"

She pulled another long swig. "Only if I murder them."

"Paul and Lawrence?"

"Mostly just Paul." Her brow furrowed. "You're right. I'd have to do them both. Lawrence wouldn't let me get away with it."

"Okay." I grabbed a chair from the breakfast table, set it in front of her, and sat. "Why are we murdering the neighbors?"

"On second thought, he's so darn nice he *might* let me."

"I repeat: why are we murdering the neighbors?"

She tilted her head. "It's sweet that you said *we*."

"You're not murdering anyone by yourself. I respect my elders and help them when they need it."

She guffawed and slapped my knee before taking a smaller sip. "Paul is incredibly boring."

I chuckled. "You don't enjoy stories about vegetables and napkins?"

"You missed the one about picking paint. And then"—she raised a finger—"he literally described what it looked like while it dried. The man told a story about watching paint dry."

"That explains why they're so nice."

She stood and slammed the bottle on the counter.

I jumped.

"That's it! That's why they're so nice. No one would put up with this level of boredom if it weren't impossible to turn them away."

"So then . . . murder. Were you thinking . . . ?" I mimed bludgeoning someone with the weight still in my hand.

"Where did you get that?"

"I thought you needed help, so I grabbed it from your workout room on my way down."

"You're sweet."

"They're clearly fond of you."

She tapped a finger. "I can't beat them on niceness, but I can liven up this party a little bit. What they need is a little fun."

She grabbed three glasses from the cabinet and poured a measure of whiskey into each. "Let's get this party started."

She wobbled back to the family room, the bottle squeezed under one arm and glasses pressed together between her hands.

I stayed put.

"You coming?"

"Maybe later. I have an idea about the case."

A moment later, the sound of clinking glasses filled the air, followed by blasts of music and laughter.

Vera's epiphany had hit me as hard as it had her.

I'd been trying so hard to be like Ivy, to prove that I was successful, responsible, and worthy of her attention. Maybe I had something to contribute by doing things my way.

I parked my car smack in the middle of the circular driveway. My black sedan had seen many road trips, and its weathered exterior probably cut Isabel's property value in half.

She could afford it.

A camera mounted not-so-subtly on a light post at the corner of the driveway and the garden path stared down at me. I waved.

The last time I was here, Isabel gave me the Wi-Fi password. Like a good little girl, I'd used it to connect to the web and run a search.

But I could do more, especially now that I didn't have to worry about Ivy's judgment staring over my shoulder.

I grabbed my laptop from the backpack in the passenger seat and opened it. Montgomery Manor was enormous, so it probably had several access points inside to spread the range across the entire property.

Isabel's Wi-Fi popped up as available with a strong signal. On my road trips, I could always count on the biggest house on any block to have the strongest signal, and Isabel's manor didn't disappoint. It was on a block all by itself.

I banged in the password and connected. The next step was to gain administrative access to the router that provided this wireless signal. For that, I would need *another* password.

My custom software would handle that. I initiated the dictionary-attack software and let it do its work.

My phone rang, and I glanced at the screen: my mom.

I answered. "Hey."

"Did I miss your call?" Her voice crackled on the other end.

"Mom? I can barely hear you. Where are you?"

"I'm on a cruise ship! The reception out here is awful."

"Since when do you go on cruises?"

"It was last minute. Hal surprised me with a vacation. We're in a huge balcony suite. The view is incredible."

I forced a smile, even though she couldn't see it. "That's great. I'm happy for you."

"I meant to let you know before we got on the boat, since we have our dinner this weekend. But you missed the last one, so I figured you'd probably miss this one too, and then it was a whirlwind getting on board . . ."

I felt a pang of disappointment. I had actually planned to be back in Atlanta by then. But Mom deserved a boat full of love and fun, and so far, Hal had been more reliable than her last boyfriend. "That's great," I said again.

"So what are you up to? Hal is taking a nap after last night's dancing."

The software running on my laptop popped up an alert that it had cracked the router password. "I'm in the middle of something. Can I call you back?"

"The least you can do is talk to your mother for three minutes. I carried you for a lot longer than that, and my back hurt the whole time."

"Mom . . ." I put the phone on speaker and set it on the passenger seat. "Three minutes."

I filtered the router's connection history to show only data from 1:00 p.m. to 5:00 p.m. on Tuesday, the timeframe for Eliza's murder.

My mom's voice poured from my phone as she rattled on about Hal and the cruise ship. "Anyway"—she took a breath— "I should have told you more about Caleb when you were growing up. Then you wouldn't feel the need to check him out yourself. I didn't realize you were curious."

"It's not your fault I'm here. I make my own choices." I tried to keep my side of the conversation light so she wouldn't worry.

"They're not always the *best* choices. I'm just saying I wish I'd been more open with you."

I steered the conversation away from my history of questionable choices. "I like Willow Lake. The people are nice. Nosy, but nice."

Her home in Atlanta was only a few hours away. I hoped the local news there hadn't been talking about Anna's and now Eliza's murder. I didn't mention them because the worry about my presence here would multiply if she knew.

"I've never been," she said.

"You mean Caleb didn't invite his mistress to his hometown? Shocking."

"Rose!"

On my computer, thirty or so MAC addresses appeared on the screen. Each one was associated with metadata telling me what kind of device it was.

"I know," I said. "You didn't know."

Her muffled giggle came across the line. "I can laugh about it now, but that man broke my heart." Her voice became serious. "He's not a good person, Rose."

I filtered the list of devices down to only mobile phones and took a screenshot. I didn't care about computers and cameras that were connected during the murder. I cared about people, and people were attached to cell phones.

"I'm sure he's not all bad," I said.

She sniffed.

Interesting. Eliza's phone had left the Wi-Fi network at 1:03 p.m.—I recognized the model number on the list because it was the same as mine. Her phone had been busted next to her body, probably destroyed in the struggle. That meant she'd died within minutes of 1:03.

That also meant the demise of Liam's alibi. He would have had just enough time to drive the three hours from the Montgomery guesthouse to North Ridge Resort and still check in by four thirty. I filtered the list of mobile phones on my screen to just the one connected to Isabel's Wi-Fi at 1:03 and grabbed another screenshot.

"Have you met the wife?" Mom asked, her voice crackling.

"*Ex*-wife—Ivy's mom. He's remarried." One of the phones that had been connected during Eliza's murder was using a lot of bandwidth at the time. I clicked through to investigate that device's history on the network.

"Have you met her?"

"Mm-hmm," I mumbled. The question registered, and I added, "Faye is great, actually. She's been really friendly."

"She probably feels guilty that you grew up without a dad. And Ivy?"

I kept my focus on the screen. With that kind of bandwidth, the phone in question had to be video streaming. Based on its history, that was a regular thing for whoever this was.

I imagined Isabel, in a white designer suit with red-bottomed shoes, streaming videos of K-pop stars to her phone.

But this person was an uploader, not a downloader. They were recording and streaming their own footage live. Maybe Isabel was streaming ultra-high-definition boudoir videos of herself in diamond-studded lingerie.

I burst out laughing.

"What's so funny?" My mom laughed, too, even though I hadn't told her the joke.

I hesitated long enough to come up with a lie, something that had nothing to do with murder. "I was just remembering how Faye said the same thing about Caleb. Neither of you think he's a good person." Faye had said no such thing, but given that he'd cheated on her and had a baby out of it, I imagined she would.

"I guess that's something else we have in common," my mom said.

"Mom, I have to go. I'll call you tonight."

"As if I don't have plans."

"Love you, Mom. Talk soon."

We disconnected, and my finger hovered over Ivy's number. I should tell her about Eliza's phone leaving the network and what that meant. After a second, I pressed down and placed the call, holding my breath. Ivy's voicemail picked up.

I disconnected without leaving a message.

Movement caught my attention, and I looked up to find Blake stomping down the front steps of the manor. He waved like I couldn't see him. I tilted my head back down at my laptop.

"Roll down the window, please," he said, all prim and proper.

I pretended not to hear him, but I closed the browser window I'd used to access the manor's router. If he saw, he would report it to Isabel, and I'd have to talk my way out of getting fired again.

"Rose." He rapped on the window with the back of an open hand.

I didn't look up.

He bent his long frame and pressed his nose near the glass. "I am not invisible. It is rude to ignore people, even ruder to loiter in someone's driveway without invitation."

Without looking up, I reached out and pressed the button to roll down the window. With the glass barely below my face, I said in a tone just as formal and proper, "Don't you know it is rude to bang on people's windows?" I rolled the window back up.

Red-faced, Blake sputtered on the other side. "You can't— you can't just . . ."

I put the window down two inches. "I'm busy. Could I have some space, please?" I sent the window back up.

"I will call the sheriff. Loitering is illegal."

"The sheriff is trying to solve two murders. I promise he doesn't care about loitering at the moment." I faced the window. "You do care about Eliza's murder, don't you?"

"Of course I do!" Although his eyes were dry, the edges of his eyelids were red and puffy.

Maybe he actually did care. In that case, I should stop tormenting him.

"I'm going." I closed my laptop, slipped it into my back-pack, and started the car.

It sputtered to life, and I followed the circular driveway back to the long stretch that led to the rest of Willow Lake.

I had what I needed for now. It would be too lucky for Eliza's murder to have been captured on video and streamed, but it wouldn't hurt to track down the streamer anyway.

CHAPTER 33

IVY

As I pushed open the door to the local bar, the smell of beer and liquor engulfed me. I breathed it in. Bars weren't normally my scene, but I liked this one. It had character.

The bartender was wiping down the counter. The only other patrons were two middle-aged men nursing beers at the bar. One wore a baseball cap, the other a beard that reached down his chest.

Dad's wife, Pearl, sat in the same seat at the end of the bar where she'd been camped out during my last visit here. Her hair fell in loose dark waves, framing a low neckline.

I made my way to the opposite side of the bar and sat.

The bartender approached. "What can I get you?"

I started to ask for the same as last time, but it wasn't a red-wine kind of day. "Vodka tonic."

He went to work.

I leaned back in my chair and closed my eyes. This was

what I needed. Peace and quiet and enough alcohol to dull my problems.

When I opened my eyes, Pearl stared at me across her pink drink, head tilted to the side as if asking a question.

I sighed and stood. I should have gone to a different bar—if there even was a second one in this town. I circled the high top and slid onto the stool beside her. The bartender set my drink in front of me.

Pearl and I drank in silence. The vodka burned down my throat. The picture on the wall behind the bar was crooked. It needed to be straightened. When Pearl finished, she set her glass on the bar top and eyed mine. I pushed it her way.

She grabbed it and gulped. "How are you holding up?"

I laughed.

She slammed down my glass, and clear liquid sloshed over the side. "Can you not?"

I laughed again. "I'm not doing anything."

I waved for the bartender and pointed at Pearl's empty glass. He nodded.

"Give me a break," she snapped. "You haven't liked me since the start. I'm not trying to replace your mom. I just want to be friends."

"Friends." I tested the word. It tasted sour. "When you had that first affair with my dad, he and my mom were still married."

"I was young and dumb. I'm not that person anymore."

I eyed her up and down. She was less than a decade older than me, and she looked the same as she had back then. Same pouty lips emphasized by lip liner, same tight clothes, same attitude that the world should love her.

"You think because I dress this way, I'll always be a home-wrecker."

I shrugged.

"I thought they would have taught you better than judging people by their clothes at all your fancy educational institutions."

They had, actually, but that didn't extend to Pearl.

She squirmed under my gaze. "I wasn't innocent, but your dad pursued me. After all of it, we got married because we love each other."

The bartender set a green drink in front of her and took her empty glass away. She pushed the remains of my vodka tonic back toward me.

"When did you order something else?" I prided myself on my observation skills, and she hadn't placed a new order since I walked in the door. If he were going to give her a refill, it would have been the same pink one.

She sniffed the drink, smiled at it like it was prey, and gulped. "He knows what I like."

I cranked one eyebrow upward.

"Don't be rude. Not in a sexual way." She dabbed at her mouth with a napkin. "I think he was cheating."

"Past tense?"

"Anna." She stared at her drink. "Caleb wasn't always up front about where he was going or what he was doing. He said he was working late a lot, but his office was closed when I stopped by."

"You checked up on him."

"He's my husband, and his stories didn't add up, and . . ."

"And he had a history of infidelity."

She waved a hand in confirmation. "He seemed nostalgic lately. Talked about the past a lot."

"Like what?"

"He pulled out his old case files and reread them, talked about them." She gestured toward me. "Talked about you, mistakes he made with Faye and . . ." She snapped her fingers. "Rose's mother."

I reached for the name but came up empty.

Pearl waved her hand. "It doesn't matter."

"Did you notice anything else that changed in his behavior?"

"He seemed sad, like he was regretting things."

The bartender poured a beer and slid it in front of one of the regulars. He set a new vodka tonic in front of me, even though I hadn't finished the first one yet. He was used to his customers sticking around for a while.

I lifted my first drink and sipped. "Sad, how?"

She licked the rim of sugar on her glass. "Off the record, okay? I'm not stupid. I know you're investigating."

I nodded.

"Dragging his feet, staring into space. Not complimenting my clothes." She fluffed her hair. "I've bought a lot of new dresses lately. Lots of hair appointments too. I was trying to win back his attention."

"Anything else?"

"The safe." She toyed with her glass, turning it on the bar top. "Caleb usually keeps a gun and cash in our home safe. He took them out."

"You saw him?"

"He was near it when I came into the room, and he hid

something behind his back. I checked later, and it was empty —except for the passports, life insurance documents, that stuff. The cash and the gun were gone."

"Why do you think he did that?"

She didn't answer, just raised her glass to her mouth and set it down without drinking.

"What about money? Did he empty your accounts?"

"You think he killed her and ran?"

"I'm hoping he ran—beats the alternative."

She flinched. The alternative was that whoever murdered Anna killed him too.

"Whether he killed her is a different story. Any chance he just left you? He wanted out, so he took off?"

"No way. If he wanted to end our marriage, he would tell me to my face. I know you don't think I mean anything to him, but our relationship is over a decade old now. I'm—"

"I'm well aware of when your relationship started."

She narrowed her eyes but let that slide. "We have a good life. He wouldn't abandon me."

"But you think he would cheat with Anna?"

"Men aren't always rational when it comes to sex."

I restrained myself from making another crack about their affair.

She gulped her drink. "Neither of us has been entirely faithful."

"I'll bet."

She shot me a murderous look that snapped my jaw shut.

"Despite that, we love each other. We forgive each other. There was no reason for him to take off." Her face looked sincere, but that was all. No signs of lying, no signs of hatred.

Pearl had as much motive as anyone to kill Anna and get rid of Caleb, but if she did it, she was an Olympic-class liar.

"You're not angry at him for going wherever he went?"

"I'm trying not to be."

I stayed quiet. People often kept talking when given space to do so.

"As far as I see it, there are three—maybe four—options." She set her drink down and raised one finger. "Caleb killed Anna and fled town to keep from being arrested." She raised a second finger. "He didn't kill her, but he fled for fear of being accused." A third finger, and she hesitated.

I inhaled a long breath. "He's dead," I filled in.

She nodded, her lips trembling. "Or his disappearance is a complete and unrelated coincidence."

I grunted.

"I know," she said. "Fat chance."

"There's one more option. Whoever killed Anna was after him too, and he ran away to escape. If so, he anticipated this. That's why he was acting strangely and grabbed the cash and gun from your safe. If that's the case, his life is still in danger."

Color washed from her face, leaving it cold.

"I need you to keep me in the loop if you think of anything else," I said. "You were closer to him than anyone."

"Except Anna."

"Except Anna," I echoed.

"Find him." For the first time since I sat beside her, her voice cracked. Her chin trembled.

I hated when people cried in front of me. It made me feel awkward and powerless.

The bartender approached, but Pearl waved him away. His

presence seemed to steel her, and her rock-solid facade locked back into place.

She drained her drink and looked me straight in the face. "Find him. Bring him home."

CHAPTER 34

IVY

I STORMED INTO THE SHERIFF'S OFFICE, AND THE AUTUMN WIND slammed the door behind me. The bang reverberated through the room, locking every gaze on me.

A reception desk with a computer monitor stood near a temporary wall that blocked most of the space. Behind the computer sat a plump woman with a tight bun and a forced smile, speaking into a phone receiver in a hushed tone.

She raised one finger and pointed to the tiny waiting room to my right with four uncomfortable-looking metal chairs. A woman in her forties sat on a brightly colored cushion on one of them. She clutched a magazine so tightly the paper crumpled, while one knee bounced up and down.

She'd been waiting for a while. I didn't intend to do the same.

I maneuvered around the reception desk.

"You can't go back there!" The receptionist tried to grab

me, but I dodged her. One of her hands still clutched the receiver of a landline phone, tethering her in place.

"Hey," the other woman shouted, "I was here before her."

"Sit," the receptionist hissed.

Without looking back, I heard the clank of the metal chair as the woman sat back down.

I strode down a hallway constructed from more partitions. Voices to my right told me that the bullpen was probably that way, on the other side of the barrier, so I hooked a left when the hallway ended.

Footsteps padded behind me over the thin carpet, and a hand landed on my shoulder.

"Don't touch me." I shook her off and kept moving.

The hand withdrew, and the receptionist fell into step beside me. She was shorter, so her feet had to move quicker to keep up. "You can't be back here."

In front of us, a closed door had Sheriff Foster's name on it. I stopped before reaching it. "What's your name?"

"Dolores."

"Are you going to get in trouble if I barge in there?"

She bobbed her head.

"Okay, I don't want that."

She let out an audible breath, and her shoulders relaxed.

"I'm going in there."

She stiffened.

"If it's better for you, you can go in first and announce me." I tapped my chest. "I'm Ivy Gray. I'm here to discuss the murder of Anna Baxter and the disappearance of my father, Caleb Gray."

Dolores sucked her lips in, nodded, and opened the door.

She closed it behind her. A moment later, muffled voices followed, and Dolores hurried out, looking pale. "Could have been worse," she whispered. Louder, she added, "You can go in, Ms. Gray." She took off for her desk.

As I entered the office, Sheriff Foster stood behind his desk, arms folded over his chest. His brows lowered over glaring eyes.

I hesitated for only a second before pulling the door shut after me. I mirrored his pose—arms crossed, wide stance, eyes narrowed. I didn't take up as much space, but he'd get the gist that I couldn't be moved.

We stared at each other for almost a full minute before he grunted and dropped into his leather chair. He placed two large, booted feet on top of the desk.

I sat on one of the other seats, a wobbly metal-and-plastic chair that, by my guess, served the sole purpose of putting his guests at a disadvantage.

"Why are you here, Ms. Gray?"

He knew why I was here. Otherwise, he would have dispensed with this posturing and calling me *Ms. Gray* when we'd known each other for years, even had a friendly run-in five days earlier.

"Look, Dan."

"Sheriff Foster."

"Sheriff Foster," I corrected, "you know me. I've been an FBI agent for six years. I've worked dozens of cases—"

He took his feet off the desk, slamming them on the floor. "The FBI taught you to barge into a sheriff's office and make demands?"

"I haven't made any . . ." I stopped that sentence in its

tracks. I was indeed here to make demands. "This is my father we're talking about—and Anna. You can't shut me out."

"Even if you are fully capable—"

"I am."

He waved a hand. "Even so. You are too close to this case. On this matter, you are a private citizen, and that is all."

"You haven't even heard my ask yet."

"I know your ask. You want the case file."

I did, indeed. "I want us to collaborate. I have investigative experience that your deputies couldn't get from working in this small town."

His eyes narrowed. It was a misstep to suggest his deputies weren't equipped to handle this.

I tried again. "I know my dad. I know Anna. I might see something in the evidence that your people don't see."

His eyes stayed slits, but something changed in the tilt of his head.

I gestured around the room. "This is a substation. It's not even your primary office. I'm sure you have a ton of work to do in the rest of Oak County."

No movement.

"I can lighten the load. Your people drive. I'll stay in the passenger seat, pointing out what I see. That's all."

"Not interested." He was leaning forward, though, showing interest. He needed me to sweeten the pot.

"I won't make a move without your okay."

He leaned back, examining the ceiling as if the terms of our agreement were up there, and he was checking them for loopholes.

"This is your investigation," I added.

"Strictly unpaid consulting. I'm in charge of my deputies, and they're in charge of you." He raised one hand in the air, palm down. "Me." He put the other one a few inches under it. "My deputies." He moved his top hand a foot under the lower one. "You. You understand?"

"Perfectly."

"This isn't going to end with me getting screwed, is it? If this crosses state lines, is the FBI going to barge in here and insist on an official collaboration?"

I stifled a laugh. The last thing the FBI was going to do at this point was back me up. "That's not going to happen."

He pulled his phone from his breast pocket and set it on the desk. "Give me your supervisor's number. I don't want him getting blindsided like I just did. I need to make sure he knows what's going on and agrees—up front—that this is local business."

I was suddenly aware of my heart pounding. If Sheriff Foster found out I was on administrative leave, there was no way he'd trust me anywhere near this investigation. I licked my lips. "If we're going to work together, there needs to be trust and communication. You handle your people, and I'll handle mine."

He stared at me for a few seconds, then slipped the phone back into his pocket. "As you can imagine, I'm extremely busy."

"Of course. I'll need access to my father's and Anna's computers."

"I'll think about it. This arrangement only works if one of my deputies agrees to take you on. I can't hold your hand through this investigation."

I gritted my teeth to keep from arguing with the suggestion

that I needed a babysitter. He was almost on board. Just a little more groveling.

Foster led me into the hallway. By the time we reached the bullpen, he was making full use of his long legs, and I was hurrying to keep up. The space held a collection of desks and chairs arranged in pairs, each desk facing another.

Deputies Marks and Ramirez sat at one pair. Hers was spotless, with nothing except a coffee mug, a single notepad, and one pen on its surface. Across from her, Marks nursed a pile of folders on his own desk. Around them stood two more deputies—one of whom was my high school sweetheart, Deputy Jay Matthews.

The four of them had been laughing in conversation, but they hushed as the sheriff and I strode in. Ramirez and Marks sat straighter. Jay and the other man rotated to face Foster as though they were soldiers and he was in command.

Sheriff Foster pointed at them one by one. "Jay Matthews, Kurt Givens. You've met Marks and Ramirez."

I avoided Jay's eyes, even though he was clearly trying to draw my attention. The last thing I needed was for Sheriff Foster to have another potential bias as an excuse to keep me away from this case.

Sheriff Foster clapped his hands together. "Ivy Gray is an FBI agent. She's going to be our unpaid consultant on the Gray case." He gave me a side-eye as he emphasized the word *unpaid*.

No one responded.

"She'll need a liaison in this office to keep her updated." He said *liaison* like it caused actual pain to his tongue, spitting it out.

Deputy Marks shrank into his seat as if that would make him invisible.

"Sir." Ramirez cleared her throat. "She has investigative experience, but she's already too close to this. She's called in two bodies in less than two weeks."

"Isn't she Caleb Gray's daughter?" Givens asked.

"Indeed," the sheriff said. "That's why any information earmarked to go to her will be approved by me first."

I opened my mouth to object, but his glare silenced me.

No one else spoke up.

The sheriff sighed. "I know working with consultants can be a thankless job. Think of this as an opportunity to step up for me. You'll work with me on what information she sees, and as a result, you'll be my go-to for this case when I'm not on site."

All four deputies looked at one another.

Ramirez shook her head. "It's a bad idea."

"I'm looking for a volunteer, not an opinion."

Jay inched his hand into the air.

"Deputy Matthews, are you volunteering your time or your opinion?"

"My time, sir. I'll be her liaison."

This just got a lot more complicated. "This liaison thing really isn't necessary. I can commute to your main office as needed, and—"

"It's decided, Gray." Sheriff Foster nodded at Jay. "Figure out what she needs and run it by me." He stomped away.

Jay waited until his footsteps receded, then came over to me. "Welcome on board." He stood close enough that I got a whiff of a woody scent—the same cologne he'd been wearing since high school.

I stepped away. "Let me know when you've got the case file." I turned and hurried for the exit.

Mission accomplished. It would be a little more awkward than I anticipated, but soon, I would know everything the sheriff knew about my father's disappearance and Anna's murder.

CHAPTER 35

ROSE

I unlocked Vera's front door from the inside and threw it open. On the porch, Vera shrieked, shielding her face with one arm while holding her keys like a weapon.

"It's me." I grabbed her wrist and yanked her into the house.

"Are you trying to give me a heart attack?" She pressed a hand to her chest.

"I've been waiting an hour."

"Hardly an excuse for trying to scare me to death. I'm a retiree. I do what I want and don't answer to people less than half my age." She slipped her key ring onto a hook by the door.

I snatched the keys back and pushed them into her hands. "That's a terrible place for these. Keep them in your purse or your room."

"So I can lose them like you do?"

It was a fair dig, so I took it. "If I can't find them, neither can a burglar."

Vera huffed but dropped them into her handbag. "I thought your thing was computers. Now you're a home security expert too?"

"I'm trying to keep your home safe. We don't need any break-ins."

She put her hands on her hips. "Tell me you didn't stalk my doorway for the last hour to make sure I didn't leave my keys by the front door."

I flapped a black envelope in her face. She tried to take it, but I pulled it back and slipped out the interior black card with gold-foil lettering before waving that in her face too.

"Enough with the buildup." She grabbed my wrist, snatched the card, and inspected it. "This is an invitation to tonight's auction."

"I assume it's from Irving Greenfield. He called Gray Investigations after the vand—" I hadn't told her about the vandalism and didn't want to scare her. "He wanted to make sure Ivy and I knew that Isabel's Monet would be on the auction block. He wants us to solve the case."

"Because it makes him look bad?"

"Something like that."

Vera flipped over the card to reveal a gold-foiled logo. "Fancy."

"Right? If the invitation is that luxe, I assume the guests will be just as fancy."

She handed the card back. "It's black tie. I've driven past during an auction. Everyone's in long, sparkly dresses and tuxedos."

I sucked in a breath.

"Ah." It dawned on her. "You have nothing to wear."

"I could wear this." I laughed down at my wide-legged jeans and fitted tee shirt. "But I need to fit in."

Eliza's co-conspirator—and murderer—would be at this auction. If they wanted the painting once and killed Eliza over it, they still wanted it. I couldn't investigate if I didn't blend in. More importantly, whoever worked the door wouldn't let me over the threshold dressed like this.

Vera hooked her arm through mine. "Let's go shopping."

I didn't usually care about high-end clothes. I wore what I liked, what showed off my curves and personality. If Ivy was invited too, she'd dress impeccably in a sleek black gown, making me look like an amateur.

"The auction's in an hour." Panic seeped around the edges of my words.

"I meant upstairs in the closet." Vera patted my hand. "It's okay. We'll get you there."

Twenty minutes later, in her son's old bedroom, Vera had me in a shimmery black jumpsuit. The V-neck was daring but not risqué. The straight pant legs ended in faux leather hems, the same material lining the sleeveless arm openings.

"It's a little badass," I admitted.

Vera turned a circle in the closet, muttering, "Accessories, accessories, where are you hiding?"

I pointed at an open box in the corner.

Vera peeked inside. "Just some scarves and gloves. A few handbags." She pulled out a plain black clutch with a long strap. "This isn't bad, but it looks like she took the rest of the good stuff."

"She left thousands of dollars in clothing. I can't imagine how much her jewelry was worth. Can't blame her for taking it with her."

"My understanding was that her parents were wealthy, and she was an only child who got whatever she wanted." Vera scowled. "Probably why she was such a b—"

"Vera!"

She waved a hand. "I was going to say *brat*."

I cocked my head.

"Don't you worry about what I was going to say. Does Ivy have something you can borrow?"

"No," I said too quickly. And admit that I couldn't do a simple thing like dress myself without her managing me? Absolutely not.

Vera narrowed her eyes but didn't push. She knew better than to pry into family drama.

"You can't go like that," she said. "You'll freeze, and your neck looks too bare. A bare neck is the sign of a woman who doesn't know how to accessorize."

"It's fine."

She ignored me and spun another slow circle like accessories would suddenly appear. "Stay here. I'll be right back." She shot out the door.

I flopped onto the bed and sank into the mass of pillows piled against the headboard. Two books stacked on the side table looked like self-help on making money and staying focused. Behind them sat a small, framed photo of Vera's sons, one with his arm around his brother's shoulders while they grinned at the camera.

Vera's voice reached me from down the hall. "No! She has to be there in forty-five minutes, so stop arguing." She came into the room, phone pressed to one ear, and waved at me. "Don't make me call your mama. Get your rear over here." She disconnected before the other person could object again.

I sat up straight. "Who was that? Who's coming over?"

"My nephew. He has good fashion sense and a limousine."

"He has a limo?"

"He bought it at a police impound auction and fixed it up. He'll drive you so you blend in with those rich folks."

"I'm not sure a limo is the way to blend in."

She shushed me. "He'll pick up jewelry too. He's resourceful, and I told him what you're wearing."

Thirty minutes later, Vera and I were sitting in the living room, watching the front door like it was the best thing on television. My hands tangled together in my lap. Any longer, and I'd be late. Were auctions like church, where, if you arrived after the start, you had to wait outside until the ushers let you in?

The lock clicked, and the door burst open. Adrian strode into the room like he owned the place.

I jumped to my feet and yanked Vera behind me. "What the hell?"

He grinned a kind of half-apologetic, half-mocking smile. "Rose, good to see you." His words slid out like oil, too smooth.

Vera tried to step around me, but I held her back.

"Rose." She shoved me aside. "This is my nephew, Adrian."

"Your—your . . ." I sputtered. "Adrian is your nephew?"

She squinted at me. "You've met?"

"Unfortunately."

Adrian's grin widened. "Usually, women find it fortunate to meet me."

Vera's phone rang an upbeat tune, and she pulled it from her pocket. She hopped in place as she checked the display. "It's Carl. I have to take this." Grinning like a schoolgirl, she kissed me on the cheek, then Adrian, before half-running away into her sunroom.

"Hello," she said before her voice faded into the distance.

I glared at Adrian, and then an epiphany slammed into me so hard I almost fell over. I pointed at him. "You left that threatening photo on the coat rack."

"It wasn't threatening . . . *per se.*"

"It wasn't threatening?" I hissed. "You skewered it on a hook—a photo of me and my sister that you could only have taken if you were stalking me."

"I wasn't stalking you. I had a pickup."

"A pickup?" My voice screeched, and I wished I could dial it down to a more human level.

"I collect vehicles—buy them up at auctions, mostly. I have a van and two trucks. Sometimes, people pay me to pick things up and drop them off."

"You broke into my home."

"I have a key." Adrian dangled his keys in the air, still grinning like a chump—although I suspected I was the only chump in the room.

He tucked his keys into one pocket. From the other, he extracted a long, thin silver chain with a tasteful rectangular pendant. I snatched it from him and pulled it on over my head.

It caught in my curly hair. Adrian reached out to help untangle it, but I smacked his hand away. He pulled out a pair of dangly silver earrings. I jabbed out a hand, and he dropped them into my palm. I looped them into my ears.

He looked me up and down and nodded. "It's a good look."

"They're fine," I admitted. The pendant fell just above the V of the neckline, framing my collarbone and elongating my torso. "It's okay."

He gestured toward the door. "Don't be late."

"We're not done. Why would you leave that photo here if not to scare me?"

"To scare you," he confirmed in a tone that was matter-of-fact.

I lunged at him but stumbled as one high heel caught the carpet fibers. That gave him enough time to dodge to the other side of the couch.

I waved in the direction of the sunroom and hissed, "I was scared for her life."

He dipped his head. "I didn't know you would show it to her."

"I didn't." I lunged again.

"Hey, hey!" Vera ran back into the room.

I froze, inches from his neck. He was lucky I didn't want his aunt to watch me rip his throat out. "Did you see him in the video that Lawrence sent over? You watched the whole thing."

"Of course." Vera slid between us. "He visits me a couple times a week. Why?"

I pointed at Adrian. "He put—"

"Hey," Adrian cut in loudly. "You don't want to be late for this auction."

So he didn't want her to know. "Embarrassed?" I smirked.

"What did I miss?" Vera asked.

Adrian crossed his arms, causing the suit jacket to crinkle around his shoulders and show off admirable muscle tone.

"Why are you wearing a tux?" I asked.

His brow crinkled as he looked from Vera to me and then back. "Aunt Vera said to get dressed because you have a plus-one."

"I don't have a . . ." I patted my hips, but the pockets of my jumpsuit were empty.

Vera whipped out my invitation and handed it to me. *Rose Gray and Guest*, it read. I growled at it.

"If he's driving you, you can't expect him to wait outside," Vera said.

"I don't need him to drive me!" I shouted.

"You plan to drive that bucket of metal parked out front?" Adrian jerked his thumb at the door and then gave me a slow once-over, starting from my feet and lingering at the V-neck. "Wearing that?"

"You said you wanted to blend in," Vera said.

"I'm not going anywhere with him until we talk." I stomped toward the kitchen. "In private."

He followed.

"You're going to be late," Vera called after us.

When we were alone, I circled the breakfast table to put space between us and crossed my arms over my chest. "Explain."

He rubbed the back of his neck. "I told you. I wanted to scare you. You eavesdropped on a private work call, and I didn't want you involved in . . . what I'm involved in."

"So this was an attempt at chivalry?"

"Don't make it a sexist thing. I would have done the same for a man."

I raised an eyebrow.

"It had nothing to do with Isabel Montgomery."

"I'm supposed to believe on your word alone that it's a coincidence we meet on her property and then you threatened me about something else entirely? Convince me."

He shrugged. "I can't."

"You're gonna."

"It had nothing to do with Mrs. Montgomery's painting or whatever got Eliza killed."

Sparks danced across my nerves, setting them on fire. "Do I look like some simpering flower you can threaten, and I'll go away because you said so? Tell me what you're into, or I'm telling Vera you left a stalker photo in her home to scare me."

He widened his stance as if blocking my way to his aunt.

"Explain," I said in a low voice.

"I'm self-employed. I do a lot of odd jobs."

I waved for him to continue.

"Sometimes . . . I'm hired to collect debts. My current client sells marijuana."

"You work for a drug dealer?"

"Only marijuana." He kept his voice low.

I sniffed. "It's still illegal in this state." I didn't have a problem with it, but that wasn't the point. I wasn't the one on trial.

"My client wants to get out of town fast and needed me to collect for him. That's all."

"So what? You were going to break Eliza's legs if she didn't pay up?"

"Usually, the threat of violence is enough . . . except that one time, but it was only a finger, and the guy healed fine. He was an asshole and had it coming. Honestly, I would've broken his finger for free—job or not."

I closed my eyes for a second to process that. "On your call, you told your client he didn't have to do whatever he was thinking because Eliza would complete her payment." I looked him in the eye. "You work for someone who was threatening to hurt her. How do I know *you* didn't kill her on your boss's orders?"

"You've got it wrong." He raised both hands, palms out. "He's a softie. I don't work for killers. He was threatening to dock my fee if I didn't get what she owed. That's all."

Eliza's murder was connected to the Monet. We knew that because she had it in her possession. Adrian's story made more sense than the theory that he stole the painting—and then killed her. He didn't seem the type to frequent auction houses and deal in million-dollar art.

Adrian lowered his hands. "Are we good?"

I stomped past him toward the door. "Just drive. Don't talk."

"Have fun," Vera called as I threw the front door open.

I couldn't deal with Adrian right now. I needed to find a killer.

CHAPTER 36

ROSE

I LOUNGED IN THE BACK SEAT, SINKING INTO THE BUTTERY LEATHER AS Adrian slowed the limo outside the auction house. Luxury cars filled most of the parking lot, but this section looked reserved for chauffeured rides. Adrian pulled up beside several others.

"Who knew there were so many filthy-rich people in town?"

Adrian turned in his seat. "Anyone with eyes."

In most of the other limos, the drivers still sat in the front seats, reclined or reading. One driver stood outside his car, leaning against it while sucking from a vape pen.

"I guess you're supposed to stay here with the chauffeurs."

He glared at me before popping his door and sliding out. He slammed it so hard the whole car shook.

"You're not going to get my door?" I shouted. "All the other chauffeurs get their chauffees' doors."

He stuffed his hands in his pockets several feet away.

I sighed as I climbed out of the lush interior. I might resent

Adrian being my driver, but I couldn't complain about the accommodation.

"*Chauffee?*" he asked.

I shrugged. "You know what I mean."

The Lakeview Luxe Gallery looked grand at night. Its white stone facade gleamed under the spotlights, giving the whole setup a magical glow.

A line of people in their finest attire waited to get in. Men wore black tuxedos or custom-tailored suits, with a few daring colors sprinkled in the mix. The women wore sophisticated updos, their gowns in rich tones or classic black. Jewels glittered on their wrists, necks, and fingers.

As we approached the entrance, Jake Thompson held up the line. Unlike the others, he wore a sport blazer and slacks. He gestured with both hands, and his voice carried across the lot.

"I need to be in there!" he shouted.

The two security guards, including Rigsby's nephew Lamar, spoke to him in low tones.

Jake half-turned to walk away and then lunged toward the gap between the two men. Lamar grabbed Jake by one arm and the back of his collar and hauled him to the end of the line. He marched Jake past me to the edge of the main parking area.

"Don't think that because I'm wearing this suit, I won't tune you up," Lamar said.

Jake gave him a last defiant look, took in the other man's grim expression and thicker frame, and slumped his shoulders.

Lamar smoothed Jake's jacket, turned, and strolled back to his post at the entrance as if nothing had happened.

I turned to Adrian. "Stay here. I'll be right back." Before he could protest, I hurried after Jake, who was heading for the far end of the parking lot.

"Jake!" I called.

He stopped, turned slowly, and eyed me through slitted lids as I caught up. He sagged like a popped balloon. All the fight had left him.

"We haven't met officially, but we saw each other at Isabel Montgomery's the day before yesterday."

His expression stayed blank.

I stuck out my hand. "Rose Gray. I'm investigating Eliza's murder."

His eyes narrowed. "Look, I don't know what Isabel has told you, but I loved Eliza. I would never—"

I lifted the hand he'd refused to shake and gave him a dismissive wave. "Isabel has biases, just like the rest of us."

He searched my face. "She hired you?"

"Initially, to find the Monet. You said you just arrived, but I saw you stalking Eliza at the festival on Saturday. You were in town long enough to have killed her."

Jake's face paled. "I didn't—"

"Maybe you were here when the Monet was stolen too," I pressed. "Were you and Eliza partners all along?"

His face crumpled.

I waited. Ivy told me that sometimes, when people wanted to talk, I should shut up and let them. Now seemed like one of those times.

"I was a terrible husband." His voice was so quiet I had to lean in to hear. "All she wanted was my time, but I was always moments away from winning my next big case or gaining a new client that would set us up for life." He paused, his gaze distant.

"Jake?"

"The only thing I know about the Monet is that it caused Eliza's death, and they're selling it tonight. I was her partner in every way that mattered, but we didn't steal anything. That's a lie."

"We found it in her home."

"Then somebody tried to frame her."

"What's the point of framing someone and then immediately murdering them?"

He choked on a sob.

I needed to pick my words more carefully. Jake was either a brilliant actor or innocent, and the last thing I wanted was to add more pain to an innocent man's trauma. "Why were you following her on Saturday?" I asked more gently.

He swallowed and then answered. "I was here—I admit it." His gaze fell on my collarbone as though he'd rather tell his truth to it than to my face. "Eliza kept going back and forth on whether she wanted a divorce. It was breaking my heart and hers, so I decided to free her. I signed the papers. I came to give them to her, but . . . she was so beautiful."

"You lost your nerve," I finished.

He nodded. "I just wanted her to be happy, even if that meant signing off on the divorce. I never would have killed her." His attention returned to my face, and his expression tightened. "I don't know anything about that painting except that it killed her. I want it gone, sold, as far away from Eliza as possible."

"Rose?" Adrian appeared and stood shoulder to shoulder with me. "Everything okay?" He looked Jake up and down.

"I'm fine."

"I just want to make sure it's gone," Jake said before

turning and heading off across the parking lot, away from the light and the auction.

"What was that about?" Adrian asked.

"A man with a broken heart," I murmured. "Let's get inside."

We walked toward the Lakeview Luxe Gallery entrance and its dressed-to-impress patrons.

Isabel's chef, René, loitered by the door in plain black slacks and a black button-down. He chatted animatedly with Lamar, who was back on duty—kind of. Unlike the other guard in a similar unadorned tuxedo, who stood sentry on the opposite side of the entrance, Lamar split his attention between checking invitations and watching whatever was on Chef René's phone.

As we approached, neither looked up. Lamar burst out laughing and pointed at the screen.

The other guard glared.

Despite Lamar and Chef René breaking the vibe, the entrance looked snazzy with the spotlights and tuxedoed bouncers.

Adrian and I joined the back of the line. He draped an arm across my shoulders like it was the most natural thing to do.

"Do you want to lose that arm?" I hissed through the gritted teeth of a fake smile.

"I thought you wanted to blend in."

"If I punch you in the face, would that help us blend . . . or not?"

He dropped his arm.

"Invitation?" We'd reached the front, and the tuxedoed guard held out his hand. He was all business, offering a stiff posture and a warm smile.

To our left, Lamar waved two women through the entrance without checking their invitations. He peeked at their butts as they strolled past, then returned his attention to whatever Chef René was showing on his phone.

I pulled my invitation from my clutch and handed it to the guard. He compared it to his tablet, took in Adrian, who stood so close to me that there was no question he was my plus-one, and waved us through.

The inside was more impressive than the outside. The auction house's high ceilings and spacious layout gave it an immediate sense of grandeur. The overhead lights were dimmed, but lights lining the bottom of the walls shined upward, making the royal blue walls look even more luxe.

Another change from my last visit was the setup. A massive, blue velvet curtain blocked the windows to Irving's office. In front of it stood a low stage that appeared to have risen from inside the floor itself.

A small collection of chairs faced the stage. Not enough for everyone, so Irving expected a standing-room situation to increase the urgency and exclusivity of the moment.

Smart.

I caught a glimpse of Irving standing at the side of the room, talking to a group of well-dressed people. He wore an impeccable blue tuxedo in a stunning shade somewhere between royal and navy.

"You want a drink?" Adrian pointed to a bar set up on one side of the room.

"Wait here," I said. "I'll be right back."

I would *not* be right back. Adrian could stay or leave—he wasn't my concern right now.

"Excuse me." I elbowed my way into Irving's small-talk huddle.

The conversation halted, and Irving turned to me. "Can I help you?"

"Can we speak in private?" I whispered, even though everyone in our circle could hear me.

"In a moment."

He had invited me here, knowing I had no money to spend, but his blank expression kept that under wraps. He didn't want his guests to know he had anything to do with me—in case I caused a scene.

Which I just might do.

"Irving," I said louder in an exaggeratedly posh, slightly British accent. "So lovely to see you. Could we speak in your office?"

His eyebrows lowered, but he offered the rest of the group a dignified nod and led me into his office. From here, the blue curtain's back side blocked the view of the main space.

Stiff-backed, Irving circled his desk and sat on his chair. "You have three minutes." He checked the vintage watch on his wrist.

I settled into a guest chair and dropped the sophisticated act. "You can't sell that painting tonight."

He looked around the room as if examining the space and then back at me. "And here I was thinking I owned the place."

"It's evidence in a murder."

"The sheriff has given me no indication of that."

"That's because the painting disappeared from the crime scene. Isabel took it."

"It's hers to take . . ." He glanced at his watch again. "For another half hour."

"You can sleep at night knowing you let a murderer go free?"

He sighed. "Ms. Gray, you know as well as I do that I invited you here to keep that from happening, but this conversation"—he pointed between us—"does not instill me with great confidence."

"Have you at least confirmed the one you're selling isn't the forgery?"

"Of course," he shouted. He cleared his throat and lowered his voice. "Don't tell me my job."

I leaned forward and stripped the fight from my tone. "Please. You knew Eliza. She came here often to preview art for Isabel. Don't you want to do everything in your power to help us find her killer?"

"I believe I have. I cannot stop Mrs. Montgomery from selling the Monet—I have already tried. If I don't auction it, someone else will. And that someone will perhaps be her go-to auction house in the future. I enjoy having Mrs. Montgomery as a customer, and I intend to keep it that way."

"What if you postponed for a week or two?"

"There is an art auction scheduled for tomorrow less than a hundred miles from this spot. I'm sure Mrs. Montgomery has done her research and has that as a backup plan."

"You could keep the painting in your secure room under the guise of needing to authenticate it."

He shook his head, stood, and smoothed his suit with a hand so quick that it snapped across the fabric. "Now, please." He gestured toward the door.

As if on cue, the office door burst open, and Ivy stepped through.

She wore a sleek feminine tuxedo with tailored pants that

hugged her hips and made her legs seem endless. Her updo featured curls pinned upward from the nape of her neck. The look was both elegant and daring.

She and I locked eyes for a split second before she turned her glare on Irving. "What the hell are you doing?"

I shrank into my chair.

"I'm . . . I'm . . ." His mouth opened and closed like a dying fish. "Ms. Gray?"

She slammed the door and marched up to him until they stood Oxfords to pumps. "You cannot sell the Monet."

He met Ivy nose to nose. "What is it with you Gray women telling me what I can and cannot do on my own property?"

"If you sell that painting," Ivy said with her chin jutted forward, "Rose will tell everyone how she sneaked in your back door and poked around in your delivery truck, and no one stopped her. Who will trust the security of their valuables to you after that?"

He paled and stepped back.

"Isabel is selling the painting today or tomorrow," I said. "If Irving doesn't sell it, another auction house will."

Ivy didn't even spare me a glance. It felt like a serrated blade in my gut.

"It's already on their books as a tentative late addition," Irving confirmed.

I jumped up from my chair. "Give us until the end of the night then. Make the Monet the last item up for bid."

Irving looked between the two of us and nodded. "That won't give you much time."

"We'll make it work," Ivy said. I liked hearing her say *we*.

"We'd better."

CHAPTER 37

ROSE

TEN MINUTES LATER, I WAS IN THE MAIN AUCTION HALL. IVY HAD
bolted like a cat in a thunderstorm the moment we left Irving's
office. I perched on a cushioned bench, my back rigid as I
scanned the room for anything weird. Adrian sat beside me,
looking relaxed and smug.

I wanted to smack that grin off his face.

"Can we finish our conversation?" he asked.

"It's finished."

Irving clapped his hands twice as he climbed the stage, and
the sound bounced off the high ceiling. "Gentle people, if I
could have your attention, please. It's time to begin the
auction."

"I guess we'll talk later then," Adrian said.

"Not if I'm lucky," I muttered.

"Please make your way to your seats." Despite having no
microphone, Irving's voice boomed through the auction house.
"Let me introduce our esteemed auctioneer."

Adrian stood and offered me his hand, but I slapped it away.

The small collection of maybe twenty chairs faced the low stage. With twice as many guests as seats, Adrian and I hovered toward the back of the seating area while Irving talked. We'd have a better view from here anyway.

"What's the plan?" Adrian whispered.

I didn't answer, not because I wanted him to scram—which I did—but because I had no plan. My goal was to find Eliza's killer, but how to do that still escaped me.

Ivy stood near the last row of chairs on the opposite side, staring straight ahead, hands clasped behind her back.

She probably had a plan.

I tried to catch her eye, but her gaze never wavered from the stage.

The audience members filed into seats, most clutching champagne flutes or short glasses of dark liquor. Hushed conversations evaporated.

I sidled over to Ivy and glared at Adrian when he followed. "You got a plan?" I asked her.

No answer.

"Because I don't."

She cut a look at me before returning her attention to the stage.

"Can we talk for a minute?"

Still nothing.

Isabel found a seat on the front aisle, and Blake stood beside her like a self-important sentinel. He noticed me, wrinkled his nose, and whispered something to his boss. Isabel was pale but placid. I imagined a cocktail of diazepam was involved in that.

At the back of the room, Thomas Rigsby stood near the door, hands clamped in front, ready for action. He gave me a cool look but otherwise didn't acknowledge me.

Several feet away, on the other side of the entrance, Lamar stood with Chef René. Both men were still laser-focused on René's screen.

"What do you think that's about?" I nudged Ivy with my elbow.

She sighed but rotated to face me so she could see René in her peripheral vision. She cocked her head to one side.

"What?" I asked.

"Chef René pays a lot of attention to his phone."

"How do you know that?"

A pause and then, "When I interviewed him, he seemed irritated he had to get off it to talk to me. Then he made me chop vegetables like it was a punishment."

"Any chance he was uploading live video?"

"It's possible." Her eyes narrowed. "Why?"

"Someone was streaming video when Eliza was killed."

Ivy closed her eyes briefly. "And you know that because . . . ?"

"Instead of trying to find fault, maybe listen to what I'm saying."

Her jaw worked for a moment. "Assuming that's true, Chef René could be your streamer."

"So we should talk to him, right?" I pushed. "I doubt he murdered Eliza while uploading it all to the cloud, but he might have caught something useful."

"Without further ado," Irving boomed. With a flourish, he handed a leather-bound notebook to the auctioneer, who took his post behind the podium at center stage.

In the corner, the back door where I'd first met Thomas Rigsby opened, and two men in black suits came through. Between them, they carried a large rectangular something covered in a lush blue cloth.

When they reached the stage, they set the object down and rolled it to the center. Irving grabbed the drape and ripped it off.

The crowd oohed and aahed.

A glass box held a towering statue carved from Carrara marble and polished to a gleam. Its flowing robes, serene face, and gold leaf accents wowed on top of a black granite base.

Even I couldn't help but gasp, although I wasn't sure if it was the showmanship or the art that ripped my breath away.

"Whoa." Beside me, Adrian leaned forward, just as awestruck as everyone else.

"You can't afford that," I whispered.

"Don't worry about what I can afford." His return whisper was a low rumble.

"Let's get started with lot number one," the auctioneer shouted before rolling into a spiel about the statue, its artist, its provenance, and its estimated value.

"Excuse me." I headed for the front entrance, my sights on Chef René.

He was still bent over his phone screen with Rigsby's nephew, Lamar. As I neared, René pointed at the display, and both men burst into laughter. René spotted me, shushed his friend, and slipped the phone into his pocket.

"Chef René," I said.

Ivy came up beside me.

"Why did you hide it?" I pointed to the pocket.

"We were just watching the game." He backed up a step.

Ivy tilted her head. "What happened to your accent?"

René looked down at his shoes, which, unlike every other pair in the building, showed actual scuffing.

"That explains why it sounded muddled," Ivy said.

"My accent is *parfait*!" he hissed, then looked around and lowered his voice. "It is perfect. My mother is French."

"Uh-huh," Ivy said. "You're watching the Falcons?"

"Yeah . . . yes, I think they're going to take this one."

"The Falcons don't play tonight," Ivy said, quick as a laser. "They play on Sunday."

"You're live-streaming the auction," I said.

Chef René shuffled backward.

"It's not a crime," Ivy said. "We are, however, trying to solve a murder. We don't care about what you're doing and have no intention of telling Isabel you're broadcasting her life online."

"Or maybe we do," I chimed in. "It depends on what you say next."

Chef René huffed. "People pay big money to see how the rich live, and Isabel pays peanuts. This stuff is gold."

"The French accent is for your audience?" Ivy asked.

"They eat it up. When we first met, I was live on camera. You'd already heard the accent, so I kept it up."

Ivy's face pinched. She had a bug up her butt about liars.

"You were live-streaming when Eliza was murdered too," I said. "At 1:03 p.m." To Ivy, I added, "That's when her phone left the Wi-Fi. It was broken next to her body."

René paled. "I . . . I might have been."

"We need to see that video," Ivy said.

His hand pressed his pocket closed. "I'm not a suspect. I had no reason to kill her."

"No one said you are. We still need to see it."

"We don't think you killed anyone." I stepped closer, and he backed up another step. "Eliza stole the Monet, but she had a partner. Whoever she was working with was looking for the painting when they killed her. Your video might tell us something—if nothing else, it would help exclude you and whoever else appears on it."

Lamar nudged René with his elbow. "Show it to them, man. This is no joke."

"So give us the phone." Ivy's tone was as sharp as mine was smooth.

René shrank under her glare, then pulled out the phone and unlocked it. "Let me find the one."

I snatched it and scrolled through the clips until I reached the day Eliza died. I hit play. The video started with a close-up of René speaking in his French accent, which earned him a scowl from Ivy.

On the screen, René must have flipped the camera, and the view showed an expansive closet almost as big as my Atlanta apartment.

The camera panned over a collection of designer shoes, each pair aligned on lighted shelves like a museum exhibit. Dresses and suits hung in color-coordinated sections. Tags still dangled from some pieces, and others remained wrapped in protective plastic.

Ivy leaned closer to the phone. "Isabel's closet."

René shrugged. "Mrs. Montgomery was out for a walk, and my followers had been requesting it for ages." He pointed at the screen. "I almost doubled my numbers with that."

He reached for the phone, but I twisted away from him, scrolled, and selected another video. The clip played, showing

Isabel's garden. Liam strolled from the back of the frame toward the front driveway, his confident stride and ponytailed dark hair unmistakable even at a distance.

Eliza caught up with him. When he saw her, he yanked her into his arms and hugged her. She laid her head on his chest. After a moment, he kissed her forehead and left.

"What the hell?" I mumbled.

René snatched the phone away. "That was weeks ago, and I wasn't spying on her."

"No more than you spied on everyone else," Ivy noted. To Lamar, she added, "Isn't that right?"

Lamar cut his eyes to one side and didn't answer.

"So, Liam and Eliza?" I asked.

René shrugged. "Liam is handsome and charismatic. Many women find him attractive."

"Isabel said he's barely at the house anymore," Ivy said.

René scoffed.

Rigsby stepped into the center of our circle and squared up with his nephew. "Keep pushing me, and your aunt won't be able to convince me to keep you."

Lamar cocked his head and looked up at the taller man, not backing down an inch. Rigsby had his hands full.

Rigsby turned to Chef René. "Do you have an invitation, or are you on your way out?"

Unlike Lamar, René didn't stand up to the larger man built like a fortress. He ducked his head and hurried for the exit. A gust of wind swirled through as the door opened and closed behind him.

Lamar sauntered back to his post next to the door while Rigsby muttered something under his breath.

For the first moment in days, Ivy and I were alone. We

stood as still as the statue that had just left the stage while we faced the auction, now in full swing. We didn't have all night to be awkward. We were running out of time.

"The necklace Olivia stole," I said finally. "Do you think it was Eliza's? It's not Isabel's taste—too simple."

"Mm-hmm," she agreed. "Liam has some explaining to do."

CHAPTER 38
IVY

THE AUCTION WAS IN FULL SWING. THE AUCTIONEER RATTLED OFF head-woozying dollar amounts while Irving stood next to a painting that took up most of the stage's width.

"Do you see him?" Rose hissed.

We marched across the room toward the chairs and the patrons, both standing and sitting, paying rapt attention to the stage.

"Irving reserved a seat for him in the front row," I whispered.

There he was, front and center. As usual, Irving had treated him like royalty and assigned him a throne with the best view of how to spend his money.

I pointed.

"Liam!" Rose hissed.

I flinched as several patrons looked our way. I started to shush Rose, but an older woman with a scalp-pulling bun scolded her as if she were a child. I scowled back at the woman —it wasn't her business to silence Rose.

"Liam," Rose called again.

He did a double take as he spotted her. Rose gestured wildly for him to join us until the people on both of his sides shoved him in our direction.

He stood and scrambled past the others in his row to reach us. "Rose, Ivy," he said with more than a dose of annoyance. "What's this about?"

I jerked my head for him to follow us away from the auction.

"We know Eliza died at exactly 1:03 p.m.," Rose said once we were out of earshot. "That left you plenty of time to drive to North Ridge Resort after killing her. Murder Eliza at one, drive three hours, check into the hotel by four thirty—no problem."

"No . . ." Liam's face pinched as he worked out that math. His eyes widened. "No! This is ridiculous." He moved to step around her, but I slid into his path, arms folded in front of me.

"You have two motives to kill her," I said. "Hiding your affair with Isabel, which Eliza surely knew about, and reacquiring the Monet. The sheriff would be interested to hear this. You'd be their number one suspect."

"If he's not already," Rose added. She tilted her head, and I could see her readying another bomb. "Actually, you have a third motive too—to hide your affair with Eliza."

Liam gaped. "What—what are you talking about?"

"Chef René caught you two embracing—and kissing," Rose added.

The kissing part was an exaggeration, but a good one, designed to test Liam's reaction. I kept quiet, letting the statement hang between us.

Liam swiveled his face around the room as if checking for witnesses, then bent closer. "Eliza and I were never like that. We were friends. We grew close when I was with Isabel."

"Friends who kiss?" Rose asked.

"We never—" He lowered his voice. "Just cheeks and fore-heads. She was like a daughter to me."

That tracked with the nature of the kiss in the video.

"Isabel forbade me to come around after I broke things off," Liam said, "so my friendship with Eliza involved some sneaking after that."

"And the necklace?" I asked. "It wasn't for Isabel. It's too simple for her taste."

"The one with the circular pendant?" He swirled a finger at his throat.

I nodded.

"A gift. For Eliza's birthday. She was insecure—thanks in part to Isabel always putting her down. I wanted her to know she was loved."

"Why didn't you tell us this before?" Rose asked.

He hissed, "You know why."

"You didn't want to look guilty," I said, "but now you do. You were close with Eliza, and you forged the Monet. How do we know you two didn't plan all along to switch it with the original?"

"When she hid the painting from you—maybe she had a change of heart about selling it—you killed her," Rose added.

"I would never—" His words came out in a shout. Noticing the gazes pointed his way, he stomped farther from the auction setup.

Rose and I followed.

"I would never hurt Eliza." His voice shook. "I cared deeply for her. She was sensitive. She loved art. She loved life. I wanted to save her from Isabel." His eyes watered. He turned his face away.

A piece of the puzzle fell into place. "You and Isabel broke up before the Monet came into the picture. You forged the painting for Eliza, not Isabel."

He hesitated, swiped a hand over his eyes, and nodded.

"So, another lie."

"Technically, I didn't lie about that. I told you it was a gift. You assumed it was for Isabel."

I played back our conversation in Liam's home, and I couldn't recall him saying he'd made the copy for Isabel in particular. He'd said it was for display so that Isabel could enjoy the authentic one exclusively. Indeed, making a gift to Eliza would allow Isabel exclusive enjoyment of the real thing.

Rose held out her hand. "Let me see your phone."

Liam stepped back. "Absolutely not."

"I have a list of every device connected to the Montgomery Manor Wi-Fi at the time of the murder. If you want to be excluded as a suspect, hand it over."

Liam hesitated only a second, then reached into his pocket and withdrew the phone. He handed it over. She checked it against something on her own phone, grunted, and passed it back.

She nodded at me.

"Just so we understand," I said, with a heaping pile of skepticism, "you admit to making the false painting for Eliza, but you claim she swapped it with the original on her own—or with someone else."

"I claim no such thing. I don't believe Eliza would steal from her aunt. She loved Isabel, whether Isabel deserved it or not." The way his upper lip curled made it clear he did not think Isabel deserved it.

"Why did you break up?" Rose asked. "You and Isabel."

"The woman is a harpy." Liam scowled. "She can't go two seconds without insulting someone."

I waved Rose aside to get back to the point. "Eliza and a partner swapped your forgery with the original."

Liam shook his head, disgust on his face. "Absolutely not. If someone swapped the paintings, it was not with her knowledge."

"Then who else knew about the forgery?"

"Please stop calling it that. When I gave her the copy, Eliza displayed it on her mantel. Anyone who entered Eliza's home would have seen it."

"Thanks, Liam," I said. "Sorry for pulling you away from the auction."

He bowed his head and moved back to his seat, maneuvering past other patrons.

Rose looked at me. "That should narrow down our suspects."

"It *would*," I said, "but we don't know who came and went from Eliza's place."

Rose narrowed her eyes. "We might, actually. Isabel sent a link to her video footage in the cloud. There's a camera pointing out to the driveway and another to the garden. We should be able to tell if anyone who parks goes right toward Eliza's, or straight toward the main house. And the garden camera will let us see anyone going from the main house to Eliza's."

"That's a year's worth of videos."

"I didn't say it would be easy, but I might be able to . . ." No, there was no time.

"What?" Ivy asked.

"And now," Irving's voice boomed from the stage, "the moment many of you have been waiting for."

Two security guards rolled the current treasure, an abstract painting in metallic paint, off the stage. Its paint sparkled in the spotlights as the men carried it through the door to the back.

"I must apologize and ask for your understanding regarding this next piece," Irving continued. His voice lowered to a hush. "Given the extraordinary uniqueness of this next piece, we must conduct this bidding with prudence."

Every person in the room leaned forward as if pulled on puppet strings.

Irving's long pause sent every gaze to the back door. I held my breath, expecting it to reopen, re-welcoming the security guards and the next piece of art.

The door remained shut, but a large, glowing, three-dimensional image appeared above the stage. The audience gasped, and Irving couldn't hide his pleased grin.

A hologram of the Monet floated on the stage. I'd never seen a hologram so rich in its colors, transparent yet appearing solid. Irving hadn't blown it up to massive size. The image was no larger than the true piece, a mere eight inches on each side, but it glowed as if made from some priceless metal.

"Fancy," I mumbled.

Rose scoffed. "It's just showmanship to cover the fact that he's too scared to bring the painting out here."

"You're not giving him enough credit," I said. "It's a smart move. There's a ninety-nine percent chance the murderer is in this room. Why bring them what they want?"

"I'm sending each of you more specific details about the piece—its dimensions, colors, year, and place of origin." He waved his hand in a circle to indicate that even more information would be coming.

Phones buzzed throughout the space, and people reached for their purses and pockets. Soon, everyone's phone was out, and guests stared wide-eyed at the colors and details on their displays.

While everyone was distracted, now was the time to check on the Monet. If I were the killer and I still wanted it, I would consider this my opening.

I leaned closer to Rose's ear. "We should go—" My clutch vibrated.

Irving was a born showman, but despite my curiosity about what he'd just sent to my phone, now was the time to act.

Adrian strolled over and slung an arm around Rose's waist. She jabbed her elbow into his side, and he folded like paper.

"Hey." I grabbed him by the shoulder and spun him to look at me. "Hands off."

Adrian raised both hands in the air. "Easy. I'm her date."

"He accompanied me," Rose said. "It's fine. I've got this."

I moved toe-to-toe with him anyway. Rose's judgment was better than I'd first thought, but maybe she couldn't see past this guy's pretty face. "He threatened us on the phone," I reminded her. Even in my heels, I was a few inches shorter than him, but with my training and his ego, I could take him down easily enough if the situation called for it.

"You bugged my car." He stepped behind Rose and propped

his chin on her shoulder, avoiding the confrontation and taking the opportunity to touch her. "Illegally. I had every right to warn you off."

Rose shrugged him off. "He's harmless." She emphasized the word to make it clear she intended it as an insult. "But he thinks that because he's good-looking, he can convince me to accept his apology."

Adrian perked up. "You think I'm good-looking? Thanks." He grinned a sly smile. "I wasn't sure you noticed."

"Don't say thank you. You can't take credit for genetics." She added in a hiss, "Touch me again, and I will make your identity disappear."

"You can do that?" He sounded more impressed than scared.

Rose had things handled here. She should stay put to see how things developed. We could cover more ground by splitting up anyway.

I slipped away from them to find Lamar. Now that Chef René had been exiled, Lamar leaned against the wall by the entrance, his expression cool. Rigsby was nowhere in sight.

I positioned myself right beside him with my hand open between us. "Give me your key card."

He snorted. "Why the fuck would I do that? Your sister squealed on me about buying shoes on duty."

"Your uncle is one more infraction away from firing you, nephew or not. He didn't notice you letting attractive women in here without checking their invitations. I watched you do it at least twice. I'm guessing there were more." I nodded toward a table with hors d'oeuvres and drinks.

One of the women Lamar had waved through stood in front of it, her small plate piled to tipping with food. In the other hand, she held a tall glass of champagne—probably not her first.

"Rigsby is loyal to this auction house," I added. "He won't appreciate your freeloading friends."

Lamar's jaw clenched. He slid his hand into his jacket and placed the key card in my palm. "Bitch," he mumbled.

"Nice doing business with you."

I headed toward the security door that would lead to the back of the auction house. This case would be over tonight, one way or another.

CHAPTER 39
IVY

WHILE IRVING LAUNCHED INTO A SPEECH ONSTAGE ABOUT HOW Monet's upbringing shaped his art, I swiped the key card and slipped through the door into the employees-only area of the auction house.

According to Rose, this long hallway ended at the loading dock. The first door on the right would be the treasure room, secured by a fingerprint lock.

A security guard in a nondescript black suit stood outside the locked door. He leaned against the wall with his right hand hovering by his side, ready to grasp the gun hidden under his jacket. His gaze scanned the space and locked on me.

He pushed off the wall as I approached. "Only authorized personnel back here."

"I'm Ivy Gray. I—"

He held up a hand. "Mrs. Montgomery's investigator?"

I stiffened.

"It's no problem. Mr. Greenfield said one of you might come back."

"Did he?"

"He said I should show you around the lockup if you want." His intonation slid upward in an implied question.

"Sure." I tried to keep the surprise out of my tone. Apparently, I'd misjudged Irving.

The man pulled out his phone.

The door behind me opened, and I spun to find Mina hurrying down the hall on pointy high heels that tapped across the floor. "Ivy," she said, out of breath. "I'm glad I caught you."

The guard's brow pinched. "Is everything okay? I wasn't expecting you back so—"

"Fine. It's fine." She stopped in front of us. "Irving needs you on stage. He'll want you prepared to chat as soon as he's finished with the Monet."

The guard didn't move.

"Trevor." She clapped her hands. "He's almost finished."

He slipped his phone into his pocket and ran down the hall.

I moved toward the fingerprint lock that controlled the door. "Trevor was just going to let me peek around."

She shook her head. "That's not happening."

Her stiff expression could have cut stone. I squinted at her. "What's going on? Did you run back here only to stop me from entering that room?"

Her chest rose and fell as she caught her breath, but no answer came. That was fine—I didn't need one. Her actions were answer enough.

"You're the insider who made sure security was just relaxed enough to allow someone to swap those paintings a year ago."

She stayed stone-faced. At least she knew her denial would sound like bullshit at this point.

"Let me see your finger." I reached for her hand.

She slapped mine away and stepped back, hands raised in fists.

"You don't want to do that," I said.

"You don't know me." Her tone was too calm. This wouldn't be an easy fight.

I lunged for her. She sidestepped and grabbed my arm. Her other hand shot out, aiming for my throat. I blocked, but her grip on my arm tightened as she twisted it behind my back.

I stomped on her foot, and she yelped, enough distraction for me to twist out of her grasp. She swung a fist at my face.

I blocked it with my forearm and drove my elbow at her chest.

She dodged and hit me in the face with an open palm. The blow stung. I shook it off and went on the offensive, springing at her, but she sidestepped and kicked me in the stomach. I staggered back, wheezing.

I aimed a kick at her flank. Her leg left the floor at the same time, and her foot crashed into my knee. I screamed and went down.

Mina raised her leg, and I rolled to keep her stomp from landing on my head.

I scrambled to my feet off balance, with my knee screaming in pain. Mina took advantage to kick me in the chest. The blow landed with a loud smack that echoed down the hall. I crashed backward, and my head bounced off the drywall.

The world spun.

Okay. She was short but a kicker, and my best kicking leg

was out of commission. I could adjust to that. I just needed to get in close and stay there.

I shook my head to clear it. Mina's fists were clenched at her sides. Her chest heaved with each breath.

I leaped in close. My knee wobbled but held. Her foot came up, but I smacked it down before it got above her other knee.

She swung.

I dodged. *I* swung.

She dodged. She grinned. "I can do this all night."

I didn't have all night. Irving would finish his auction, and then his entire security team would be back to collect the goods. I guessed that whoever else was involved was already inside the locked room, so Mina was here to keep me out.

I lowered my fists a fraction below my face, enough for her to see the opening.

Mina cocked back her hand and rammed it forward, putting her whole weight behind it. She was cocky—too arrogant to pass up an easy win. I slid to the side and grabbed her wrist with my right hand, twisted, and tucked her arm under my left.

She screeched and tried to yank her arm back, but I had it locked down. I swept my left leg into her right, and she lost her balance. At the same time, I yanked her forward. She stumbled, and her fist uncurled.

"Thank you." I slammed her thumb on the keypad.

She screamed.

I released her, and she crumpled to the floor, cradling her right hand. "You broke my thumb, you bitch!"

The door beeped, and I pushed it open. "Yeah, that's my bad."

I hobbled into the room, ignoring the searing pain in my right knee.

The room was as large as I'd expected, with a high ceiling and a skylight letting in natural light. It smelled of dust and paint, telling me this place held pieces of art and history.

The space was divided into sections. To my left were paintings leaning against the wall, none stacked on each other. Each treasure had its own personal space, all wrapped in protective paper or plastic. A few sculptures stood on the floor, also wrapped.

In front of me was a line of glass display cases holding smaller sculptures, artifacts, and jewelry. The pieces looked like they came from every corner of the world—a mask that might have come from Africa, a small bust with intricate designs shining with gold and jewels, an ancient book with a faded cover.

As much as I wanted to stay and explore, I had a purpose— and I was on the clock.

I limped across the room. As I rounded the first display case, a noise stopped me.

In the corner, Blake stood tucked between two plastic-wrapped paintings as if he thought they could hide him. He clutched the miniature Monet painting in one hand.

The other hand held a screwdriver.

Above his head, an open vent cover dangled by one screw.

"Well, this doesn't look suspicious." I pointed at the vent. "Let me guess. You figured you'd hide the Monet from Irving and return for it after the search died down."

"Stay back," he said. His voice was tight with tension, and his chest heaved with each quick breath.

Gone was the poised assistant I'd met a week ago. This

person wore a mask of red-rimmed wild eyes and tension that cut deep crevices in his face. Or was it a mask before, and this was the true man?

I stepped forward. "Blake—"

He lunged toward me with the screwdriver extended like a sword. I dove to the side. My injured knee collapsed under me as Blake barreled forward.

A woman's voice boomed from behind me. "Stop!"

Blake jumped over me and tackled the security guard in the doorway. She grabbed him around the waist and took him down with her. The Monet tumbled to the floor. I cringed as it bounced against the carpet with a crack. Blake fought to his feet as she tried to grab his ankle. He kicked her in the shoulder and scrambled away, scooping up the painting.

He hooked a right outside the doorway.

"He's heading for the loading dock," she shouted.

I pushed to my feet as quickly as my knee would allow and limped after him.

CHAPTER 40

IVY

MY KNEE ACHED WITH EACH STEP, BUT I FORCED MYSELF TO MOVE.

I didn't have the luxury of time. If Blake escaped with that painting, Isabel would keep her secrets, and I might never see my father again.

There was only one exit in this direction: the loading bay door. I hobbled toward it and pushed it open. It whooshed shut and clicked closed behind me.

The loading dock had only a few overhead lights casting pools of illumination in the dark. I stood on a small cement platform with a short set of stairs leading down to the main space. The air smelled of oil and metal, a stark contrast to the refined atmosphere of the auction inside.

I froze and listened, but silence greeted me. With an auction in progress, there were no deliveries this time of night, and the place looked deserted. Several giant crates dotted the space below, most with their tops pried off and insides bare.

Stacks of pallets were piled in a corner, and a forklift sat dormant near the garage-style loading door to the outside.

A metal ladder led up to a narrow balcony that ran along the left wall, likely for accessing the upper shelves of tall storage racks lining one side of the bay. The racks held display supplies—pedestals, decorative stands, lighting.

The closed loading door offered no escape. Blake had to be in here.

I withdrew my phone and dialed 9-1-1 with one hand without looking down at the keypad. I kept my gaze forward, on guard.

After one ring, a dispatcher answered, "What's your emergency?"

"This is Ivy Gray." It didn't matter if Blake heard me—it might be better if he did. Then he'd know there was no way out of this. Escaping me wouldn't free him from law enforcement.

"What's the emergency?" the woman asked again, kind but urgent.

"I'm in the Lakeview Luxe Gallery loading bay. I'm alone with Blake Anderson, who I suspect killed Eliza Thompson. Send someone now."

"Okay, Ms. Gray. Stay on the line with me."

I disconnected and slid the phone back into my pocket.

I didn't need to give her updates or keep me calm. I needed to be on alert so Blake didn't catch me off guard.

If I was lucky, he and I would stand here in silence until the deputies arrived. The status quo favored me, and Blake's time was running out.

Blake's silhouette appeared directly in front of me. Close. *Too close.*

I backed into the door, fingered its surface for the handle.

Tension squeezed my chest in a vise. My breath went shallow, and my heart slammed to escape.

Blake leaped. His outstretched hand slammed into the door behind me, forcing it to stay closed. The other hand hovered near my face, an unspoken threat.

"Where's the Monet?" I asked.

"I don't know what you're talking about." His breath was hot on my forehead.

I ducked under his arm and darted to one side. My knee wobbled.

Instinct hit, and I reached for my hip.

No gun. I hadn't carried one since before my administrative leave. Somehow, with no gun and a bum knee, adrenaline had thrown me into this chase without the good sense to stop, wait, breathe.

Blake slammed into me, and we stumbled backward. Sensing the platform's edge, I twisted before we sailed over it.

We went airborne. My breath slammed out of me as Blake's back hit the rubber floor, and I landed on top of him.

"Bitch!" he coughed out, rolling onto his side.

I scrambled away, but he grabbed my foot and yanked me back.

The metal balcony above would be my safe haven—if I could get there. The storage racks up there held a ton of small, heavy items I could pelt down on Blake to hold him off until help arrived.

I flipped onto my back and kicked with my free foot. My heel connected with his cheek, and he stumbled back. I scrambled to my feet and propelled myself toward the ladder.

Blake shoved to his feet and shot after me.

My foot clanked on the lowest rung. I climbed to the second, then the third. My knee locked, and I grunted in pain.

A hand clasped my ankle and yanked.

My hands fought to hold on, but he pulled again, and my knee gave way. My grip broke, and I fell into a heap at the ladder's base.

I kicked. Blake's nose crunched under my heel, and he screamed.

Braced against the wall, I pushed to my feet, then backed away with both arms out in front of me.

He kept coming, one hand covering his nose, blood dripping through his fingers. "You've got this all wrong." Red painted his teeth and sprayed from his lips.

He was attacking *me*, and *I* had it wrong? I forced a soothing tone despite the pain making my voice waver. "You're right. Let's talk this through. I'm here to help."

He froze.

That was what he needed—someone on his side. "I'm on your side, Blake. I can help you get out of this. Tell me where the Monet is, and we can return it to Isabel. You two have a long history. She'll forgive you."

His wild-eyed gaze darted from side to side, unfocused. Red eyes.

"Are you sleeping?" I asked in a voice I hoped sounded soothing despite my tension ratcheting upward, and my pulse threatening to drown out everything else.

"I sleep fine." His breath reeked of alcohol. He leaped forward.

I spun away, but my knee buckled, and I slammed into the side of a crate. The rough wood bit into my shoulder. Blake grabbed a crowbar from the floor and swung it at me.

I dropped and rolled.

The metal whooshed above my head.

"Don't play games with me, Ivy." He advanced, crowbar raised.

I crawled across the floor, testing whether my knee would hold my weight and scanning for a weapon. I reached a stack of pallets, grabbed one, and flung it at Blake.

It smashed into his shins. He stumbled, and I took the opening to push to my feet. My knee wobbled but held.

"No games." I raised both hands as I backed away. "We're just talking. What did you do with the painting?"

"Shut up about the damn painting!" He hurled the crowbar at me.

I ducked. It clanged off something behind me.

My knee screamed as I lurched behind the forklift to put its mass between us. "Blake, talk to me. We can figure this out together."

He said nothing but followed in my footsteps. Unlike mine, his breathing was silent. I was wearing down, and he wasn't even out of breath.

"Blake." I hurried around the forklift as I spoke, keeping it between us. Now back on the other side, I continued the circle. This forklift was the best cover I'd have in here. "It's just a painting. You'll probably get no more than a slap on the wrist, maybe community service."

"Just a painting?" he shouted. "Claude Monet was a genius. His work with light was perfection. Every brushstroke formed a perfect Fibonacci sequence."

Interesting. True or not, Blake admired the painter for his diligence, a trait he himself could aspire to. Only lately, Blake hadn't been as on point with his duties as when I first met him. Something had led him to spiral.

"Claude Monet was an innovator!" Blake's steps quickened as he circled the forklift, and I struggled to keep up.

My knee burned. Dizziness spun my head and focus. I reached out, keeping one hand on the forklift's cool metal as I hurried around my designated circle. It would keep me grounded, balanced.

"No one told him what to do. He rejected his field's norms and chose to paint outside in nature. The piece Isabel bought was the peak of that. Its mathematics are perfect. Even the dimensions create the perfect formula."

I'd never heard anything about Claude Monet and math before. Either I'd missed that in Art History, or Blake was seeing what he wanted to see. The latter didn't bode well, since I was trapped in a dark room with him.

Delusions. Wild eyes. Recent mood changes and duty dereliction.

Withdrawal symptoms?

Eliza hadn't wanted Blake to drink at the Autumn Festival, and he'd agreed. Now, he was drunk and a lot less poised.

That was the connection between Blake and Mina. Both had become perfect little soldiers a year ago—and now they weren't. They had changed back to their actual selves, only this time with withdrawal symptoms to boot.

"So you admire Monet's genius. I get it." I tried to keep my tone even, but pain slurred my words.

"Don't pretend to understand me."

"That's why you took the painting," I huffed out. I needed to keep him talking. "Isabel didn't appreciate it."

"Isabel never appreciated what she had. Do you know she

hasn't given anyone on her staff a raise in four years? Four years!" It was the first time I'd heard him use her first name.

"Isabel doesn't care about the people around her. She wants to own them—like the painting. She wanted to hide it away so she could exclude other people." Had I just said that? Words swam around the pain, and I couldn't make sense of them.

"You're not listening!" He darted forward in a burst of speed.

My knee wobbled as I tried to keep up, but Blake slammed into me. My fingers slipped off the forklift, and we tumbled to the ground.

I scrambled to my feet, but he gripped my ankle and pulled. I landed face down, spread-eagle, my breath whooshing out of me. I coughed and rolled over.

"Blake," I said. "Let's talk. We're having a good conversation. I want to hear your side."

He leaned over me, his breath stale with alcohol. "I'm not playing your game."

I kept my hands up where he could see them. "What were you taking, Blake? Whatever it was—it's your excuse for any crimes you committed. Don't make it worse now."

He blinked, caught off guard.

"A stimulant? An amphetamine?"

His face morphed into fury.

I rolled to the side just as his fist came down where my face had been. I struggled to put my feet under me, but Blake grabbed my leg again.

I screamed as pain hammered my knee.

He stood over me and pushed one boot down on my chest. The pressure was a weight on my lungs, pulling me down.

I squirmed. His face grim, he leaned into his foot until my breath hitched. I stilled. The pressure lightened.

"No more games, Ivy."

The crowbar lay on the ground beside us. Blake swiped it up. He bounced it in his hand as if testing its weight. Wild, red eyes stared at me as he raised the metal bar above his head and prepared to bring it down on my face.

CHAPTER 41

ROSE

ADRIAN FIDGETED BESIDE ME AS IRVING YAMMERED ON ABOUT THE childhood, life, and times of Claude Monet. Meanwhile, I had my nose glued to my phone, searching for a program to sift through the thousands of hours of Isabel's manor footage.

I needed everyone who entered the guesthouse in the past eleven months, since the day Isabel brought the painting home.

"Consider, if you will," Irving rattled on, "the sheer audacity of Monet's quest to capture the fleeting moments of existence—the play of light upon water, the dance of shadows across meadows, the whispers of wind through trees."

I leaned over to crack a joke to Ivy about rich people and their ramblings, but her spot was empty. I turned to Adrian instead. "How long has Ivy been gone?"

"You're talking to me now?"

"Only to ask you—how long has Ivy been gone?"

A woman in a silver sheath dress gave me a glare so chilly I got frostbite. I grabbed Adrian's arm and pulled him several feet away from the crowd.

"I was trying to watch the show," he grumbled.

Irving was still going on about Monet. "In his relentless pursuit of truth and beauty, Monet sought not merely to replicate reality but to distill its essence—to distill the very essence of nature itself—onto the canvas."

I hadn't thought much of Irving before, but he was a master of stalling. He should teach a class.

"Did you see her leave or not?" My words came out sharper than I meant.

Adrian shrugged.

From here, I could spot two exits—one near the stage to the back of the auction house, and the other the main entrance. Opposite directions. Worry gnawed at my gut, but I pushed it into a corner.

Ivy was more than capable. Ivy was fine.

"Do you know which direction she went, at least?"

"I'm not your sister's keeper."

I searched the seated guests, hoping she'd snagged a chair. There was Liam, Isabel, no Ivy . . . I squinted.

The spot next to Isabel's aisle seat was empty. Blake no longer stood by her side like a low-budget body monitor.

Blake.

He and Eliza were Isabel's scouts for new art. They were friends—he had touched her back when he introduced her, and she had checked on him at the Autumn Festival. He spent most of his time at the manor, so he must have visited Eliza in the guesthouse at least once.

Now, he and my sister were both missing in action.

I headed for the door near the stage.

Adrian grabbed my wrist, his grip firm but warm. "She's fine."

"I need to check on her."

"She's an FBI agent in an auction house packed with witnesses. I promise you—Ivy is fine." He was right. She could kick Blake's ass if she needed to, but my worry continued to gnaw and grow.

I looked down at my wrist until he released me, then crossed my arms over my chest. "What makes you think you know her so well?"

He mirrored my pose. "I'm pretty good at reading people."

"For the record, you are still a suspect in art theft and murder. I have no reason to trust you or your opinions about my sister."

He looked down at himself—a Black Latino in a tuxedo that hugged him in all the right places. Tight curls a little too long but gelled into place. The beginnings of a beard spoke of rough edges to be explored. "Do I look like an art thief?"

He looked like a snack.

I pressed my lips together to keep from saying that.

"Well?"

"People aren't always what they seem. I've been in town for two weeks and received two threatening notes and one stalker photo. What were you trying to do with that?"

His brows lowered, and his voice dropped. "What threatening notes?"

"Come on. You can't bullshit a bullshitter."

"Only the photo was from me, to keep you out of my private business. There were—"

"What private business?"

"*Private* private business."

I started for the door again. My unease wasn't going away, and Adrian was a distraction.

Again, he grabbed my wrist. "There were no notes."

"Liar." I shook him off.

"Why would I tell the truth about one thing and lie about others? How many threats are you getting?"

I searched his face, and he looked away. "You didn't leave anything telling me and Ivy to back off the case?"

"I couldn't care less about some rich lady's art."

I squinted at him, trying to see the truth under the posturing. "For the same reason you left the photo."

He threw up his hands. "I didn't leave any notes!"

I checked the door near the stage and then the main entrance—still no Ivy.

"Fine. Wait." He reached for my wrist again, thought better of it, and stuffed both hands in his pockets. "My employer is a private guy, and our contract requires me to do everything reasonably within my power to protect that. I was trying to scare you into leaving me alone."

For the first time, he didn't look away.

"But I promise—I left you the photo and nothing else. No other threats."

"I don't care!" I shouted. Heads turned, so I lowered my voice. "Believe it or not, you are not my primary concern. You are *nowhere* on my list of concerns. There is a killer in our immediate vicinity, and my sister is missing. Help me find her, or shut up."

Adrian clamped his mouth shut. I stomped toward the main entrance, shoulder-checking him on the way. Fear and worry expanded from their private corner in my belly.

His shoes tapped the floor behind me.

Security nodded as we passed, and Lamar glared, still salty. It wasn't my fault he was a terrible security guard.

We pushed through the front door into the parking lot.

The spotlight that had lit the entrance was off now, and evening had turned to night. A cool wind whipped through my hair, and I hugged myself.

Adrian reached out to put an arm around me.

"I will cut that off and feed it to my dog."

He withdrew the arm.

We were alone except for a few chauffeurs chatting and smoking at one corner of the building. Their limousines sat dark and silent near Adrian's. Other than that, the lot was empty. Where was she?

"What kind of car does she drive?" Adrian asked.

"Dark blue sedan." I gave him the make and model, the words tumbling out in a rush.

"License plate?"

I couldn't summon the number, so I shook my head. "I have a good memory for numbers, so I'll know it when I see it." I hoped so, anyway. Why couldn't I remember?

"Bumper stickers? Rearview mirror decor? Stuffed animals in the back window?"

"It's a rental, so it's pretty nondescript." Focus. I squeezed my eyes shut, trying to picture the vehicle.

He jogged down one aisle of cars. I did the same on the other, my pulse speeding me forward. Only two light posts stood at the lot's edges, casting long shadows. I squinted at every dark car, blinking back tears as worry took over.

"Here!" Adrian called after a moment.

I ran and stumbled in my high heels, cursing under my

breath. When I reached him, he was standing near a dark sedan.

"This it?" He pointed.

"Yeah." The license plate looked familiar. Tension tightened in my chest and clenched like a vise.

"Maybe she was in the bathroom."

"For ten minutes?" I shook my head. "She must have gone the other way."

I hurried back to the entrance and yanked open the door to the auction house. My heart slammed double-time with each step.

Lamar stood on the other side, blocking the doorway. "Invitation?" His face was blank, like he hadn't just seen us in here.

"You know us." I looked around for Rigsby, but he was by the stage now, deep in conversation with another suited underling. I had to get back in there *now*.

"It's my job"—Lamar spoke calmly, each word deliberate —"to check every invitation before letting people through. I wouldn't want to be derelict in my duties. Would I?"

Adrian stepped toward him, jaw clenched, but I held him back.

"It's fine," I snapped. "Don't make a scene." I ripped my invitation from my clutch and slapped it into Lamar's hand.

Slowly, inch by inch, he extracted his phone from the pocket inside his suit jacket, navigated to the guest list, and confirmed my invitation.

He handed it back. "Enjoy the auction," he said.

I shoved past.

Adrian was already ahead, moving as quickly as he could without drawing everyone's attention.

Despite his endless ramble, Irving still had a rapt audience. We reached the back door, and Adrian knocked on the small window. On the other side, a woman in a dark suit—another security team member—stood in the alcove.

She dismissed us with barely a glance. I wanted to scream. Every second felt like an eternity.

I barged past Adrian and knocked again, repeatedly. I rapped on the window for a full minute until the woman finally yanked the door open.

"Can I help you?"

I could see a sliver of the hallway. Beyond her, Mina Lee sat on the floor, scowling at someone wrapping a splint around her thumb.

"Ma'am, can I help you?" the woman asked again. "This is a secure area."

"What's going on? Is Ivy Gray back there? Is she okay?" The words burst out of me, high-pitched and frantic. I barely recognized my voice.

The woman's eyes narrowed, and she continued to block the doorway.

"I'm her sister."

She didn't move, so I barreled through.

The door to the secure room stood open, and Rigsby and another man blocked the entry. As the other guard gestured to the room's interior, Rigsby stared on with a grim face.

"Where's Ivy?" I pressed my hands to my legs to keep the shaking under control.

No one answered.

"Where's Ivy Gray?" I shouted. My heart had been pounding since I'd noticed her missing, but now the thud of each beat filled my head. I was underwater, and everything around me was a hazy echo except for my reverberating pulse.

Rigsby looked up. "I'm in the middle of getting briefed." He turned back to his underling. "Harry?"

Harry held out his phone and navigated through what looked like video recordings of this area. Rigsby leaned down to watch.

This was getting me nowhere, and that was not my planned destination.

I spun toward Mina. A woman with a first aid kit was wrapping tape around her hand while Mina scowled at everything and everyone.

I snapped my fingers in her face. "Have you seen my sister?"

"Bitch broke my thumb!" she shouted.

"That sucks for you," I snapped. "Which way did she go?"

"I was writhing in pain on the floor after your bitch sister broke my thumb. So no, I didn't see where she went."

"Sir," called another guard from inside the treasure room.

Rigsby looked over, his expression severe, eyes narrow slits. The man shrank back.

"Spit it out."

"The Monet is missing."

Rigsby staggered backward. "What?"

If I knew anything about Rigsby, he cared about two things —his wife and his work. He rushed into the room, shoving the guard aside. His eyes widened as he looked into a corner and found it empty.

"Rigsby." I grabbed his wrist. My nails dug into his skin. "Which way did Ivy go?"

Behind me, Mina let out a string of curses so foul that

everyone in the room cringed. Conversation paused for a second and then restarted.

Rigsby patted my hand until I released him. "The Monet is my concern."

Ivy wasn't in the auction space, the parking lot, or this hall. I headed for the door at the end of the corridor.

Harry slid into my path. "You can't be back here." He pointed the other way. "Please return to the auction."

I met Adrian's eyes. He nodded almost imperceptibly and shoved Harry.

Shock flashed across Harry's face as he slapped Adrian's hand away. "What's your problem?"

Adrian slammed him against the wall. The two men grappled, arms locked in a struggle.

"Hey, hey!" Rigsby shouted.

I shot for the loading bay door. Blind panic propelled me forward.

CHAPTER 42

ROSE

I BURST INTO THE LOADING BAY AND FROZE.

Blake faced me, a crowbar raised high. Under his booted foot, her face pale in the dim space . . . lay Ivy.

"Stop!" I barreled forward and leaped off the platform's edge.

Blake slammed the crowbar down.

Ivy twisted, and the metal thunked against the rubber floor, missing her ear by a sliver.

My knees flexed as I hit the floor and stumbled forward. I raised one hand toward them. "*Blake, stop.*" I'd read somewhere that using people's names made them more likely to empathize with you.

He raised the crowbar again.

"She's a real pain—I know." I spoke in a rush but kept my voice even, using the same tone I used to coax passwords out of people. "I thought about hitting her a couple of times myself."

He froze, eyes bloodshot like he hadn't slept in days. "What?"

"Ivy." I pointed at her and inched closer. "I've known her for two weeks and fantasized about hurting her for just that long."

Blake looked down at Ivy, then back at me.

"What did she do?" I asked.

His eyes rolled upward like he was trying to remember. He looked seriously tweaked out.

"That's okay. I get it. There's just something about her."

He tightened his grip on the crowbar.

"She's not worth it, though." I could barely hear my words over the panicked screaming inside my mind. My pulse beat fast and heavy like a drum solo crashing to its finale. Still, I waved a hand like we disagreed over dinner plans. It trembled, so I held it behind my back.

His arm muscles tensed, but the crowbar lowered a fraction.

"She's bossy. Holier-than-thou. Knows everything all the time." I put one hand in front of me long enough to pinch two fingers together. "Makes you feel this big. Am I right?"

Blake's chin dipped, then rose. A small nod—but it counted.

Still lying face-up, Ivy tilted her head back to see me. Her eyes shined like spotlights in the dim loading bay.

Blake wiped sweat from his face with the back of his hand, still gripping the crowbar.

"Let her up," I said. "Nothing happened here. Nobody's upset with you."

He looked down at Ivy, his expression unreadable. Time slowed, and the moment stretched into an eternity, my heartbeat pounding out each unending millisecond. My breath stilled, hovered, waited.

He lifted his foot from her chest.

Ivy stayed frozen, arms open, palms up beside her face.

Blake shuffled away until he no longer stood over her.

Ivy crab-walked backward, then scrambled to her feet. She kept her arms raised in a show of surrender. Her right knee wobbled. Her hairdo had fallen to the base of her neck, and sweat plastered a chunk of loose hair to her forehead.

She took an unsteady step my way.

"Good." I reached for her. "That's good. No one else has to die."

Her eyes went big, and she shook her head.

Too late.

Blake grabbed her jacket collar and jerked her toward him. Her knee buckled, and she stumbled backward into his chest. He wrapped one arm around her, crowbar in hand, and gripped the other end to lock her in place. The bar pressed into her throat.

She gasped, clawing at the metal crushing her windpipe.

"Blake!" I screamed.

Ivy's eyes bulged. Her face turned red.

Blake pulled tighter, and her gasping stopped. She scratched at the metal, her fingers bleeding as the nails snapped.

"Ivy," I said in a voice on the verge of falling to pieces, "it's okay. It's okay." In my head, I chanted the same words to myself. "Blake, she's not worth it." Panic set my chest on fire, but I pushed all my will into keeping my voice steady.

"Shut up!" he hissed.

Ivy's bloody fingers scrambled at the crowbar.

"Look, I'm sorry." I held my hands up. "She's not worth it." I sounded like a scratched record, nothing new to say, and Ivy was paying the price.

Her legs straightened as she pushed up on her toes and then fell back to her heels. She kept clawing at the bar. Her mouth gaped as if reaching for air she couldn't find.

"Tell me . . ." I started. "Tell me what you're feeling."

His gaze flicked to the door behind me, then to the sides, before landing back on my face. "I killed Eliza. Everyone's going to know."

They had been friends. Something must have made him snap. "Did she hurt you, reject you?" My voice squeaked.

"She . . . No . . . She . . ."

"Eliza switched the paintings, and you got mad?"

"No! It was me. All me. I knew Liam made her a copy. Taking the real one from Isabel was so easy. She has so much expensive junk—she didn't even notice for months."

I raised my hands higher so he could see my palms. "Eliza never knew you switched them."

His grip loosened, and Ivy gasped.

Interesting. He was more interested in preserving Eliza's memory than saving himself.

"She didn't know until I came looking for the original. She was furious. Then I slapped her." He choked on the words.

"You didn't mean it."

He shook his head fast. "She just wanted me to go to rehab. When my dealer left town and cut us off, I paid for him to ship me one last bottle, but he sent me an empty box. Asshole." Saliva sprayed.

That explained why Blake had been so eager to dig into his

packages the day I followed him—and why his poise had spiraled since then.

"I went cold turkey because I had to, and . . ." Blake's gaze searched the floor as if an explanation might be there. His fingers loosened, and the crowbar sagged in his grip.

Ivy slurped in a loud breath, and tears swam in my eyes.

"Nothing makes sense," he continued. "I'm angry all the time. I couldn't remember what I was supposed to be doing at any moment, and it just made me madder."

"Us?"

He jerked his head up to look at me.

"You said the dealer cut *us* off?"

"Me and Mina. She needed it too—to stay focused. She agreed to be my lookout as long as I supplied her. When I couldn't anymore, she demanded I switch the paintings back, or she'd give me up."

"Is that when you started threatening Ivy and me?"

"I didn't—" His grip on the crowbar tightened, and again Ivy clawed at it. A ragged gasp escaped and died, leaving her mouth opening and closing in a silent scream.

"Of course you didn't," I said over the panicked pounding in my chest. "You just wanted to make things right."

A tear slid down his face and settled above his lip. "I don't even know what happened."

"You would never have hurt Eliza on purpose."

"She was my best friend. I loved her."

"It was the withdrawal," I said.

He nodded fast, his head bobbling like a doll.

"You don't want to hurt anyone else, right? Eliza wouldn't want that."

He shook his head just as fast.

I pointed at Ivy. "She can't breathe."

He stared down at the top of Ivy's head, then up at me. He dropped the crowbar like it was on fire.

Ivy stumbled toward me, her hand on the bright red skin of her throat. She ran several steps past me before she slowed and returned to my side.

Her breaths came in long, ragged pulls.

I reached out and grasped her hand. She squeezed me back, and I released her.

With a bang, the door slammed open, and deputies Marks and Ramirez burst through.

"Who's dead?" Marks shouted. His face was red, and sweat dotted his forehead. He held his gun low.

Ivy, Blake, and I all threw our hands up.

"No one," Ivy shouted. Her voice was desert dry. She coughed and pointed at Blake. "He confessed to killing Eliza."

Blake's shoulders slumped. He didn't fight as the detectives pushed him to the floor and cuffed him.

Ivy leaned into me, and I wrapped my arms around her to hold her up.

CHAPTER 43
ROSE

I paced the worn rug of the waiting room inside Gray Investigations.

Rusty, my giant puppy, sat on his hind legs, his furry head moving left to right to keep me in his sights.

I had a lot of energy to burn. I'd spent some of it swinging by home to get Rusty. If I was sticking around, I wanted my baby with me. For the first time in days, I didn't feel like I needed to be doing something—snooping, questioning people, checking out crime scenes.

Now, it would all pay off.

My bank account was ten bucks north of another overdraft fee, but Isabel's information could be priceless. With it, we could find Caleb, and I'd get everything I had coming to me.

"Would you stop that?" Ivy called from Caleb's inner office.

She was sitting on a chair in front of a filing cabinet, a stack of folders to one side. Her left knee was bent under her, the other leg extended with the heel on the floor. A black brace supported her right knee.

The painkillers must have worked because she'd been elbows-deep in organizing this office all morning. She'd already cleaned up most of the vandalism mess. Shiny magazines dated this century now decorated the coffee table in the waiting room, and the table's legs were all upright and intact. A vase of fresh flowers sat on Anna's desk.

I stopped pacing. "Do you really think Blake didn't trash this place?"

Rusty stretched his front legs and lay down.

"He confessed to everything else." Papers rustled as she worked. "Why admit to threats and murder but lie about vandalism? The note was his—the ransacking wasn't."

"Maybe he forgot. He wasn't exactly in his right mind. Withdrawal is a bitch."

"You know from experience?" The crinkling-paper sound stopped.

"If you want to know about me, just ask. Don't be all coy-FBI-agent."

Ivy went back to her organizing. "You're right. Sorry."

I went back to my pacing. Rusty watched me but didn't get up.

"Would you sit? You're making me nervous."

"You could just not look over here."

The door banged open, and Isabel swept into the room like a queen visiting peasants, her chin up and gaze down at us mere mortals.

Rusty shot to his feet. The hair on his back stood straight up.

Isabel shrieked and darted back through the doorway. One

foot stumbled on its high heel, but she kept moving. "Whose beast is that?" she called from the hallway.

I rubbed Rusty's head and whispered, "Such a good boy."

He lumbered to the doorway and curled on the floor beside it. From there, he could relax or chew off an unwanted visitor's arm—it was a prime spot.

"It's fine, Mrs. Montgomery. He won't bother you."

"If he bites me, I will sue," she shouted, still out of view.

"He's a softie. I promise."

Isabel inched into the room and hurried past. She'd pulled her black hair back tighter than usual, and her dark suit was all business.

"Ms. Gray." She headed for the door to Caleb's office.

Ivy hobbled out and guided Isabel in the other direction. "Let's talk out here. I'm in the middle of a reorganization project."

"I'm sure Caleb won't mind if we use his space. We'll be more comfortable."

"You can go in there if you want . . ." I said, drawing out my words so she'd sense the warning.

Isabel froze.

"But you should know Anna died in there."

She wrinkled her nose.

"Her brains were all over the wall. You enjoy artwork, though, so maybe you're into that." There was no need to kiss Isabel's butt anymore. We solved the mystery, so she had to pay us as agreed, whether she liked me or not.

Isabel edged toward an armchair in the waiting room, equidistant between Caleb's office and Rusty. She lowered herself into it. "Very well."

I sat across from her.

Ivy eased herself behind Anna's desk, careful not to jostle her injured knee. "You received our report?"

"Of course." Isabel shifted in her seat and blinked several times, still recovering from the thought of Anna's corpse. "It was very thorough."

Ivy cut me a glance but said nothing. She'd written the entire thing herself, even the part I'd agreed to handle.

"Thank you," Ivy said. "We're glad you're pleased."

Isabel glanced around the room with an appraising look that, for once, wasn't steeped in disapproval. "Sheriff Foster returned my Monet from where Blake hid it in the loading area." She gestured toward me. "And I hear your gentleman friend was not arrested for starting a scuffle."

"He's not a gentleman," I muttered, "or a friend."

Ivy raised an eyebrow.

"I understand Mina will do well if she cooperates with authorities," Isabel continued, "although Irving must choose better about whom he trusts."

I could have said the same for Isabel, but I decided to be my best self instead.

"I assume you would like to be paid."

I leaned forward.

Ivy leaned forward.

Isabel's mouth snaked into a smile.

She opened her handbag, a bubblegum-pink piece of art that must have cost twice Vera's monthly mortgage, and withdrew an envelope. She held it out to me, snapped it back before I could grab it, and stood to hand it to Ivy.

I stuck my tongue out at her impeccably dressed back.

Isabel clasped her bag closed and smoothed her suit. "I trust this concludes our business."

Ivy grabbed a letter opener from Anna's desk and slit the envelope open. Whatever this was, it had better be worth all the trouble. Ivy slipped out a single piece of paper and read it. "What the hell is this?" Her professionalism cracked like a cheap vase.

Isabel shrugged one delicate shoulder. "As promised, one page from the file on Caleb's desk the day before Anna died and he disappeared."

I swiped the paper from Ivy's hand. It contained only two scribbled notes—an address and a name.

CHAPTER 44

IVY

"Daniel Foster," I said. That was the name on the page Rose was flapping inches from Isabel's face. I gripped Rose's shoulders and walked her back a few feet.

My hands and legs tingled with energy. I knew this sensation—the feeling of having a clue that led in a dangerous direction. Daniel Foster was the sheriff. My dad couldn't have been investigating him—or could he?

Isabel pointed at the address under the name. "That's not the sheriff's office."

"Then what is it?" Rose snapped.

"I suggest you run a web search and"—she made air quotes—"investigate."

I snatched the page from Rose and waved it in Isabel's face. "You told us you had indispensable information relevant to our father's case."

"I assume that's true."

Rose grabbed the paper and held it close to Isabel's nose. "This is what we get instead of payment?"

I took the note back and tucked it in my pocket. The last thing we needed was Rose hitting Isabel with it and ending up in jail—again.

"This was the bargain. I will also send a check for your itemized expenses." She turned on one high heel and strode out, leaving Rose and me staring after her.

I closed the door and pulled out my phone to search for the address on the note. It popped up on the map. I zoomed in. "It's a storage facility."

"Maybe Sheriff has a rental space there?"

"We can stake it out tomorrow," I said.

"Low chance they'll just tell us if we call and ask?"

"Zero chance. But it's one hundred percent that whoever answers will immediately tell Sheriff Foster we asked. That would kill any advantage we might have."

A knock sounded at the door. Rose and I looked at each other.

"Isabel?" she whispered.

"That woman has never knocked in her life. She's more of the barge-in type."

"Are you expecting someone else?"

Another knock.

"It's not locked," Rose called.

The door swung open, and a young man in a polo shirt walked in, a messenger bag slung over his shoulder and a bike helmet attached to the strap.

Rusty raised his head from his spot near the door.

The man stiffened.

"He's just a puppy," Rose said.

"A massive puppy." The man inched backward out the doorway.

Rusty sniffed his knees, then his waist, before lumbering away. He dropped back to the floor and curled up.

"Congratulations," Rose said. "You passed."

He gave a stiff laugh but stayed on the other side of the door. "Are you Ivy Gray?"

I met him at the threshold so he wouldn't have to come any closer. "That's what my driver's license says."

"From Deputy Jay Matthews in the sheriff's office." He reached into the bag, pulled out a folder closed with a cord, and pushed it into my hands.

"What's this?" Rose asked.

"I just deliver. I don't know what's inside." With a backward wave, he took off.

I limped to Anna's desk and tipped the contents of the folder onto the desk. Out slid a small stack of papers and two flash drives. One drive had a piece of tape stuck to it labeled *Anna's computer*, and the other *Caleb's computer*.

Rose leaned over my shoulder. "Papers from the sheriff's office?"

"Flash drives, too." I pushed them in her direction. "I'm officially-unofficially working with the sheriff on Dad's case. Foster promised to send over the file."

We both went silent at the mention of Foster's name, and my gaze slid to the coffee table, where the page with his name sat.

"And you were going to tell me *when*?" Rose asked after a moment.

I pointed between the two of us. "We haven't exactly talked much in the last few days."

"Whose fault is that?"

We stared at each other, then shrugged at the same time—a silent agreement that now was not the time to rehash that argument. We *would* need to rehash it, though.

Rose grabbed the papers from me.

"Hey."

With a pointed look, she split the stack and returned half to me. "Teams work together."

Sure, that was fair. Still, I frowned down at my stack. "What do you think?" I asked.

A pleased smile spread across Rose's face. "You want to know what *I* think?"

"You're smart, and you see things differently than I do. Don't make me repeat that—ever."

The grin stayed locked in place, glowing. "It may be easier to scan everything and run a program to surface key details. Do you trust me to do that?"

She needed assurance that we were in this together. And we were—for now. "We're partners until this is finished. I'll return to work as soon as they let me, and I'd like to have everything squared away before that happens. We can finish this more efficiently as a team."

Her face went solemn.

"Let's talk about what we know," I continued, "which is not much. Thankfully, Isabel will sing our praises all over town, we'll get more clients, and more people will feel comfortable talking to us, just like they are with Dad."

"We know Caleb disappeared before Anna died, and it was probably his blood on the letter opener *before* she died. So the sheriff's theory about Caleb killing her and then running to avoid getting caught is bullshit."

I raised a finger. "Anna only thought he was missing. He could have still been in town, hiding out with a mistress after cutting his hand while opening mail."

"That's a stretch."

"Fair enough. But my point stands—at the moment, we have no way to verify what Anna told us is actually true. It could be a coincidence that she couldn't find him, or she could have had an ulterior motive for calling us here, or a hundred other possibilities that we need to methodically consider before we jump to a conclusion."

"But you don't think he killed her?" Rose asked.

"I don't think anything at the moment. I don't want to exclude options based on bias."

Rose looked down at her hands. "I don't know the guy, so I don't have any biases."

"Everyone has biases. The fact that you don't know him is a bias."

"Hold on." Rose hurried out the door.

Rusty raised his head and whined.

"She'll be right back, big guy," I assured him.

He seemed content with that and lowered his head.

I leafed through the pages in my stack and frowned. Interviews with me and Rose at the scene of Anna's murder. Interviews with other people—with thick black lines marking out portions of the text and names.

Rose returned, pushing a wheeled corkboard as tall as she was. She stopped it in front of the wall opposite Anna's desk and dropped a bag of pushpins on the coffee table. "Supply closet down the hall. Now, we can create a murder board. Isn't that what y'all call it?"

"I don't work murders. You know that." But her grin was

infectious. "Evidence boards aren't usually a thing in real life. Each agent works multiple cases, and we can't just fill the office with boards."

Rose propped her hands on her hips. "At the FBI, do they teach you to be a buzzkill, or is that something you do naturally?"

"A little of both."

She clapped and jumped in place. "You made a joke!"

"I'm offended by how delighted you are." I grabbed a photo of Caleb from my half of the file and pinned it to the center of the board. "We need to look through Dad's case files. Most likely, whoever did this is a client of his."

"Or a client of Anna's," Rose said.

I leafed through my pages for a photo and pinned Anna next to Caleb.

"She had a birthday party the night before she died," Rose said. "We need a complete timeline of that party."

I tapped my stack of papers. "There are guest interviews in here, but a lot of it is redacted."

She flipped through her own pages and cursed.

"I'll follow up with Jay to see what we can get un-redacted. And we'll need to go through these thumb drives."

She snatched them off the desk. "What else? Any suspects?"

"Everybody who looks bad in any of Dad's cases is a suspect." I gestured toward the office, where I'd been organizing the files. "That's one of the reasons I'm trying to implement a logical organizational system."

"So basically, we don't know squat."

"We have a lot of work to do. TV and movies make investigations look glamorous, but mostly it's pounding the pavement, talking to people, correlating information."

"Sounds exciting," Rose said, her voice pancake flat.

"We'll know more soon enough."

Rose swiped the note Isabel gave us off the coffee table and tacked it under Caleb and Anna. "Sheriff Daniel Foster."

I stared at the board, at the name of an old friend who was now the most powerful man in this town—and might have something to do with a murder and my missing father. "We'll start with him."

MORE TO COME

Get inside information and hear about new releases, discounts, and other bookish stuff. Plus, get a free book when you subscribe to my newsletter.

www.writeralicia.com/links

ACKNOWLEDGMENTS

Yellow Tape was a journey I couldn't have completed without the support and encouragement of my people. I write mysteries all the time, but they are usually in science fiction or fantasy settings. I'm proud to call this my first contemporary novel. It was an adjustment, but one I'm thrilled to have made.

If you're a science fiction fan, don't worry. I have more in the works.

Thanks to my partner and the rest of my family for being a constant source of support. Thanks to my community for appreciating my need to write multiple genres and advising me. Thanks to Bruce Tamanaha, Lauri L., and others for their awesome beta reading. Finally, to all my readers—your support means so much. I hope this book brings you as much joy and intrigue as it did me.

Yellow Tape is the first in a series. I hope you're ready for more.

ABOUT THE AUTHOR

I decided to write books about ten minutes before graduating from law school.

Now, I'm an Atlanta attorney moonlighting as an author, electronics junkie, and secret superhero. With two degrees in computer science and an MFA in Writing Popular Fiction, I love creative problem-solving, especially as it relates to high-tech things.

I write mysteries, sometimes for young adults, sometimes in fantasy or science fiction settings, and sometimes in the real world.

amazon.com/author/writeralicia

bookbub.com/authors/alicia-ellis

facebook.com/writeralicia

instagram.com/writeralicia

x.com/writeralicia

goodreads.com/writeralicia

patreon.com/writeralicia

Printed in Great Britain
by Amazon

45071401R00212